W9-AHL-657

*Of course.
He'd tackle this whole marriage
question from the other end.*

Why hadn't he thought of that before? He'd *start* by asking someone he really wanted to spend his life with, love or no love. *Nina.* He'd start there, and if she turned him down, why then he'd maybe move on to Donna or someone else.

Dear Nina, he'd write. *I know you've never considered something like this before, but I thought I'd ask anyway…. We've had a chance to get to know each other over the last few months, writing letters the way we have. And I think maybe we could work out a pretty good life together.*

By the time Cal drove into the ranch yard, he had it all thought out. The only thing he needed to do was find a piece of paper and a stamp.

① Keep
2-'08

MARRY ME,
Cowboy

THE RANCHER'S RUNAWAY BRIDE

Judith Bowen

Secrets!

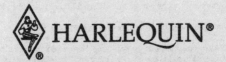

HARLEQUIN®

TORONTO • NEW YORK • LONDON
AMSTERDAM • PARIS • SYDNEY • HAMBURG
STOCKHOLM • ATHENS • TOKYO • MILAN • MADRID
PRAGUE • WARSAW • BUDAPEST • AUCKLAND

If you purchased this book without a cover you should be aware
that this book is stolen property. It was reported as "unsold and
destroyed" to the publisher, and neither the author nor the
publisher has received any payment for this "stripped book."

HARLEQUIN BOOKS
225 Duncan Mill Road, Don Mills,
Ontario, Canada M3B 3K9

ISBN 0-373-65352-2

THE RANCHER'S RUNAWAY BRIDE

Copyright © 1997 by Judith Bowen.

All rights reserved. Except for use in any review, the reproduction or
utilization of this work in whole or in part in any form by any electronic,
mechanical or other means, now known or hereafter invented, including
xerography, photocopying and recording, or in any information storage
or retrieval system, is forbidden without the written permission of the
publisher, Harlequin Enterprises Limited, 225 Duncan Mill Road,
Don Mills, Ontario, Canada M3B 3K9.

All characters in this book have no existence outside the imagination of
the author and have no relation whatsoever to anyone bearing the same
name or names. They are not even distantly inspired by any individual
known or unknown to the author, and all incidents are pure invention.

This edition published by arrangement with Harlequin Books S.A.

® and TM are trademarks of the publisher. Trademarks indicated with
® are registered in the United States Patent and Trademark Office, the
Canadian Trade Marks Office and in other countries.

www.eHarlequin.com

Printed in U.S.A.

JUDITH BOWEN

Judith Bowen was born in Edmonton, Alberta, Canada, and grew up in a logging camp in the Rocky Mountain foothills. She had many friends who lived on farms and ranches, a fact to which she attributes her love of the outdoors and of rural life.

Judith bought her first horse at age twelve with money saved from allowances, gifts and odd jobs—the horse only cost sixty dollars and was fresh off the range! Luckily he was a sweetie, and she trained him and rode him until she left high school.

She and her family currently live in Ladner, British Columbia, and she spends most weekdays at her word processor, writing the stories she loves. Weekends and summers are for family.

Judith's "Men of Glory" miniseries for Harlequin Super-romance arose directly from her experience of going to school in a small town and living in small towns all over Canada. She has lived in many of Canada's provinces, from Prince Edward Island to B.C., and writes from the heart about people who live on the land that she knows best.

Before writing fiction, Judith worked for newspapers and magazines. She holds a bachelor's degree in English Literature from Carleton University in Ottawa, and is a member of many writing and arts organizations.

Please address questions and book requests to:
Harlequin Reader Service
U.S.: 3010 Walden Ave., P.O. Box 1325, Buffalo, NY 14269
Canadian: P.O. Box 609, Fort Erie, Ont. L2A 5X3

To my daughter, Alison Claire,
who showed us what joy there is in loving animals

and

To Marena G. Bahala, R.N.,
who reached out and grabbed on to a star

CHAPTER ONE

If only Louisa Twist had kept her nose out of her nephew's private life...

"HIGH TIME you found yourself a wife, McCallum."

Cal froze, his fork halfway to the plate of hot buttermilk biscuits his aunt had just set down on the table. "Oh?"

Louisa Twist eyed him over her bifocals and blew a wisp of graying hair from her forehead. It had to be ninety degrees in the kitchen already and not yet nine o'clock. An Indian summer to end all Indian summers.

"You heard what I said. Buy yourself some new clothes. Go get a haircut, for heaven's sake, and get out there and start looking."

Cal proceeded to fork himself a biscuit before settling back down onto the hard wooden chair. He frowned. Where had this come from all of a sudden?

"No question, big brother," Jeremiah drawled. "Time you settled down."

Henry guffawed.

Cal gave his foreman a mild look. Henry, too? He calmly split and buttered the biscuit he'd speared, then reached for the coffeepot. He gave his aunt a weak grin. "You know what they say about a house with two women in it, Lou."

"You can save that fifty-dollar look for someone else, McCallum," his aunt said severely. "A *wife* is what you need. Somebody to take charge. Just look at you—all of you." She waved one corner of her apron. "Since the haying crew left, nobody even bothers to put on a shirt anymore—"

"Heck, Weezie," Jeremiah interrupted, lazily scratching his bare chest. "You know it's too hot."

Cal frowned at his brother. Lou had a point. Jeremiah wore nothing but a pair of old jeans, as did Cal. Henry had on a frayed sleeveless undershirt, which revealed grizzled chest hair and a dozen scars on his arms and shoulders, the legacy of a lifetime spent wrestling ornery cattle and restive horseflesh. At least Henry wore boots, Cal thought, guiltily curling his own bare toes under the table.

But then, as far as he could remember, he'd never seen them off. For all anybody on the Rocking Bar S knew, Henry J. Hilton took a bath with his boots on.

Still, he wished Jeremiah'd kept his big mouth shut. Lou hated being called Weezie. On the other hand, Cal wasn't exactly sure what Lou was getting at—

"Ha!" His aunt's face wore an expression he'd seen before. Her mind was definitely made up about something. "I don't know how much longer you can count on me, that's all." She glanced down at her plump hands and airily inspected her nails. "S'pose you can look out for yourselves, hmm? You're big boys now. Manage somehow, I s'pose."

Cal stared. His aunt's face was flushed. "Just what exactly does that mean, Lou?" he asked slowly.

"Means George Edward has been plaguing me for

an answer for months now," she blurted. "Means I'm about ready to take up his offer, that's what."

"Hot damn!" Jeremiah dropped his fork.

"You gettin' married?" Henry chimed in. Cal thought the pair of them had never looked so foolish.

"Could be," she said, bright spots of color in both cheeks. "I'll be sixty-eight next May, and I'll have you know that's not beyond getting married again, young Jeremiah. What I *am* saying, though, is it's high time McCallum made some other domestic arrangements."

Jeremiah and the hired man turned as one to stare at Cal. "Cal?"

"Now, hold on here," Cal began. He raised both hands and cleared his throat. "Everybody—just hold on. Of course you're not beyond getting married again, Lou. We all know that," he said soothingly. "In fact," he said, pinning the other two with a hard look, "in fact, George Edward is one helluva lucky guy and I hope he knows it."

Henry and Jeremiah both nodded solemnly, as if on cue.

"But what I don't rightly see," he went on carefully, "is what any of this has to do with, well, me getting married."

"Married!" Jeremiah broke in. "Hell. You gotta *meet* women to get married, Cal. When's the last time you got serious with a woman? All's Weezie's saying is, high time you started looking." He shared a significant look with Henry, who seemed about to burst with some private inner amusement.

"I date," Cal objected. He reached for the honey

jar. "What about Glenda Sawyer? We went out quite a bit last winter, as I recall."

"Glennie! Why, she gave up on you months ago, McCallum," his aunt said sharply. "She's engaged to Brent Williston from the Oarlock Seven, and they're getting married next month in Black Diamond. Didn't you hear?"

Maybe he had. Someone must have told him. Cal couldn't exactly remember.

"And I took Jen Farmer to the harvest social only a few weeks ago," he continued, somewhat lamely. He liked women, all right. He just didn't have time for them lately. Too busy. It was tough enough running a foothills ranch during good times, and these past couple of years had been hell on cattlemen all over southern Alberta.

"Fer cryin' out loud, Cal, Jen Farmer don't count," Henry scoffed. "She's the preacher's sister and she went back to Winnipeg last week."

Cal decided the conversation had gone far enough. His marriage prospects—or lack of them—were nobody's business but his. "Well, if Lou does decide to leave, I'll hire someone to take over here. Damned if I'm going to up and get married just so you two can have a live-in housekeeper and cook. We can do our own cooking if we have to."

They'd come to count on Aunt Lou in the ten years since Uncle Will had died. He couldn't quite remember what it had been like at the Rocking Bar S before that. "Put an ad in the paper maybe," he added, and reached for another biscuit.

"*Ha!*" That was his aunt again.

"Why not? Somebody's sure to want a steady job cooking for an outfit like this." Cal glanced up. "Jobs are tight all over."

"Cooking, maybe," Louisa said. "But what about cleaning and washing up and laundry? What about shopping for groceries and plantin' the garden and mendin' socks? What about letting any old cow-puncher in dirty boots drift through that screen door looking for a meal, day or night, and…and…" She seemed at a loss for a few seconds. "And putting up with you fellows coming to the table in your…in your *underwear* on a Sunday morning, that's what!"

She dabbed at her eyes with a balled-up handker-chief. "You and Jeremiah's blood kin, and I suppose I have to put up with it for the sake of your dear dead mama, God rest her soul. But darn it, Henry ain't!"

"Now, Lou," Cal said gently with a guilty look at the other two. "It hasn't been that bad around here, has it?"

"We-ell…"

Cal didn't doubt for a moment that his aunt loved them all, even Henry. She just felt bad having to break the news to them that she might be leaving. *Married!* That sly old son-of-a-gun neighbor of his, George Edward Robison. Buried two wives and now hunting for a third.…

"Face it, Cal," Jeremiah said, shrugging one bare shoulder. "Lou's right. What're you waiting for? You're thirty-five years old. Sure, you're no Romeo, we all know that. But you're steady. Real steady." He shot a mock-serious look at Henry. "Women go for that, don't they, Henry?"

Henry mumbled something. Jeremiah turned away, obviously stifling laughter.

Cal stared at his brother, then at Henry. Jeremiah, younger by nine years, had always had an easy way with women; so did Henry, even though the old fool had to be seventy if he was a day. He was as cagey about his age as he was careful about his feet.

Hell, Cal had always thought *he'd* been pretty good with women, too—when he took the notion. He'd dated over the years. Plenty. Was it his fault nothing ever came of it?

Cal took a deep draft of his coffee, which was almost cold—and rearranged his knife and fork on his empty plate. The truth was, he'd never quite figured women out. They were a mystery to him. In his experience, everything always moved too fast with women. Either you got the impression they wanted you to pop the question on the third date, or they dropped you for some guy who did.

Sure, he'd always planned on getting married one day. He had to admit he liked the idea: a partner in his struggle to keep the ranch afloat, company for the long winter evenings—he was tired of looking at those two across the table from him—regular sex. Maybe it *was* time he got serious about looking for a wife. What he didn't like was Lou and Henry and Jeremiah setting the agenda for him.

Most women he knew didn't want just marriage. They wanted love. And that was where he always seemed to go dead wrong. He could say he'd been fairly serious about maybe half-a-dozen women over the past fifteen years, but he couldn't say he'd been in love even once.

Love…hell. Come right down to it, *that* was the part he didn't have the time or inclination for. Courting, flowers, candy, going to the movies, all that mushy romantic stuff women seemed to thrive on. It just didn't come natural to him.

Not that he didn't think he could handle the hearts and flowers if he really put his mind to it. If he had to. Haying was over, roundup was a couple weeks off… Cal looked up. His aunt met his glance. She looked hopeful. Expectant.

It made him nervous.

"Could be I'm just too particular," he said, rubbing his unshaven jaw with one hand. He'd noticed that Jeremiah hadn't shaved for a couple of days, either. Nor Henry. Maybe Lou was right. Maybe things *were* getting slack at the Rocking Bar S. After Lou left, there'd be just the three of them, cowboy bachelors. Another few months, and what woman in her right mind would want to move in?

"Could be you're just too rusty, big brother," Jeremiah responded with a grin and a broad wink at Henry.

"Nope." Cal stood and reached for his hat. "I don't believe I am." He ran one hand through his hair and settled his hat on his head. "Truth is, you boys are starting to aggravate me. Maybe it's time I showed you just how wrong you are."

He stalked out onto the porch, letting the screen door slam. As he jammed his bare feet into his boots and cussed halfheartedly at the assortment of dogs lazing on the porch, careful not to disturb any of them, he pretended not to hear the chorus of cheers behind him. He even thought he heard Lou's shrill "Whoopee!"

Damnation. Had it *really* gotten as bad as all that around here?

IF ONLY NINA O'SHEA O'Sullivan hadn't been driving a fancy foreign car that fine September day. You could get parts in *any* small town for a Chev or a Ford....

BUT SHE HAD a foreign car, a cream-colored honey of a Targa, brand-spanking-new, and it drove like a dream. Well, there *was* that funny little thumping noise when she accelerated. It didn't happen all the time, but maybe she should let the Porsche dealer have a look at it once she got back to civilization.

The trees here had started to change color already, the poplars bright pools of gold against the dark serious green of spruce and pine. And everywhere, the backdrop of those fabulous mountains. The Canadian Rockies—there was no finer sight on earth. You might not be able to call this part of southern Alberta civilization, but it was gorgeous country. Thank goodness she'd managed to snatch a week from her hectic schedule for a short road trip. All by herself. Her idea of heaven. She planned to do the loop—Vancouver to Calgary through the Kicking Horse Pass, then up to Calgary and Banff, over the Crow's Nest Pass and back home again to Vancouver.

Nina had the top open, and the wind filled her lungs and streamed through her hair. At the moment she was playing one of her favorite games from childhood, something she often did when she traveled alone— pretending to be someone else. Right now she was a race-car driver. Scott Goodyear, Mario Andretti, Jacques Villeneuve. She leaned into each curve, her body one with every vibration of the superb machine. The speed, the power humming beneath her hands— all those horses harnessed under the hood just for her. She loved not knowing what was around that next bend. Or the next. It was part of the game.

She tipped her wrist to steal a glance at her watch. Just past four. She'd have to think about stopping soon for the night. There'd been a sign a while back: Glory, 47 kilometres, Calgary, 153. Glory—what kind of place was that? Maybe she'd have something to eat there, then carry on to Calgary.

No one knew where she was, not even Leo, her business partner, and she told him everything. Well, *nearly* everything. For this one stolen week, she'd managed to free herself from all the trappings and constraints of being an O'Shea-O'Sullivan, and it felt terrific. Having an outspoken retired federal politician for a father and a high-profile criminal lawyer for a mother, not to mention a half brother who was in and out of civic politics, meant her life had always been very very public.

And Nina knew she'd not been the most biddable of children. Bringing her up had been a trial to all concerned, especially her mother, Nina thought wryly, pulling the Porsche through a hairpin twist in the road.

Poor ma! Busy defending every rapist and serial murderer in the country, yet worried sick because her only child, a premenopausal impulse but dearly loved all the same, skipped school once in a while or ran with a distinctly *un*preppy crowd or brought home the homeless for a hot meal and a warm bed and a shower from time to time.

Thunk! Thunk! Nina frowned and studied the dashboard instrumentation. Nothing unusual there. Maybe the temperature was a bit high, but that was to be expected considering the hills she'd been climbing and the speed she was traveling—wasn't it?

Nina loved cars, but she was no mechanic. A breakdown out here wouldn't be much fun; she hadn't seen more than three or four vehicles since she'd left the main highway an hour ago.

The car coughed once, then again, and Nina realized to her horror that, although she was still traveling just over the speed limit, the Porsche's engine had died. Gingerly she touched the brake, checked quickly in her rearview mirror and stepped harder on the brake pedal. The power-assist from the engine had vanished and she could barely steer the car. She could still brake, but with difficulty.

Luckily there was a slight incline ahead. Swallowing her panic, Nina wrenched the wheel to the right and practically stood on the brake pedal. The car slowed, then stopped, then—*dear God!*—began to roll gently backward.

She knew she had to get off the road and onto the gravel shoulder before the car stopped altogether, which, somehow, she managed, steering blindly backward. She pulled the hand brake as far as it would go and fell forward, gasping, against the steering wheel.

Her hands shook. Her blood hammered painfully in her ears and at the back of her neck.

She raised her head and stretched her fingers slowly. They'd been glued to the wheel. She heard her knuckles crack. It was that quiet. Only the soft breeze moved, enough to stir her hair slightly. Her knees felt weak, her thighs still vibrated from the effort to brake.

Nina turned the key in the ignition a couple of times, not really expecting success. Dead. Did this kind of thing ever happen to the Andrettis?

She smiled to herself and got out of the car and leaned against the gleaming fender. The air was warm and light, a glorious afternoon. High high above, a hawk circled lazily in the porcelain blue sky. She swore she could actually smell the distant mountain pines. The silence of the landscape seemed to reach inside her, and for a few long seconds Nina rested, mind blank, breathing the pure warm air.

Then she thrust a hand into the driver's compartment and pulled the hood release. Now why, she wondered, did opening the hood always seem like such a good idea when a person had car trouble? She gazed at the mystery of wires and tubes and stinking hot metal. In the distance she thought she heard the whine of another engine. In this silence, if a car was coming, it could still be a mile off.

She walked around the car and took her cell phone out of the canvas tote on the passenger seat, then flipped down the visor and slowly punched out the number of the automobile association. She'd never had to call for help before. Her father would be pleased to know his insistence that she keep up her membership had finally paid off. She hunched her shoulders and listened as it rang three times before being picked up.

"Where are you, ma'am?"

Nina looked down the road she'd just driven on. She thought she could still hear that distant engine. "Uh, I'm not sure. Somewhere between Coleman and Calgary."

"Can you be a little more specific? Are you on Highway 22?"

What had that sign said? "About a hundred kilometers or so south of Calgary. Southwest," she quickly added. "I think."

"I've got a listing here for a towing service with… Walt's Garage," the voice came back doubtfully. "In Glory. Are you on the Glory road?"

Glory! That had been the other name on the highway sign. Nina balanced the phone on her shoulder as she dug deep in her bag for a pencil and paper. "Uh-huh, that'd be it." She tore a check from her checkbook. "Thanks. Just give me the number." She scribbled it on the back of the check.

Whew, it was hot! Nina lifted the hair from her neck. She *had* heard a vehicle. A station wagon sped past, camping gear lashed to the roof. The sound of the engine rapidly fading into the distance made her shiver.

She dialed and let it ring a dozen times. No answer. Wouldn't *that* be great if old Walt decided to close up early on a Saturday? She dialed again. No answer.

She crossed her arms and took a couple of deep breaths. No problem. If she didn't get through, she'd just call some outfit in Calgary, although it was a long way off. Or back in Coleman or Pincher Creek. Somebody around here had to have a tow truck.

Another vehicle appeared in the distance, this time a late-model pickup truck. It was dusty and had two men inside. The truck slowed.

Nina stood a little straighter and was ready when the truck stopped beside her. She took a deep breath. Was she nervous? Not really. This was rural Alberta, she reminded herself. The driver hadn't even bothered to pull off the road.

"Trouble?" asked the passenger, a handsome, black-haired, blue-eyed cowboy-type.

"Overheated, I guess. I've called a tow truck."

The passenger consulted quickly with the driver. Nina couldn't see him very well against the glare.

"Guess that'd be Walter Friesen, huh?"

Would it be? She nodded with a confidence she didn't feel. "Walt's Garage. In Glory."

"Uh-huh." The passenger said something to the driver again, then opened the door and stepped out. "Hop in, miss. We'd better give you a ride into town."

Nina could see the driver now, although he hadn't done much more than turn to study her briefly, then tilt his head to check the rearview mirror. He seemed bored. She had the impression he was a little older than his passenger, a little more reserved, not quite as handsome. He wore a denim jacket, as did the man who'd spoken to her, and a faded plaid shirt. Jeans, of course. Broad-brimmed hats, both of them.

"Oh, I'll be fine." Nina waved a hand. It was one thing for a woman not to feel too nervous about being alone with a breakdown on a lonely stretch of road; it was quite another to get into a pickup truck with two strangers. "Thanks, anyway. Walt'll be along any minute now."

The cowboy seemed surprised. "You got hold of him?"

"Uh, his line was busy," she lied, not sure how much she should reveal about her predicament to these men. "I'll try him again in a minute or so." As she spoke, she punched in the numbers. Might as well let them know she wasn't completely defenseless out here. A woman with a cell phone never was. The phone rang and rang.

"Me 'n' my brother'd be more than happy to give you a lift," the cowboy continued. "It's only a couple miles. In fact, we're headed right there. We got a rig to pick up at Walt's. Getting the brakes overhauled."

Nina heard the distant whine of another vehicle and felt mildly relieved. She wasn't alone. All of a sudden this Glory road was Grand Central Station! She shook her head. "I'll just stick with the car. Thanks, anyway." Why was she being so stubborn?

"Suit yourself." The cowboy shrugged and got back into the truck. He raked the lines of the Porsche in a once-over nearly as appreciative as the one he'd bestowed on her, then leaned out the open window as the driver put the truck in gear. "We'll tell Walter."

She stared as they drove off. Tell Walter what?

ONLY A COUPLE of miles, he'd said. Nina realized, too late, that her sandals weren't the best choice for walking any distance. She was hot, hungry—and thoroughly annoyed. She'd tell the automobile association a thing or two about this Walt's Garage and they'd have his hide. Still no answer! What kind of way was that to run an emergency road-service business?

And, after the virtual traffic jam of three vehicles within ten minutes while those two cowboys were stopped, there hadn't been another car or truck in the last half hour.

Hey! What was that? Ahead of her she saw the distinctive outline of a tow truck. Elderly, rusted, but nonetheless definitely a tow truck, and it was coming around the bend.

Walter! Irritation forgotten, she stepped out onto the middle of the pavement and waved her arms. The truck stopped. A round smiling face wreathed in wild gray hair and topped by a greasy mechanic's skullcap appeared at the window.

"Why, you must be the young lady that had the breakdown. Well, well. Now run around and hop in. We'll have that car of yours fixed in a jiffy—"

Nina didn't wait to hear what else he had to say. She was so relieved to see him she could've hugged him. She climbed carefully onto the torn vinyl seat of the truck, avoiding the worst of the wicked-looking springs that had popped through.

"—and the Blake boys was in, McCallum and Jeremiah, and they sez, well, actually it was Jeremiah who come out back to get me—I was working on that binder Sal Drucker's been havin' trouble with—well, anyways, Jeremiah sez, there's a young lady been trying to raise you on the telephone—"

"Yes," Nina broke in. She realized she'd have to

interrupt if she was going to get a word in edgewise. "Why didn't you answer your phone?"

"—she's stuck out there the other side Tommy Gardipee's lower pasture. Ain't Tommy's actually." He beamed at her and winked. "It's his cousin's, see? But Tommy takes the hay off, and around here we always call it Tommy Gardipee's lower pasture— Eh? Eh? What's that?"

Walt had finally noticed her desperate hand gestures.

"The phone. Why didn't you answer the phone?" It dawned on her that Walter was hard of hearing. *"The telephone!"* she shouted.

He touched his ear with grimy fingers and fiddled with something, managing to fill the cab with a shrill whistle that made her jump. "You'll have to speak up, miss. I don't hear so good."

Nina groaned. Dear Lord, she prayed, let Walter take care of her beautiful shiny new car and bring her safely to a decent respectable hotel in Glory with a hot meal and clean sheets on the bed and—

"—'course the doc says that ain't all bad when you're in the line of work I'm in. There's a lotta loud noises that could damage a fella's hearing if he wasn't already deaf, he sez, and that's never been a worry for me, no sir— Oops, sorry." Walter gave her a big gap-toothed grin, eyes shining. "No, *ma'am!*"

CHAPTER TWO

NINA FIRST NOTICED the man who'd been driving the pickup when Walter dropped her off at the Wild Goose Inn. He'd just stepped off the sidewalk in front of his pickup, and she assumed his polite nod was for Walter.

She spotted him again an hour later as she hovered at the entrance to the dining room. There were several tables with older couples, locals no doubt celebrating anniversaries—it was that kind of place—and, to one side of the room, several tables of men in dusty jeans and boots and green nylon vests. Oil-exploration companies frequented the hotel, she'd been told at the desk. The parking lot was full of their mud-spattered four-wheel-drive crew cabs.

The cowboy sat at a table by himself, and Nina took the opportunity to observe him a little more closely. Not that she could see much beyond a lean broad back and, judging from the slightly paler line of skin at his nape, evidence of a recent haircut. Without the broad-brimmed hat, she could see his face more clearly. Well, his profile, mostly. Strong clean lines and—it was hard to tell at this distance and this angle—yes, a little careworn. Where was the other guy, his handsome blue-eyed passenger?

"Are you dining alone, miss?" The hostess smiled

warmly. "Right this way," she continued, turning in response to Nina's quick nod. Nina followed her, spine stiff, aware of the interest from the drillers. There was dead silence as she walked across the dining room, then loud guffaws after a mumbled comment from one of them.

Louts. She ignored them, taking a seat at her table and looking around with a show of casual interest. The hotel decor was fundamentally Fifties Western with some strong Hunting and Fishing influences, but the room she'd been assigned was clean and fresh. The sheets were spotless—she'd already peeked—the bathroom was modern and there was plenty of hot water. The Wild Goose Inn would do for a brief visit, anyhow. Tomorrow was Sunday, and Walter had said it'd be Monday before he could get the part he needed sent out from Calgary.

It remained to be seen what the dining room offered. She'd regard her weekend in Glory as serendipity, an unexpected holiday in Alberta's cowboy country. Nina raised the menu, excruciatingly aware that the man she'd been studying earlier had noticed her—not only noticed her, but was staring unabashedly. She tried to ignore him, as she'd done the drillers, but found it much harder to do. Heat crept up her neck and into her cheeks.

Annoyed, she chose at random and gave her order to the waitress. She glanced up, tapping her water glass with one finger. Hmm. Should she order a carafe of the house wine? She could just imagine what was on offer…

To her horror, she discovered she was looking

straight at *him*. And he was looking straight at her. She glanced away, but not before he'd smiled.

This was ridiculous! He would think she was coming on to him.

When the waitress returned, Nina made up her mind and ordered a carafe of wine, after all. One of the drillers lurched by on his way to the men's, presumably, and mumbled something. A woman dining alone was apparently quite a novelty in Glory, Alberta. She drummed her fingers on the tablecloth, wishing she'd brought a magazine with her. *Anything* to keep her mind off the man two tables over.

Then, to her vast relief, she saw him stand and bend slightly to pick up his hat from the seat of the chair beside him. Thank goodness!

But he wasn't leaving.

"Mind if I join you, ma'am?" At the same time, he reached for the back of the chair across from her. She looked up, stunned. He made a careless gesture in the direction of the waitress who was approaching with a carafe and one wineglass on a tray. "Jeannie here'll vouch for my good character, won't you, darlin'?"

"You're asking an awful lot from a lady, McCallum Blake, you surely are," the waitress teased, setting down the tray with a thump. Her eyes twinkled, though; in fact, the waitress actually blushed, and she had to be at least twenty years older than this cowboy!

"Uh, I don't think—" Nina began hesitantly.

But he'd already sat down. "McCallum Blake, ma'am." He extended his hand across the table with a slow smile that did weird wiggly things to her breath.

"My brother and I offered you a ride to town this afternoon?"

"Of course." She nodded and automatically put out her own hand. "Nina O'Shea." His hand felt hard and warm and very…nice. She withdrew hers quickly. Well. Did they move fast in these poky little cowboy towns or what? Still, what harm was there in having him join her—and it would at least put the drillers' minds back on their meals.

"Shall I bring another glass?" the waitress asked, beaming. Nina had the strangest feeling everyone in the room had some kind of inside knowledge, a handle on what was going on—everyone but her.

"Certainly," she said. Why not? "That's if…if Mr. Blake would care to join me…"

"Cal," he said simply.

"Cal," she echoed, beginning to feel rather stupid.

"You can bring me a beer, Jeannie. Big Rock lager," he said to the waitress, who moved off, beaming. He gave Nina an apologetic look. "Thanks for the offer, but I'm not much for wine."

For a very long moment, a moment during which Nina thought she just might stand up and scream if something didn't happen soon, he just looked at her, still with that same half smile that was driving her crazy. His hair was a rich dark brown, wavy and thick. He was deeply tanned and freshly shaven. An outdoors man. As she'd suspected before, he'd had a recent haircut. Even his shirt looked brand-new, because now, up close, Nina could see several telltale fold marks in it.

Finally, to her huge relief, he sat back and stretched

out his legs and carefully settled his hat, which he'd kept in his left hand, on the seat of the chair between them. "Walt look after you all right?" he asked easily, as though they'd known each other for years.

"Yes. He's getting in a part on Monday. From Calgary." She leaned forward. "Why didn't you tell me he was deaf?"

"Figured you'd find out soon enough. Monday, huh?" Cal Blake repeated, his eyes on hers.

"Yes." *Two nights.*

"So you're stuck here for the weekend?"

"I don't have much choice, do I?" She took a sip of the white wine she'd ordered and made a face.

"Wicked?" He grinned.

Inexplicably Nina found herself smiling back.

"You could say that." Then she laughed. There was something about this man she liked. And she'd never met a genuine cowboy before, either. She might as well relax and enjoy herself. "Listen, do you always do this?"

"What's that?" He seemed puzzled.

"You know." She gestured vaguely. "Just get up and invite yourself over to join a lady at dinner?"

"No."

"No?"

"Believe it or not," he said, "this is the first time I've ever done it."

"You're kidding!"

"Nope."

"So…why me?"

"Well, it isn't as though we're totally unacquainted. After today, I mean. With your car." He sounded apologetic. "And, well, I just thought you looked like an interesting person. Someone I'd like to meet."

That was straightforward enough, and it seemed sincere, too. Her cheeks warmed under his gaze as she realized that her initial annoyance was mixed with a large dose of something else—something more like old-fashioned male-female awareness. Hormones. To her shock, she discovered that, yes, it was true, she was physically attracted to a man she'd met only fifteen minutes ago. You couldn't count this afternoon. She'd barely noticed him then.

Slow down, girl, slow down. This kind of thing doesn't happen. Not to you.

Jeannie brought his beer and her first course, then left. The interruption gave Nina time to try to collect her thoughts.

"So. I presume you work on a ranch somewhere around here?" she asked, starting her salad. That had to be a safe topic. Surely she could handle a simple dinner conversation with this man, attraction or no attraction.

"The Rocking Bar S. Up in the hills. We're about twenty miles west of town."

She glanced up. "You and the guy I saw you with today?"

He nodded. "We raise Herefords. Some mixed stock, exotics. Hay. Feed grain. A few horses." He shrugged. "The usual kind of thing."

"I wouldn't know," she admitted. "I've never met an honest-to-goodness rancher before."

"You've never been to this part of Alberta?" he asked, obviously surprised.

"Never." She felt sad suddenly. Wistful. She hungered for this kind of ordinary conversation. It happened too rarely in her life. Wasn't that why she stole off once or twice a year on these short solitary holidays where she could be exactly the Nina O'Shea she knew she really was inside? Not the privileged daughter of famous wealthy parents. Not the sister of the flaky mayoralty candidate.

How many times had she wished for a truly private life, the kind she imagined other people had? How many times had she wished her father was a plumber and her mother worked in a bakery, the way other people's parents did? Now, as an adult, she believed it had been that deep desire to be her very own person that had fueled the rich imagination that had gotten her into trouble more than once as a child. Just Nina and her trusty dog and a leaky rowboat setting out on a huge adventure that meant pretending the swimming pool was the stormy North Sea. Or perhaps she was a penniless orphan forced to make her way in the world selling flowers stolen from the garden. Or a bandit princess locked in a tower that was really no more than her barricaded tree house at the bottom of the orchard. Murray, her half brother, was so many years older that he'd never been her companion. She might have been an only child.

"Where you from? If you don't mind me asking," he added quickly.

Nina hesitated. She didn't want to tell this man the whole truth about who she was. Even out here in cow country people had heard of Big Jake O'Sullivan, the maverick B.C. politician. Big, brash, powerful. Nina doubted there was a person in Canada who hadn't heard of him at one time or another, associated with this or that backroom scandal. As for her mother, Meredith O'Shea had defended some of the country's most notorious criminals in the past decade. She'd been in the headlines all her professional life. Even Murray, poor screwed-up, three-times-divorced New Age Murray, even he'd been news since he was a college football star, when she'd just turned ten. Sometimes it was tempting to tell a passing stranger like this a completely made-up story—be someone she wasn't just for a few hours.

"I'm from the Coast," she said quietly. That was the truth. Their meals arrived and Nina thought, for a moment, that the question had been forgotten. But after he'd taken a few bites of his steak and she had assuaged the worst of her hunger with her chicken marengo—which, she had to admit, wasn't bad—he raised his glass to her.

"To city girls," he said.

How had he known? Impulsively she raised her own glass. "To country boys," she returned, and could have bitten her tongue.

He nodded and drank, not breaking eye contact for a second. Something fused between them. With an effort Nina dragged her eyes away.

Dear God—this was ridiculous!

"Well!" She glanced wildly around the room. The drillers were just leaving. One waved and leered, but she pretended she hadn't seen him. A middle-aged couple nearby, obviously a little high on the anniversary bubbly, held hands across the table and exchanged big boozy smiles.

"Vancouver?"

She met his eyes, stricken. He was curious about her. And why not? But did she have to tell him the truth about herself? The whole truth? It was only natural for people to make assumptions, put her in a certain social slot when they found out who she was. Not who *she* was, she corrected herself firmly—her family. For once she wanted a man to take *her* seriously.

This man.

Nina O'Shea, free spirit. Her own person. Someone with an ordinary life all her own. Not someone who'd been created by a world with different expectations, a world on the other side of the mountains. But when she answered him finally, she answered truthfully.

"Yes, Vancouver." Nina picked at the rest of the food on her plate. She wasn't hungry anymore. She wished this good-looking cowboy had never sat down at her table and reminded her of things she longed to forget. She remembered how she'd pretended to be Mario Andretti in a Formula One race earlier this afternoon. Really, sometimes she could be so pathetic.

"I guess your car'll be ready sometime Monday," he said slowly. The state of her car was a safe topic; had he realized she didn't want to talk about herself?

"If Walter gets the part in, yes," she said. She wasn't entirely sure Walter would know what to do with it when it *did* come in. Then a crazy childish impulse seized her throat. "It's not my car."

"No?" Eyes on hers, curious, he waited for her to go on.

Nervously Nina continued, "No. I'm just driving it here. I'm, uh…" She looked up at him. *Surely he'd know she was lying through her teeth.* "I'm delivering it to some rich guy in Calgary. It's my job, delivering specialty cars to clients for my boss in Vancouver. He's an importer. I'm, uh, I'll be flying back." Shocked at how easily the lies spilled forth, Nina stopped abruptly.

"Nice job." He smiled, and Nina breathed again. *That's all there is to it?* Was it as easy as this to lie to a stranger? Was it because she knew she'd never see him again? Nina shivered. She'd never let her little fantasies spill over into the real world before. She'd never involved anyone else. Would the gods strike her dead now for the lie she'd told? The silly harmless lie…

After a brief hesitation, he said, "I'm staying in town tonight, too."

"You are?" Surprised, she let her eyes cling to his. She read interest there, *real* interest, and more— warmth, appreciation, good humor. He seemed solid, someone she could trust. How could she feel all that in less than an hour? He wasn't even flirting.

Was he?

He frowned and turned away to study a rather stern-looking moose head mounted on the wall by the bar. McCallum Blake had the most interesting eyes, somewhere between brown and green, she decided, kind of a soft hazel color. Warm, tawny…*sexy.* She was glad, suddenly, that she'd lied. She was glad she was spending this short time with him. As far as he was concerned, she was exactly the person he saw in front of him. And that was exactly who she *wanted* to be.

"Uh, fact is, I'm waiting on a part, too. For one of my tractors. It's coming in on the morning bus. I could go home but I thought I'd stay over and drive back tomorrow." He shrugged. "Just something different to do."

They'd be staying in the same hotel—maybe even next door to each other.

"That's quite a coincidence, isn't it?" she said softly.

He paused, his eyes never leaving hers. Then he nodded and grinned. "I suppose it is."

"So," she said, waving away Jeannie's offer of a second cup of coffee. She felt unaccountably happy. Free. Reckless. "I guess you can tell me what happens for excitement on a Glory Saturday night."

"Not much," he replied lazily. He leaned back and crossed his arms over his chest. His eyes narrowed as he considered. "Let's see…"

Why, he is *flirting with me,* Nina thought, feeling a flicker of dismay.

"There's the bowling alley. Charlie Mah's Café and Pins. They'll be going full tilt till midnight. Pretty regular crowd there." His sideways glance caught her gaze and they both smiled. "There's usually something happening at Maude's, but you don't want to know about Maude's."

"I do!" She reached out one hand involuntarily, but pulled back before she'd touched his arm.

"You don't," he assured her firmly. "Then there's always the show. Want to go to a movie?"

He was asking her out—on a date, more or less. Well, a *movie*...

"How many theaters in town?"

"One," he said with a pained look. "The Stardust."

"What else? If we don't go to a movie?"

"Well, there's the dump," he said seriously, but Nina could see the gleam in his eye.

"The dump?" She frowned.

"We could drive down to the dump and flash the headlights and scare a few skunks. Haven't done that since I left high school."

"You're kidding."

"I'm not."

"That settles it." She could barely restrain her smile. "Let's go to a movie." *You only live once, Nina O'Shea,* she told herself. Why *not* spend an evening with this man? He's handsome, considerate, good-humored. As for the fib—if you *hadn't* told it, he probably wouldn't be asking you out.

As for the other thing, the simple attraction she felt toward him, that was serendipity, too. She was almost thirty years old; she was nobody's fool. Nor was he. Probably lonely, just like she was. Going out with him would beat watching some dumb TV movie or trying to read a paperback novel to put herself to sleep. "What's on?"

"The Lion King," he said with a sheepish grin. "Rerun. Still want to go?"

SHE DID.

He bought her popcorn and red licorice twists, which she confessed she'd always loved. He indulged her when she said she wanted to sit in the exact middle of the mostly empty theater. There was an entwined teenage couple half a row over, who didn't see much of the movie from what she could tell, and a lot of smaller kids toward the front.

Cal seemed perfectly content. He smiled at the people who greeted him in the lobby and introduced her to the red-haired boy who took the tickets, saying he'd gone to school with his uncle. He placed his hand casually on her shoulder to escort her down the steeply pitched aisle to their seats. The theater was old-fashioned, with a big screen and heavy curtains and wide wooden seats upholstered in faded maroon velvet.

And he sat beside her and watched the Lion King find his kingdom. He even offered his big navy blue polka-dot handkerchief when she started to sniffle, but she refused, digging blindly through her handbag for a package of tissues. She always cried in movies, and for once she wasn't a bit embarrassed that someone had caught her doing it.

On the way back to the hotel—they walked—Nina was a little surprised when Cal took her hand in an easy gesture and tucked it under his elbow. But then she thought about it. Why not? It felt right. She moved closer to him, welcoming the warmth of his body next to hers, the faint masculine scent of his skin, his hair, the scarred leather jacket he wore…

This is crazy, she said to herself.

No, this is fun. This feels like the beginning of a holiday romance, except it isn't Mexico or Greece.

Can't you pretend for a little longer? Besides, come Monday afternoon, it's history. Even the goofy lie you told him won't mean anything.

The thought made her feel strangely sad, but by then they were at the hotel. "That was great, Cal. Thanks for suggesting the movie." She looked up at him. "It would have been pretty boring hanging around here all evening with nothing to do."

They walked up the stairs together and down the hall to her room. Cal hadn't said anything. What if he kissed her? What if he wanted to come in? What if...

At her door, Nina pulled her room key out of her pocket. He made no move to take it from her and open the door, thank goodness. She'd always thought that particular gesture the height of male silliness. But neither did he make any move to leave.

When she had the door ajar, she hesitated. "Well. Thanks for everything." Her mind raced. She didn't want to say goodbye.

"Look, Nina..." He'd been leaning, shoulder casually propped against the door frame. Now he straightened and touched her arm lightly. She froze.

"Y-yes?" Her heart was skittering about in a frantic unfamiliar way.

"I've been thinking..." He cleared his throat and Nina realized he was almost as nervous as she was. "If you've never been to this part of the country before, maybe you'd like to see a real ranch before you leave?"

"Wh-what are you saying?" Nina began to shake her head. At the same time... Perhaps she *wouldn't* have to say goodbye, not yet, anyway.

"Why don't you come with me tomorrow? Spend the day at the Rocking Bar S. I could bring you back after supper." His voice was rough, attractively rough.

Yes, she wanted to scream. *Yes, I'll do anything you want, cowboy. I'll be anything you want. Go anywhere you want me to go…*

"That's very kind of you," she managed to say. "You sure it wouldn't be any trouble?"

"Nope." He grinned suddenly, that trademark grin of his that had her grinning back like a crazy woman. "No trouble at all. We'll head up after the bus comes in with my part, say around ten."

"Great. I'd love to go. I'll be ready."

"Maybe I'll see you at breakfast."

"Maybe. Well, uh…good night."

He said nothing for a few seconds. A few endless agonizing seconds. If he bent toward her, if he made even the tiniest first move, Nina knew she'd fly into his arms. She ached to feel his arms around her. She ached to feel his body against hers, solid and warm.

"Good night, then." He touched his hat briefly. "Sleep well." He walked down the hall and Nina closed the door behind her, locking it.

Sleep well? She didn't think she'd sleep at all.

THEY'D DRIVEN eight or ten miles from Glory, through some of the most beautiful country Nina had ever seen, when Cal pulled off the gravel road onto a grass track. More a cow path, really.

He switched off the ignition and for a moment Nina wondered just what she'd gotten herself into. The fact was when it came right down to it, she didn't know this man from Adam. Now here they were, miles from nowhere, miles from any kind of help if she needed it, and he'd stopped the truck.

"What's going on?" Her voice didn't sound nearly as firm as she'd hoped.

He shot her a quick glance, then nodded toward the front of the pickup. "Nice view of the valley from here."

Nina felt like an idiot. "Oh!" It really was wonderful. To the left rose the panorama of the Alberta Rockies, grand and glorious. Straight ahead and to the right swept the sage-brown foothills and rolling prairie landscape. A few trees followed what she presumed were hidden rivers or creeks, but most of the vista in front of her was wild windswept rangeland.

He cleared his throat. He was frowning slightly and seemed a little ill at ease. "There *is* something else."

"Yes?"

He braced his left arm against the steering wheel, his right stretched out on the back of the bench seat between them. Nina was aware of his hand just inches from her shoulder. "I've got sort of a favor I'd like to ask you." He looked extremely uncomfortable all of a sudden.

"What kind of favor?"

"Well, it's tough to explain," he began. He gazed out the windshield for a few seconds, then continued, "I ranch up here with my brother, as I told you, and our foreman, Henry Hilton. There's a couple regular hired hands on the place and there's my aunt who keeps house for us.

"Damn, Nina," he said suddenly with a pained grimace that turned into a lopsided smile. "This is hard."

"What is?" She was completely confused.

"I'm getting to it. Well, uh, a while ago my brother and Henry and Lou—that's my aunt—started ragging me about, well, about women."

"Women?" Dear Lord, what in the world was he trying to say?

"Yeah. You see, they think I'm pretty well washed-up with women. At least, Jeremiah and Henry do. My aunt thinks I should get married, now that George Edward has spoken to her— Hell!" Cal ran a hand through his hair and swore under his breath. Then he jammed the pickup into gear and turned the key. "Forget it."

"Forget it? How can I forget it—I don't even know what you're talking about," Nina said. She grabbed the armrest as the pickup jolted back to the relative smoothness of the gravel road.

"Forget I mentioned it," he said tersely. "It was a dumb idea."

Suddenly a light went on in Nina's head. "You want to introduce me as a…a girlfriend," she guessed.

He gave her an embarrassed look. "Something like that."

"What did you have in mind?"

"Well, not girlfriend, exactly. I don't know what, maybe you can just pretend—"

"I'll do it," Nina said impulsively. "If you want me to."

"You will?" He seemed surprised.

What was wrong with that family of his? What was

wrong with *him?* Didn't he realize what an attractive man he was? Didn't he realize it wasn't going to be any hardship at all to act as though she liked him? She *did* like him. Very much.

Besides, from the sounds of it, this brother of his and the aunt and that Henry character deserved whatever Cal managed to send their way.

"Sure." She smiled and her heart lurched again at the look in his eyes as he smiled back. "Why not? After *The Lion King?* I owe you."

CHAPTER THREE

CAL NEVER TIRED of rounding that last bend. No ranch had the layout the Rocking Bar S had, set as it was on a gentle rise at the base of a long sweep of rolling range, the Horsethief Hills, that had its highest point in the rugged peaks behind. But then, this was home. Perhaps he had a bias.

"Oh!"

The woman beside him gasped audibly and Cal felt his chest swell. Pride, accomplishment, commitment— he felt it all when he was in this corner of the country he loved so much. And somehow the thought that this woman responded to it, too, without his even having to point anything out to her, the best features, well, it made him feel even prouder. He could be in the hole two years out of three, but his feeling for the land never changed. He loved every rock and dry creek bed and every golden eagle that soared above. He loved every spindly-legged calf he'd ever raised here, and when the calves got to weaning age and were big enough to hold their own, he didn't even mind the coyotes. He couldn't imagine lying in bed and not hearing their thin lonesome song each night. The coyotes, the magpies, the mountains and the big blue Alberta sky. Nope, McCallum Blake had never wanted to live anywhere else on earth.

But what would it look like to a city woman? A woman who was used to concrete sidewalks and who drove other people's fancy cars for a living? Cal sneaked a sideways glance at his passenger as he braked on the gentle descent that ended in a hard turn at the bottom. He bumped onto the wooden bridge that crossed the Horsethief, the creek that marked the boundary of the home ranch.

Did she see that the frame outbuildings could use a new coat of paint? Or did she see the shiny new Quonset hut he'd put up just last year to protect the tractors and binders and the rest of the expensive machinery it took to run a ranch? Did she see the long grass that had turned dull and summer brown, laced with daisies and dried goldenrod heads alongside the lane—or Jeremiah's three newborn foals frisking in the pasture by the barn? Did the big two-story, turn-of-the-century house look old-fashioned to her? Or did she admire the way it nestled into the land, comfortable and settled, its veranda wide and welcoming, as it had always appeared to him?

Did she take note of the Virginia creeper, now beginning to turn color, on the old wooden porch? Or did she just notice that the Rocking Bar S had too damn many scruffy-looking dogs, Cal thought sourly, slowing as half a dozen bounded out to greet the pickup, tails waving, tongues hanging.

"This is wonderful, Cal," she said. He glanced at her, suspicious of her enthusiasm, but all he saw were those blue eyes and a smile that made his bones ache, made him wish he'd started looking for a wife years ago. Why couldn't he meet a woman like this around here?

Sometimes life played damn poor tricks on a man. It wasn't fair.

Alert for signs of activity—and relieved not to see any—Cal brought the pickup to a halt at the side of the garage, thirty yards from the house. He squared his shoulders, took a deep breath and tightened his fingers on the wheel. Then he relaxed and turned to Nina. He forced a smile. She watched him, waiting, it seemed, for him to speak. He caught her gaze and was glad he'd mentally prepared himself.

"You scared of dogs?"

She laughed. "No," she said, then, mischievously, "Are you?"

He grinned and got out of the pickup, walking slowly around the back to open the door for her. He thought he saw the flutter of a curtain at the kitchen window. Lou would be back from church by now and would have heard them drive up.

He noticed that Nina had opened the door slightly. Had she started to get out, then realized he intended to open it for her? *Yeah, you're a real ladies' man, Blake.* He threw the door wide with a flourish and offered her a hand down.

"Might as well do this right," he muttered. She giggled softly. Truth was, he was having second thoughts. It was one thing to invite her out to the ranch for the day. But he should have kept his big mouth shut about the rest of it. He was asking for nothing but trouble, especially if Jeremiah and Henry got wind of what was going on. They'd never let him forget it. Somehow he'd have to trust her to pull this off.

Was he crazy? He'd only met this woman yesterday!

"Nice dogs." Nina bent to pat an ecstatic Tim on the head, then straightened. "Are these all yours? What do they do—herd cattle?"

"Henry's dogs," Cal said flatly. "Far as I'm concerned there's too many, but every time I tell Henry he ought to get a few of them fixed, he comes up with some new notion about breeding."

"Breeding?" Nina frowned slightly, a tiny change of expression that brought definition to her features.

"They're no particular breed," Cal said, "as you can see. But Henry's an optimist. He's got his own theories." He adjusted his hat for the angle of the sun, then reached down and scratched Tim's ears. "You'd have to ask him. They're fine cattle dogs, mostly. And he generally gets a good price for the pups. Just doesn't sell enough of them off, in my opinion."

They continued toward the house. To his surprise, Cal felt her slip her hand into his. She smiled up at him, squinting in the sun. "We're more than friends, remember?" And she nodded her head significantly in the direction of the barn. "Isn't that someone you want to impress?"

She was right. There was Henry, leaning on the corral fence holding a three-pound hammer, his hat pushed way back on his head. He stared at the two of them as though they'd just landed from another planet. Cal grinned. Damn, this was going to be more fun than he'd expected. He squeezed Nina's hand and pulled her close. "You're right," he whispered, aware of the warm scent of her hair. It was the color of honey, streaked with amber and sunshine, and she wore it loose and swirly on her shoulders. She carried that big-city canvas purse thing on her shoulder and had on tight jeans and a big yellow shirt that she'd tied in a loose knot at her waist. She looked good. She looked *damn* good.

They continued toward the house. Cal glanced down. He had to admit it: he liked holding Nina O'Shea's hand.

"Hey, Cal!"

He turned. Jeremiah had emerged from beneath the 'forty-seven Ford pickup he worked on practically every weekend. Wiping his hands on a greasy rag, he stared at the two of them.

"My brother, Jeremiah," he said to Nina. She nodded, eyes alight, and released his hand to slide her arm companionably along his waist. Just as naturally, he put his arm around her shoulders and they walked over to Jeremiah, who glanced at him, then at the woman beside him, then at him again. Cal sensed his amazement. Obviously he recognized Nina from their brief encounter on the Glory road the day before.

"Nina, I'd like you to meet my brother, Jeremiah," Cal said with a smile. "Jeremiah—you remember we met Nina on the way to town and offered her a ride? Miss Nina O'Shea."

"H-how d'you do, miss," Jeremiah said formally. Cal had rarely seen his brother short of words.

"How'd…" Jeremiah looked at him again, then swallowed hard, still wiping his hands on the rag. "I won't offer to shake your hand, miss." He glanced ruefully at his blackened hands. "I've just been greasing Old Moneypit here."

"I can see that," Nina said. She gave Jeremiah a friendly smile, and Cal tightened his hold on her shoulders.

He cleared his throat. "Nina and I had dinner together last night at the hotel and then…uh, then she decided she'd like to have a look at a real ranch while she was in the area." Why was he explaining?

"Uh-huh. Your car's in at Walt's?" Jeremiah was recovering quickly. He flashed her the kind of grin Cal knew women often went for—all white teeth and sexy blue eyes. Cal was pleased to feel Nina step even closer to him.

"Yes. It'll be ready tomorrow." She peeked up at Cal, then turned to Jeremiah again. "But I'm going to hate to leave."

The soft sentence spoke volumes, and Cal caught a glint of appreciation in his brother's eyes. *Whoa. Fast work, you old son of a gun*—he could just about hear Jeremiah's thoughts.

"Well, uh—" Cal nodded briefly to his brother "—I guess we'd better head on up to the house, say hello to Lou."

"Sure," Jeremiah said, then, as though suddenly remembering his manners, he nodded politely. "Miss O'Shea."

When they reached the wooden sidewalk that led to the house, Cal risked a glance back. Henry and Jeremiah were still staring. Even if nothing else went right today, the last ten minutes had made the whole foolish plan worthwhile.

CAL DIDN'T THINK he'd ever seen his aunt put the midday meal on the table faster. That was after he'd introduced her to Nina and watched with satisfaction as her eyes grew rounder and her smile grew broader.

Nina played her part beautifully, all shy and modest and sticking close to him.

He and Nina had left Glory later than they'd expected—the bus had come in late—so it was nearly noon by the time they arrived at the Rocking Bar S. Midday was a hot meal in Lou's world, even on a Sunday.

Out came a crisply pressed tablecloth that Cal had never seen before. On it went the best plates, the real glasses—no plastic today—and the ornate china milk jug that had spent most of its life on a top shelf. Today it was filled and placed beside a pair of salt and pepper shakers from Lou's prized collection: plump ceramic tomatoes, salt with a sprightly hat and pepper with a mustache and cane.

As she bustled around the kitchen, Lou kept up a steady stream of observations and proud comments on the ranch, her nephews, the generally good summer weather in the Horsethief Hills and the fact that the winters brought regular chinooks hereabouts, just when a body was getting tired of the cold—not that it ever got *that* cold, mind you!—the richness of the soil in the valley and, in particular, the reliability and profusion of her kitchen garden. She sounded as if she thought Nina was applying for a position as general manager of the household.

Nina's offer to help set the table was refused.

"You just sit there, young lady, and keep McCallum company." She beamed. "I'm used to this. McCallum? You can go ahead and ring for the other two."

"Ring?" Nina looked at him.

"You go on out with him, Nina, dear. He'll show

you how we call the boys to dinner." Lou smiled and
added a jar of her famous pickled peppers to the
bounty of potato salad, green salad, oven-baked ham,
dilled beans, boiled beans, mustard pickle, coleslaw,
home-fried potatoes and a stack of homemade bread
with butter.

Cal was starting to feel bad. He'd had no idea just
how much his aunt had dreamed of his catching a wife.

Nina followed him out onto the porch.

"Here." He gestured toward the cowbell hanging
from a post just outside the door. "You ring it."

"Really?" Her eyes were shining. "Just hang on to
this?" She grabbed the oiled leather strap that was
attached to the top of the bell.

"Yeah." Cal grinned. "Give 'er hell." He watched
Nina set her feet carefully for balance, then frown and
give a tremendous yank on the strap. The bell jangled,
two of the dogs on the porch sat up and howled, and
three others dashed off the porch and into the caragana
hedge, tails between their legs, ki-yipping the whole
way.

Cal laughed. He couldn't help himself. Nina looked
up in surprise, coloring slightly. He thought the faint
blush suited her; in fact, he didn't think he'd ever seen
such a fine-looking woman in his entire life. As he
stepped toward her, smiling, she raised one eyebrow.
"Too loud?"

Cal stopped himself just in time. *What am I—crazy?*
He'd been about to pull her into his arms. Then what?
Kiss her? The move would have fit in with their plan,
but that wasn't the reason he'd been tempted to put
his arms around her.

"No." He took a deep breath and stared out toward

the barn. *Get a hold of yourself, Blake.* He saw Henry and Jeremiah walking toward the house together, heads down. Cal had a pretty good idea what they were discussing. "They're on their way. They must have heard you, all right."

Feeling back in control, he allowed himself to glance down at her. She was grinning, her eyes bright. Damn, she was pleased with herself. Again Cal felt the urge to pull her into his arms. Instead, he simply put one hand on her shoulder and turned to go back into the house.

Lou was waiting. Cal didn't think his aunt had stopped smiling since the moment he'd walked in and introduced Nina as a friend. He hadn't exactly mentioned that she was just passing through. He knew his aunt well enough to realize how she'd chosen to interpret the word "friend." He was thankful now that he'd asked Nina to play a part in this charade; it would have been downright embarrassing if she hadn't been aware of what was going on.

"So that's how they call the staff to meals," Nina said as they entered the kitchen.

"We call them hands," Cal explained. "Or boys, or cowboys. I don't believe anybody's ever referred to any of the crew as staff, do you, Lou?"

"Never have." Exactly what they called the ranch hands on the Rocking Bar S was clearly not on her mind. "What have you got planned to show Nina this afternoon, McCallum? You'll stay to supper, won't you, dear?" Lou seemed concerned suddenly, as though Nina might consider doing otherwise.

"We-ell…" Nina shrugged and moved a little closer to Cal. He was pretty sure Lou noticed, and approved. "I wouldn't want to put you to any trouble, Mrs. Twist."

"Please call me Louisa, dear," Cal's aunt said. "Or plain Lou. Everybody else does. And don't think for a moment it'd be any trouble— Now, Jeremiah! Don't you dare come in here with that greasy shirt!"

Jeremiah and Henry had washed at the sink on the back porch. Jeremiah's face was still wet, and Henry's hair was suspiciously damp and flattened. No hat. Cal couldn't believe his eyes. The old codger had dug up a comb somewhere. He looked positively respectable. Jeremiah started to unbutton his shirt, then seemed to remember that they had a guest and awkwardly backed out onto the porch. Henry held his ground.

"Henry? I'd like you to meet Nina O'Shea," Cal drawled. "She's, uh, a friend of mine." No way he was explaining himself to Henry J. Hilton.

"Pleased to meet you, miss," Henry said with a nod. His faded blue eyes were sharp with interest. Cal put one hand casually on the small of Nina's back. Henry noted the tiny intimate gesture; Cal had no doubt about that.

"Well, let's all sit down, shall we?" Lou announced grandly. "No sense lettin' everything get cold."

Henry eyed the tablecloth as though he was afraid it would jump up and bite him. Neither he nor Jeremiah said much. Silence during meals was an old-fashioned cookhouse tradition that they didn't follow at the Rocking Bar S, since it was usually just him and his brother and Henry. Cal knew the reversion to the outdated male habit was a sign of just how rattled

Henry and Jeremiah were at his—Cal's—apparent conquest of such an attractive and desirable woman.

If the joke had stopped right here, Cal would've been satisfied. But there was no way to stop things now....

"So, I understand you and McCallum met just recently?" Lou said, passing Henry the fried potatoes.

"Yes," Nina said, with a shy look at Cal that nearly made him burst out laughing. "I had a breakdown on the road south of Glory, and Cal and Jeremiah here very kindly stopped and offered me a ride."

"Jeremiah?" Lou sounded surprised.

It was Jeremiah's turn to nearly choke on his coleslaw. "Yeah, whatever happened to your car?" he asked, recovering quickly. Lou looked severely at him, as though annoyed to find that he'd met Cal's "friend" before she had and hadn't bothered to mention it.

"It's in the garage," Nina replied simply.

"Walt's?" Henry asked, fork poised halfway to his mouth.

"Yes. He's ordered a part for it," Nina said. She seemed uncomfortable talking about the car and Cal figured he knew why.

"It's not really Nina's car," he explained, helping himself to the plate of ham. "She's just delivering it to some rich guy in Calgary."

"Hey, you drive fancy cars like that for a living?" Jeremiah whistled faintly. "Nice job." He gave her a big grin that made Cal want to kick him under the table. Of course, anything to do with machines interested Jeremiah. He'd no doubt think an actual job driving fancy imported cars was a dream come true.

"Y-yes. That and other things," Nina said. Her cheeks were pink. She seemed embarrassed.

Why? Cal paused for a moment and studied her. He watched as Lou urged Nina to try her famous pickled peppers, telling her she'd gotten the recipe from her hairdresser, a Turkish guy, who'd got it from his sister-in-law.

"Other things?" he asked casually.

"Oh, heavens!" Nina laughed. Self-consciously, Cal thought. "I've had all kinds of jobs. After I tell my boss I delivered the car three days late, I'll probably get fired from this one, too."

Too? Cal gave her a sharp glance. How many jobs had she had? There was an edge of desperation to her reply that bothered Cal. All of a sudden he wanted to protect her, to shield her from the kind of disappointment and letdown her remark implied.

But Nina's comment about the jobs she'd had was just the kind of personal remark no one wanted to follow up on, although Cal knew every single person at the table was dying to hear what else Miss Nina O'Shea had done for a living. Nina must have sensed their interest, for after a few seconds of awkward silence, she spoke. "I've delivered mail at Christmas and I've worked in a fish market and I've sold sidewalk portraits Saturday mornings at the park. I even worked in a bakery one time!"

"I saw a fella draw those pictures at the Pincher Creek Stampede once," Henry said. He gave Nina a whiskery grin, obviously impressed. "He was pretty good."

"I'm pretty good, too," Nina said with a small laugh. She seemed anxious. There was something wrong here, but he couldn't put his finger on it. Maybe they were being too nosy. Maybe she was embarrassed telling them about all the different kinds of jobs she'd had. Not one sounded like it had paid too well or lasted too long. But, heck, most people had done a lot of different things in their lives. And how old was she, anyway—twenty-three, twenty-four? She had her whole life in front of her.

"How's Old Moneypit coming along, Jeremiah?" Cal deliberately changed the subject. He decided he didn't want anyone asking her any more questions. She was his guest; he'd landed her in this nest of busybodies. If she didn't care to talk about her past, that was good enough for him, and it was damn well good enough for anybody else at this table. "I see you're working on it again."

Jeremiah and Henry started discussing Jeremiah's ongoing restoration of the ancient Ford pickup—Henry had his own ideas of what Jeremiah should be doing with it—and soon they were involved in one of their amiable wrangles. Nina and Lou began some womantalk, about knitting patterns it sounded like, and Nina made some comment about the tablecloth. Lou seemed only too happy to give her the entire history of where she'd gotten it and when, and how much she'd paid for it.

Just what *was* he going to do with her for the afternoon? Cal pushed back his chair and stretched out his legs. The talk around the table washed over him in a warm pleasant haze. All he saw was the blond woman across from him, talking animatedly to his aunt with the occasional shy glance in his direction. Was she putting it on? He couldn't tell anymore. Whether she was or whether she wasn't, he liked it. Cal took a deep shaky breath.

One thing he did know was that he wanted to have her to himself for the afternoon. He didn't want to leave her either in Lou's well-meaning maternal clutches or fending off the charms of a lady-killer like his brother. Henry would go back to fixing the corral fence for the afternoon. Henry had plenty to think about for one day.

"You ride, Nina?"

He could take her up in the hills for the afternoon. There was a piece of fence he needed to check on, anyway.

"Yes." She instantly gave him her attention and it felt real. Not like playacting. He had the idea that she really would like nothing more than to go riding with him.

"How about I show you around the ranch a little, then we'll take out some horses?" Cal saw Henry wink broadly at Jeremiah.

"Great idea," Nina said. "I'd love to have a look around. I'll just help your aunt with the dishes and—"

"You'll do no such thing!" Lou was on her feet with a handful of dishes to take to the sink. "You go on with McCallum. Off with you. Go on!" She flapped her apron at them, the way she did when the chickens got too near her strawberry beds.

But Nina insisted, and Cal left her to go down to the corral and catch a couple of horses. Jeremiah offered to help.

"Jeez, Cal, how'd you manage that?" Jeremiah started to saddle Babe, the brown mare while Cal gave Blackjack, his paint gelding, a quick once-over.

"Manage what?"

"You know what I'm talking about, man!" Jeremiah grinned at him over the mare's back. "How'd you move so fast on a hot dame like that?"

"Nina?"

"Well, he-ell." Jeremiah sounded exasperated. "Yes, Nina."

"Oh, I don't know, Jeremiah," Cal drawled. He gave his brother a mild look. "Just experience, I guess. Turns out I'm not quite as rusty as you and Henry had me figured."

Jeremiah snorted, but he didn't say anything for a few moments. "Well, some guys have all the luck, that's the only thing I can say. Too bad she's leaving Monday, huh?"

"Yeah," Cal said. He frowned and studied Blackjack's near foreleg, then bent to run his hand along the tendon. The gelding had been limping a few weeks back, but he seemed fine now. "Too bad," he repeated, straightening.

He meant it.

CHAPTER FOUR

AT THE TOP of the rise, Cal turned. Nina was a hundred yards behind him. She waved as she approached at a brisk trot, then guided the mare across the hill, instead of joining him at the summit. He watched her for a few more minutes.

What could be better? An afternoon spent riding—just about his all-time favorite activity—showing a beautiful woman the ranch he'd built up over the past fifteen years, land he knew better than anyone alive. A packed lunch rolled up in a tartan blanket and tied behind his saddle—Lou's idea of a snack. Perfect northern-range fall weather... What more could a man ask?

Nina appeared to be a fine rider, which puzzled Cal a little considering her background. Of course, you could learn to ride without living in the country, he knew that. But she was more than okay—he'd seen her coax the mare over a couple of windfalls just for the fun of it. Still... Cal shrugged. He didn't care how she'd learned to ride; he didn't care about any of her background. He was just glad she was here right now sharing this glorious Indian-summer day with him.

He liked her. And damned if he didn't get the feeling she liked him, too. He recalled Jeremiah's words about her leaving the next day and frowned.

He touched his heels lightly to Blackjack's side and reined the gelding across the hill, toward Nina. Nothing wrong with that front leg now, Cal thought, still frowning, his attention focused on the gelding's stride. But he wouldn't push him. They'd take it easy riding toward the section of fence he wanted to look at, then stop for a break and let the horses browse.

Nina held up one hand as he approached. "Over there," she whispered, shading her eyes. "What's that?"

Cal looked in the direction she pointed. "Antelope." Five—or was it six?—pronghorn antelope grazed in the distance, a good half mile away. The leader kept his head up, ever vigilant.

"*Real* antelope?"

Cal chuckled softly. "Yeah. Real antelope." He watched Nina's face as she studied the animals. Curiosity, excitement, an innocence, almost, that he found unsettling. She seemed to have no reservations about showing him, a near stranger, her vulnerable side. None at all. Lots of people would have laughed, made some smart remark, maybe would have shouted just to see the antelope dash off over the nearest hill.

Nina seemed awestruck, and Cal knew exactly what she was feeling; it didn't matter how many times he came across a group of antelope—or white-tailed deer or a family of coyotes or prairie chickens, for that matter—he got that same shivery feeling. It was part of who he was, a part he knew would never change.

"Come on," he said, nudging the gelding gently with his heels. "Let's see how close we can get."

Nina smiled, her eyes wide. "You mean they'll let us get closer?"

"Maybe. Sometimes they don't spook as easily if you're on a horse." He smiled at her. "Has to do with the four legs, I guess. They don't seem to take the same notice."

But it didn't help much. They'd quartered the distance to the antelope when something—them? the horses? some unknown scent on the wind?—caused the animals to bound away. Four or five seconds and they had disappeared, absorbed into the brown of the landscape, blotted into the faint texture of the distant hills.

"Too bad." Cal leaned forward, gazing after them.

He heard Nina sigh, a delicious sound that sent another kind of shiver down his spine. Then she let her breath out, bit by bit, as though she'd held it for a long time.

"Yes," she said softly. "Too bad."

Their eyes met. Cal put his heels into Blackjack's side again. He didn't look back, but he knew Nina wasn't far behind him. The short ride to the piece of fence he wanted to check and the twenty minutes it took him to ride that fence and dismount a few times, testing posts and wires, gave him a chance to think.

Hold up, Blake. Hold up. Things are moving a little too fast here. She's your guest for the afternoon— that's all. Just because she's the sort of woman you always dreamed would show up in Glory one day doesn't mean it's happened. She's from the other side of the mountains and she's returning to the other side of the mountains. Tomorrow.

He felt a lot better when he got back on the gelding. He even managed what he hoped came across a plain old friendly smile. "Feel like taking a break soon?

Lou wouldn't want that food she packed to go to waste.''

''Here?''

Cal surveyed the bare windswept range and shook his head. ''There's a decent spring not too far, maybe half a mile....''

''Sounds good.''

Ten minutes later they pulled up. The spring was one of Cal's regular stops when he rode this particular section of range. Somebody had once rigged up a galvanized pipe connecting to the source of water in the hillside and had dug out a shallow rock-lined pool below. A thin stream of water spilled steadily into the pool, icy cold and clear, summer and winter. The rocks below, roughly jammed together, swam with sinuous green underwater growth. Cal had often thought that one day he'd like to come up and dig out the spring and reset the rocks. No reason; just something he'd like to do.

The access was difficult, so they left the horses below. Blackjack was too well trained to stray, and Cal knew the mare would stay with the gelding. The narrow approach to the spring meant cattle avoided it, which kept the water clean and the area around the pool spongy and verdant, not kicked up into knee-deep mud and ruts.

Cal brought Nina a cup of water—her second—in the battered tin mug that hung from a nail on a nearby willow. The fact that she hadn't turned up her city-bred nose at the source of water pleased him. He'd expected she'd stick to the jug of milky tea Lou had sent along.

''Sandwich?'' Cal dug through the sack of food.

He'd settled down a few feet from Nina, who perched on a tiny knoll overlooking the valley, her knees drawn up.

"Oh, I couldn't!" Nina groaned and sent him a helpless smile. "I'm still stuffed from that fabulous lunch your aunt made."

"Me, too." Cal rewrapped the sandwiches carefully and pulled out a box of Lou's molasses cookies. "Want one?"

"Maybe an apple." Nina reached for the apple he handed her, and for a few companionable moments they both stared out over the valley, silently munching.

Cal couldn't figure out exactly what he felt. On the one hand, he felt amazingly at ease with Nina, although he had to keep reminding himself that he barely knew her. On the other hand, he'd never been more painfully, more exquisitely aware of a woman in his life: every breath she took, every glint of sun on her wind-tossed hair, the snap of the apple's skin as she bit into it, the way she tucked her feet under her, knees to one side. Dainty, ladylike, precise. Yet at the same time, he had the feeling that if he'd suggested they dig out the spring that very afternoon, she'd roll up her pant legs and her sleeves and wade in right beside him, no questions asked.

Cal stretched out and leaned back on one elbow, tipping his hat against the long afternoon rays of the sun. "You're a good rider, Nina," he said, wanting to talk about something neutral.

"I love horses," she said simply. "I've always loved riding."

Cal plucked a stem of grass and chewed the end

thoughtfully. "Wouldn't think you'd get much chance to ride, living in the city."

"Oh, I loved to spend summers at the—" She stopped abruptly and colored, and when she turned to him, her eyes were overbright, the way they'd been at lunch, her laugh a little forced.

Cal frowned. What had made her uneasy all of a sudden? Him?

"Summer camp." She smiled but avoided his eyes. "I won a trip to summer camp one year and they had horses there. And…and I had a friend who lived on a farm. I slept over at her house on the weekends and we'd muck out stalls. And ride." She tossed her hair, pulled it back into a ponytail, then let it loose again.

"How'd you win the trip?" Cal asked lazily. Was she nervous? Maybe it was all his imagination, anyway; he was altogether too fine-tuned to this woman.

"Uh, I wrote an essay on why our family always ate Superior bacon—"

"You're kidding me."

"No." She laughed and shook her head. Cal couldn't take his eyes off her. "I don't know what kind of bacon we ate. Actually we didn't eat bacon all that often." She gazed off into the distance, her expression dreamy, her face flushed. "But when I saw the contest in the paper, I decided to enter. And I won!" Her eyes shone as they met his and her cheeks were very pink. It was as though she'd just heard she'd won, right now.

Cal laughed. "That's the craziest thing I ever heard."

"It is, isn't it?" Nina dug at a half-buried pebble beside her foot, her hair hanging to hide her face from him. He studied her, smiling, knowing she couldn't see him.

"You're lucky you had a friend who lived on a farm," he continued finally, just to make conversation. He didn't know what to say. What he wanted, with a suddenness and an urgency that scared him, was to reach over and pull her into his arms and tell her she could ride every one of his horses and every one of Jeremiah's horses as much as she wanted. Anytime, she didn't even need to ask. Something about this woman brought out all the tender and protective feelings he'd ever had. Feelings he associated with the ranch and his widowed aunt Lou and—much as he hated to admit—with every rough-and-tumble mongrel litter Henry's bitches produced from under sheds and out of mangers at regular intervals.

"Yes." Nina leaned forward, clasping both knees. "I grew up in a small town near Vancouver. Ladner's Landing. On the river. My father was a fisherman. He had his own boat. One day he went out and he never came back. We never saw him again. He was lost at sea somewhere." She talked fast and her voice trembled. Cal's eyes were steady on her.

"Good thing my brothers weren't with him or we would have lost them, too." She looked off into the distance for a few seconds, then went on, "My mother couldn't handle it. She starting drinking a lot—none of us blamed her. She died just over a year later."

"How old were you?"

Nina hesitated. "When my dad died?" She ran her fingers through her hair again. She was breathing quickly.

"Yeah."

JUDITH BOWEN   63

"I was, uh, let's see, I guess I was fourteen when my dad died. Luckily he had some kind of pension from the fishermen's union or something. And insurance on the boat. The bank took most of that, but we were okay for a couple of years. I finished school and so did my brothers and sisters."

"Sisters? How many in your family?" After her earlier reluctance to speak, Cal was finding this sudden flood of information disconcerting. Poor kid, he'd had no idea she'd grown up an orphan.

"Two. Younger than me. Both nurses." Nina nodded, then said, "I have two brothers. Older. They more or less raised us. We did okay." She smiled. "We never had much money, but we had a lot of fun. It wasn't so bad."

"Doesn't sound bad," Cal said quietly. The brightness in her eyes told him something else. He couldn't quite understand the odd exhilaration she exhibited as she told what was basically a pretty sad story. Somehow he could see the kid she'd been: long blond pigtails, skinny hand-me-down T-shirts, patched jeans. He had no intention of digging further. In a way, he was sorry she'd told him as much as she had. It was none of his business. He couldn't let himself care; after today he'd never see her again. He leaned back and drew his hat over his eyes, as though he was planning to catch forty winks.

"Hey. Don't go to sleep."

He tipped up the brim. "I'm not."

"Your turn. Tell me about yourself. Who's Mc-Callum Blake, anyway?"

"Nothing to tell."

"Come on!" He felt her hand touch his arm lightly

and he pushed his hat back and met her eyes. "You're an attractive man," she continued. "Why's your family so determined to get you married off?"

"Oh, hell. *That* business." Cal felt uncomfortable. He wished she hadn't brought the subject up.

"Well?"

Cal shrugged. He wasn't all that sure himself why his family was so damn interested in his love life. "They think it's high time, I guess. That's all."

"How old are you?"

"Thirty-five."

She smiled. "So, why aren't you? Married, I mean. You must be a pretty good catch around here. Your own ranch and everything."

Cal frowned. "You think so? That's what it takes? A couple sections of good grass and water and some first-class beef? That's what a woman considers a good prospect?"

Nina laughed—a delightful sound that gave him shivers and warmed him up from the inside out.

"Let's just say it doesn't hurt."

"Maybe." Cal pulled his hat down and stretched, uncrossing his ankles. "Who knows?" He could change the subject, at least. "You about ready to head back?"

No such luck.

"So. What *is* the problem, Cal? No eligible ladies around Glory?"

"Could be." He gave her a level look. "You just never leave off, do you, Miss O'Shea?"

She laughed again and reached for a stem of grass. "No, I don't." She popped the stem in her mouth and grinned. "So you'd better 'fess up, cowboy."

He was silent for a moment or so. "Okay. You met my brother and Henry, right?"

"Uh-huh."

"Well, Jeremiah's a prime lady-killer, always has been, and believe it or not, old Henry's had a pretty good run in that department, too."

"Uh-huh," Nina said, nodding. "I can see that."

He looked at her hard. "You can?"

"Of course. Jeremiah's no mystery—he's just the type a lot of women go for. Not me, necessarily," she added hastily, "but a lot would. And Henry...well, Henry's got a gleam in his eye, all right. A woman can tell."

Cal laughed out loud. By God, if Nina O'Shea didn't have that old devil figured, and she'd only just met him. "Anyway. They don't have much appreciation for my methods, that's all. They're always trying to set me up. So the subject of marriage came up again lately—it's come up before—because now Lou's decided she might get married herself. One of my neighbors has asked her, and she figures I ought to find a wife before she leaves and— Oh hell, I told you it's way too complicated."

"So they've been giving you a hard time. Jeremiah and Henry."

"Yeah. That's about it." He slid a grin toward her. "That's why I thought I'd fix their clocks today showing up with you."

"I see. And you're just not interested in marriage, is that it?"

"I *would* be interested, definitely. No question. If the right woman came along." Cal paused, surprised at the truth of what he'd just said. "But I haven't had the time or inclination lately to pursue it. If I did—'' he shot her a sly look ''—I can tell you it wouldn't be because some woman considered me and my cows a paying proposition.''

For a few long seconds, they shared the humor of the situation they'd found themselves in, both smiling. Time to head back to the ranch. He sat up, then got to his feet and offered Nina his hand.

She stood easily, still smiling at him. Cal didn't want to let go of her hand. What he wanted—what he'd do on a perfect day in a perfect world—was to take her up to the spring and lie down with her in the sweet green moss. He wanted to kiss her and touch her, every part of her. He wanted to feel her sink into the green under the weight of his body. He wanted to imprint himself on her just as she marked the soft earth beneath them both. He wanted to kiss her and hold her and never let her go.

Crazy man. He cast a quick eye to the sun. ''It's getting late,'' he said gruffly. ''We'd better head back.''

Cal was sorry the afternoon had been so short. He knew he'd never see Nina O'Shea again. He knew, too, that he'd carry the memory of this afternoon for a long time. If her car hadn't broken down on the road to Glory…

But that kind of thing happened all the time. People's lives could change, just like that.

He felt enormous pride as they rode slowly back. He pointed out a few landmarks, marveling again, as he always did, at what made the Rocking Bar S such a great ranch. Water and grass. A rancher's prime assets were water and grass, and plenty of it, to support

the cows and calves and to give the steers a good start
before sending them to the feedlots. And these days,
with more consumers demanding lean grass-fed beef,
there was a growing new market for him right here,
finishing his own beef.

Yes, things were beginning to happen for him,
which was partly why he'd been so busy the past couple of years. The future was looking brighter and
brighter. He'd worked damn hard and he deserved
some payback. Maybe Jeremiah and Lou and Henry
were right; maybe it *was* time he found himself a wife
and started raising a family.

Cal waved briefly to Henry, still working on one of
the corral fences, as they came up to the ranch yard
at a trot. Henry waved back. Jeremiah was nowhere in
sight, and Cal noticed that the old truck he was re-
storing had been pushed back into its shed. Jeremiah
often left for town early on a Sunday evening—Cal
had an idea he was seeing someone in Glory. Perhaps
he'd already gone.

Nina insisted on helping him take care of the horses.
Cal let her brush down the mare while he went to get
a bucket of oats. After supper, he'd turn Blackjack and
the mare back into the pasture.

When he came back with the grain, he was surprised
to see Nina on tiptoe peering over the far side of the
stall with an impish grin on her face. Both horses
whuffed and snorted gently as he poured the grain into
their feed boxes.

"Psst!" she whispered, beckoning to him. "Come
here."

Cal put down the feed bucket and walked over to
the stall partition. He glanced into the dark cavern of

the barn. Nothing of particular interest that he could see.

She reached for his hand and stepped close to him, forcing him to look down at her. She placed his hand on her waist, then she slid both her arms around his.

Cal smiled a little hesitantly. "What's going on?"

"Shh. Put your arms around me."

He did. It was so natural, so good.... He held her a little closer, liking the way she felt, the slim length of her body against his. He could feel her breasts small and pliant against his chest, and the feeling made him draw in his breath. *What the hell...?*

"Kiss me, cowboy," she whispered. Her eyes danced, but there was a serious note in her voice. Cal felt like he'd put his bare hand into a hornets' nest. Maybe both hands.

"You mean it?" He frowned slightly, and at the same time tightened his arms around her. She didn't resist, not even the tiniest bit.

"Uh-huh." She nodded and lifted her face to his. "I mean it," she whispered.

Her lips were soft and firm both at once, and sweet, and he didn't think he ever wanted to stop doing what he was doing right now. Kissing her, tasting her, touching her. Drawing her scent and her breath into his body. She was soft, womanly, mysterious—all the things that made his blood stir. He kissed her for a very long time.

Finally he felt her pull back, just a little, and he dragged his mouth from hers. "Mmm," she said, her eyes dark and strangely solemn. The warmth of their breath held together, fused. They stood like that for four or five very long seconds, him holding her close, their mouths bare inches apart, eyes locked. Frozen.

"What was that all about?" he managed to ask. His voice sounded ragged. *He wanted to kiss her again.*

"Your plan," she said simply with a nod toward the barn. "Jeremiah's in there."

Her answer delivered the gut kick he needed.

"Think he saw?" Cal whispered as soon as he trusted himself to speak. Gradually he loosened his hold on her, reluctant to let go, even knowing—as he did now—why she'd asked him to kiss her.

She giggled slightly. "I think so."

"Good." He managed a smile, too, and sternly ordered his thundering heart to slow, his pulse to calm. At last he released her and stepped back.

He took a deep shaky breath, then checked on the horses one last time. *You damn fool,* he told himself. *You two-bit, gold-plated, goddamn fool.*

CHAPTER FIVE

SHE'D LIED. And one lie had led to another. Well, maybe "lie" was a harsh word; she'd told a story, become caught up in it. And once she'd started, she couldn't stop. She'd made up that whole thing, reinvented her childhood…her entire life.

But if she hadn't realized she was about to tell Cal that she'd learned to ride at the Nicola Valley ranch, where she'd spent most of her childhood summers, would she have impulsively jumped in with all that stuff about Superior bacon and summer camp and the rest of it? She'd never know. No matter how silly she felt about blurting out that fanciful story, it couldn't be undone now.

The Coquihalla Cattle Company held special memories. She'd had her own horse, Bertie, which she'd ridden during the happy summer weeks she'd spent there each year, her tiny bedroom tucked under the eaves of the ranch manager's house. Ned and Mrs. Bolton. What was Mrs. B's first name? Nina didn't think she'd ever been told.

Her father, who was part-owner of the ranch, used to join her for a week or two during the course of her five-or six-week stay with the Boltons. Occasionally, her half brother accompanied him. Sometimes that was fun—they'd be a happy family of three, her father al-

ways smiling and playing practical jokes. Sometimes—more often—he and Murray quarreled. She'd
hated that.

Murray had only shown up a few summers, when
she was still fairly young, nine or ten, and he was in
college studying law—he was ten years older—which
he'd finally quit. Nina had looked up to her brother,
saw him as sophisticated and privileged and living
such an exciting life away from home. But even then
she'd known that Murray had been a big disappointment to her parents.

Her mother never came to the ranch. Or if she did,
she'd be on her way to somewhere else. A big court
case, maybe, or a business meeting with a client in
Kamloops.

Meredith O'Shea, defender of murderers and thieves
and senior partner in O'Shea, Butler and Hasic, didn't
care for horses. Oh, she loved to watch Nina ride, she
said—and Nina had had a wonderful teacher in Ned
Bolton—but she didn't care for horses with their hot-
blasting velvety noses and their hard, unpredictable
feet. Nor, she said, did she like their manes, all bristly
and thick. They reminded her of boot brushes. Nina
always laughed. She loved it when her mother said
things like that. Boot brushes!

Big rough noisy Jake O'Sullivan—ex-logger, ex-
bush pilot, entrepreneur, maverick politician, a man
who loved a fight, physical or otherwise—and her im-
peccably dressed beautiful mother. No one who saw
the two of them together could doubt that they were
hopelessly mismatched in every way but one: they
loved each other madly.

When they were apart—and that was often—there

were phone calls daily. Perhaps Meredith confided misgivings, if she had any, about her new cases; Nina often wondered if her mother was ever less than confident about anything. Jake probably raged about some injustice he'd discovered, told coarse jokes in the confidential way that made her mother giggle and complained about his only son. Not the man's man his father was, in Jake's view. The law degree Murray had abandoned midstream was never discussed.

Why? Because Murray's intransigence had wounded their father greatly. He had thwarted his father's wishes and abused his generosity, and Nina didn't think Jake O'Sullivan would ever forgive him.

Nina realized now, as an adult, that her parents were much larger than life, and it was probably only their frequent separations that kept the marriage intact. She loved them both, but she did not enjoy the inevitable tension—four strong-minded people pulling in four different directions—when the family was together. They were together less and less often.

Nina frowned as she stared out the passenger window of Cal's pickup as he drove her back to her hotel. Come to think of it, how many months had it been since she'd seen her brother? Poor mixed-up Murray. A guy who'd been married three times and earned his living leading relationship workshops at expensive Gulf Islands retreats.

Nina considered the contrast with Cal's family. Sure, they appeared to have their noses stuck firmly in Cal's personal life on this marriage question. But they seemed happy enough. And they all seemed to like and respect one another.

Jeremiah had given them both a broad wink—a reference, she guessed, to what he'd witnessed in the barn—before hurrying off just after supper. He'd offered to drive her back, and Nina had been pleased at Cal's swift refusal. It made her think she wasn't just a guest he was obliged to return to her hotel later that evening. It had made her think he wanted to spend the extra time with her.

As she did with him. Nina allowed her thoughts to drift briefly to those few moments in the barn. What had begun as a joke had ended as anything but. She still felt the shape and taste of his mouth—fresh, exciting—the solid perfect feel of his arms around her, the warm barn scents of horses and hay, the heat of his breath on her skin…

Nina shut her eyes and tried to block out every single solitary sensation and recollection. There was no point, no point whatsoever, in dwelling on that particular incident. *No point in dreaming….*

"What's that?" She realized he had spoken to her. He was smiling, but he seemed distracted, too. He'd had a quick shower and changed, and he looked very male and very handsome in a pale blue chambray shirt and black jeans. Plain dusty boots, the hat—still definitely the cowboy.

"That big sigh." He frowned. "Worried about what your boss is going to say when you get back?"

"My boss?" Nina thought wildly, then remembered the business about the Porsche. How she regretted everything; all her lies, yesterday and today. She kept telling herself that it didn't really matter, that they barely knew each other, that after he dropped her at the hotel, she'd never see him again. But the whole thing was so darn childish. Orphaned middle daughter of a commercial fisherman! Drunken mother, drowned father, endless dead-end jobs. It was one thing to pretend to be Mario Andretti behind the wheel of her Porsche. That might be silly, but at least no one had to know. It was quite another to actually involve someone else in one of her foolish fantasies. Unfortunately she was stuck with it.

"Not really." She avoided his eyes. "It'll probably work out one way or another."

"Good." Cal concentrated on his driving. From what she could remember of the trip out, they were about halfway back to town. "I'd be a shame if you lost your job over something like that."

"Oh, well." She shrugged. "I wouldn't care. I'd just get another one." One more embellishment, but what did it matter now? She didn't want to leave McCallum Blake with the impression that she was some pathetic helpless person he'd met on the road to Glory one fine September day. The *real* Nina O'Shea O'Sullivan was a businesswoman, artist, textile designer, world traveler. There was nothing pathetic about her—or her life.

"So, what about you?" Nina smiled. She was determined to finish the day on a bright note.

"Me?" Cal frowned and wrapped his right hand, strong and tanned, around the knob on the gearshift, preparing to shift down for the hill ahead of them.

"Think this little joke of yours went the way you wanted today?" Nina wrenched her eyes from his hand.

"I think so. I appreciate you helping me out." He shot her a quick penetrating look, then smiled. "I don't think I'll be taking much more aggravation from

Jeremiah and Henry on the subject, but I'm a little sorry I misjudged Lou…''

"In what way?''

"I didn't realize how serious she was.'' He stared straight ahead at the road. "I didn't realize how much she really wants me to get married. I didn't know how much it matters to her.''

"Maybe it's because she's thinking of leaving. She strikes me as a very responsible person. Is she your mother's sister?''

Cal nodded.

"Your mother's dead?''

Cal nodded again. "Car accident, nearly twenty years ago. Jeremiah was just a kid at the time. We went to live with Lou and Uncle Will.''

"Maybe in her own mind she still feels she has to look out for you and your brother. She probably isn't convinced you can handle things on your own. Even now.'' Nina paused, uncertain of her ground. After all, she didn't know these people. An acquaintance of a couple of hours gave her no basis to make judgments.

"She won't turn down George Edward on our account, I'll make sure of that,'' Cal said firmly. "If she figures she'll be happy married to Robison, well—'' he paused, shrugged "—I'm not going to argue. I'm just going to make sure she gets the chance she deserves, that's all.''

"Even if it means taking a wife yourself?'' She was only teasing, but something about the question made her go cold and tense, waiting for his answer.

"Maybe.''

She wasn't imagining it; Cal had sighed.

"Could be they're right, Lou and Jeremiah and

Henry.'' He ran one hand slowly over his jaw. His eyes were sombre beneath the broad-brimmed hat, steady on the road. ''Maybe it's time I did,'' he said heavily.

She wished she'd kept her big mouth shut. *What can it possibly matter to you? Tomorrow morning you're out of here and you're never going to see McCallum Blake or this one-horse Alberta town again.* If only she hadn't lied...

If only. The lies, meaningless as they were, had ruined what should have been a perfect day. She felt mean and cheap and foolish.

They came to a stop in the hotel parking lot, which was almost empty. After the motion and engine noise, the cab of the pickup seemed awfully silent. Nina risked a glance at Cal.

He made no move to get out. He stared at the top of the steering wheel, frowning slightly, then turned to her with a quick grin and leaned against the door. He stretched his right arm along the back of the seat. ''Well?''

''I guess we're here,'' Nina said foolishly.

''Yeah.'' He nodded and tapped his fingers dangerously near her shoulder. ''I guess we are.''

Nina glanced distractedly out the window. The sun had set sometime in just the last few minutes, throwing the other vehicles and trees around the lot into sudden purple shadow. She shivered, although she wasn't cold.

''I want to thank you, Cal, for the lovely day,'' she began, not entirely sure she could trust her voice. ''For showing me your ranch and everything.''

''Hey.'' He touched her shoulder lightly. ''I'm glad

you came with me. I'm glad I decided to bite the bullet and ask you—''

''Bite the bullet!'' Her response sounded unnaturally loud in the confines of the pickup.

''Yeah. I almost didn't, you know.'' Their eyes held. Nina felt her breath clog her throat. ''Henry and Jeremiah are right. I'm not good at that sort of thing.'' He grinned, then added, ''Generally.''

''Well, I think they're both crazy,'' Nina said. ''You're a very nice man and very attractive, and I can't see how your family could be so wrong about something like this. They seem to be fairly reasonable people otherwise.''

Cal watched her closely. Her words hung between them. With a flash of insight, Nina realized that he was embarrassed. He wasn't used to this kind of talk. All she knew of him so far, and she admitted it wasn't a whole lot, pointed to the fact that McCallum Blake was a straightforward man. Maybe even shy. It made her like him even more.

A holiday romance? This was the strangest twenty-four hours she'd ever spent.

''I want to thank you again,'' she said firmly. She reached for her canvas carryall, which was on the floor of the cab. ''I...'' She caught his steady gaze and felt her courage falter. *Why didn't he kiss her?* ''I had a wonderful time,'' she finished simply.

He straightened, grasping the door handle. ''Hold on. I'll walk you up to your room.''

They walked to the hotel in silence, not touching. There were several people in the hotel lobby, one of whom greeted Cal. He nodded and spoke briefly, but Nina didn't hear what he said.

Then they were climbing the stairs. Nina's mind raced. She couldn't believe she'd be saying goodbye to this man in a moment or two, *really* saying goodbye, and she'd never see him again. He'd get in his truck and drive back to his ranch twenty miles from town, and she'd pick up her car tomorrow and drive to Calgary and then, probably the next day, head west back to Vancouver. Their lives had touched briefly, through complete happenstance, and now they were going their own ways again. The ridiculous sense of loss she felt at this knowledge was almost more than she could bear. She felt unbalanced. Fragile. Deeply affected by what had happened since she'd met this man the day before.

They arrived at the door to her room.

"Well...goodbye, Cal." She held out her hand and smiled, wanting the goodbyes to be over so she could escape into the neutral unambiguous safety of the hotel room. She wanted the door shut between them. It was the only way, physically, that she could regain some of the balance she needed so desperately.

"Goodbye, Nina." He took her hand briefly, a quick, impersonal touch, then nodded. "Have a safe trip tomorrow."

Mindless inanities. Clichés.

"I will."

"Can I do anything else for you? You want me to check with the garage, make sure that part comes in?"

Nina looked up at him. He seemed reluctant to meet her eyes. "Don't bother, Cal. Thanks. I'll take care of it." She was proud of herself; her voice was remarkably firm, considering the emotions that were zinging through her.

"All right." He raised one finger to the brim of his hat. "So long." He strode toward the staircase. Nina froze, unable to tear her eyes from him until he'd vanished, until the sound of his boots had faded.

At the head of the stairs he paused, one hand on the painted newel post. He hesitated. She couldn't move a muscle, couldn't say a word, couldn't wave breezily the way she knew she should. Couldn't squeeze out a last cheerful goodbye.

"Nina?" He stared at her. "You...you okay?"

His voice sounded as uncertain as she felt. She nodded and reached blindly for the frame of the door behind her.

He swore savagely, and in two long strides he was back and his arms were around her. His hard mouth crushed hers. Nina felt shock and then a joy that almost hurt, as though she were bursting. As though every nerve in her body had been asleep, maybe for years, and this man had forced them all to sudden painful blazing life again. She dug her fingers into the springiness of his hair. Clung to him with all the strength she could summon. Kissed him as he kissed her. As eagerly. As wildly. With the same primitive hunger. He was tall, straight, strong—*everything she'd ever dreamed a man could be.* She felt protected and cherished, caught in the small space between his hard muscled body and the unyielding frame of the door. Sheltered. *Safe.*

Then—she wasn't quite sure how it happened because she didn't think his mouth had lifted from hers for even a second, but perhaps it had—they were inside her room and she heard the door slam as he kicked it shut. He leaned back and pulled her against him, cradling her hips against his. She gasped. He kissed her closed eyes, her cheek, the base of her ear again and again. The tender skin of her throat. Her mind was a fog. All she wanted was *more*...

"Nina." His harsh whisper sent flame up her spine. She wanted to scream. *"Oh, sweet Nina. You're driving me crazy."*

"Cal...oh, Cal." All she could do was repeat his name helplessly. *She wanted this man. How she wanted him!* She pressed her lips to his mouth again, and he growled deep in his throat and pulled her so tightly against him she thought she wouldn't be able to breathe. He kissed her over and over until she thought she'd faint from sheer pleasure.

One arm tight around her, he slid his other hand beneath her cotton shirt and touched her bare back. She shivered. His hand was hard and a little rough and so warm. He ran his hand up the length of her back, to her nape, then down, sliding his fingers under the band of her jeans. Nina sucked in her breath.

She felt him grip her hips and frantic, she fumbled with his shirt buttons. *She needed to touch him.* Two popped open, then another...and then she felt the edge of the bed against the backs of her knees. Cal slid down onto it, supporting their combined weight with one hand, bringing her with him. He rolled over, positioning himself above her, his weight pressing her into the mattress. She was panting. So was he.

He reached down and wrenched up her shirt and they were skin to skin, her belly to his. "Oh, Cal," she whispered faintly, "that feels so good." His eyes burned into hers, dark with desire. He bent down and kissed her.

Then Nina panicked and twisted away, desperate to breathe. Cal shifted his weight onto the bed, away from her. He kept his arms around her and turned his face into the bedspread. His chest rose and fell rapidly under her cheek. They lay that way for what seemed like a very long time. Nina listened to the crash of blood in her ears, the harsh rasp of his breathing and hers. Gradually she felt her heart slow and some of the heat leave her cheeks.

Why didn't he speak? Why didn't he say something?

Cal shifted again—onto his side this time—and pulled her fully into his arms. As he stroked her hair gently with one hand, she could feel the coolness of the air reaching her damp skin. Her head was tucked under his chin. His breathing, too, had slowed.

"Cal?" Her whisper sounded cracked and aching. She wanted to cry.

"Shh." He pushed one tendril of hair from her sweaty temple. She couldn't see his face, could only feel his arms around her, his body against hers, the heavy thud of his heart against her face. "Don't say anything."

His terse order vibrated and echoed in her, through his ribs and muscles into her bones and blood. She felt quick tears smart and blinked furiously. She *wouldn't* cry. She felt so tender, so exposed...so vulnerable.

Finally Cal spoke. "How old are you, Nina?"

"I...I'm twenty-nine." His question surprised her.

"You are?" He moved slightly so he could look down at her. He smiled, that sexy smile that made her melt like warm chocolate on a summer sidewalk. "You're pulling my leg."

"I'm not." She frowned. What in the world was he getting at? "How old did you think I was?"

"About twenty-one or -two. Maybe twenty-three. Just a kid."

"Ha!" She smiled at him and took a deep shaky breath. The tears, or the threat of them, were gone. For now.

"I guess you're old enough to know what you're doing."

She knew what he meant, what he was asking. She wanted to pull him to her again, wanted to kiss that wonderful male mouth—to answer him that way. "I guess I am," she said softly, instead.

He met her gaze and Nina felt her cheeks burn. She felt shy. It was ridiculous. She'd had lovers before. She was no naive eighteen-year-old virgin.

"You do crazy things to me, Miss Nina O'Shea," he said in a low tone. "I never met a woman I wanted as much as I want you. I never met a woman I felt so much for in such a short while. I never kissed a woman who tasted as sweet and beautiful and perfect as you do."

"Oh, Cal…" she breathed, absolutely undone. Tears filled her eyes again. His relatives were nuts! This man was the sexiest man alive. What woman could listen to words like that and not want to lock the bedroom door and throw away the key?

"I like you," he said, still in that same low voice that vibrated right through her. "I like you a lot. That's why I'm going to get up off this bed and walk out of here. That's why I'm not going to make love with you."

She must have made some sound, some whimper of

protest or dismay, because when he continued, he seemed very serious, very definite that he wanted her to understand what he was saying. "It's not fair, Nina. You deserve better. A lot better. Chances are I'll never see you again, and I don't think a one-night stand is really what you're looking for. You've been taken advantage of in the past, that's pretty clear—" *lies, lies, all of it!* "—and I'm not about to add my name to the list."

"Cal—" she felt panic, felt something true and real start to slip through her fingers, like warm dry sand "—listen. It's not like that. I…I haven't been taken advantage of—not that way. I—" she licked her lips, desperate to find the right words "—I want you, too," she whispered. "I want to make love with you. Here. Now. Nobody's taking advantage of anybody—"

She stopped. She was pleading. She hated the sound of her voice.

"Nope." He bent and kissed her gently. She knew instantly that he meant what he said. Every word. He wasn't going to change his mind. "Someday. Maybe." He drew away from her and supported himself on one arm. "I hope so." He carefully pulled down her shirt to cover her bareness. "But not now."

Then he stood and shrugged his own shirt back on, not embarrassed in the slightest. She had not only unfastened all the buttons on his shirt in her fever to touch him, but had managed to push it from his shoulders. Calmly, methodically, he did up the buttons, his gaze not leaving hers.

"I'd like to see you again someday, Nina. Maybe we could write. Give me your address. Maybe…" His voice was regretful. "Who knows? If you need anything, if I can do anything for you, just let me know—''

"You could make love to me, damn it!" she broke in, suddenly furious.

He grinned, which just made her madder. "Yeah, I could. And there's nothing I'd like better. But it's not going to happen. Not now. I already told you why."

He was going to walk out that door in a few seconds and that would be the end of…of everything! Nina sprang to her feet. She'd give him her address. She'd write to him. She'd clear up all these stupid lies— somehow!—and she'd come back. Maybe in a month or two.

"Here." She banged open the drawer in the bedside table and yanked out a sheet of tired-looking hotel stationery. She scribbled furiously. General Delivery, Ladner's Landing. Wasn't that the little fishing village she'd said she'd grown up in? Another lie!

"Write to me," she said, handing him the piece of paper. He didn't even look at it, simply folded it up and tucked it inside his shirt pocket.

"I will. I promise," he said. Nina felt the tears spring to her eyes again. She gave him a wobbly smile.

"Okay." Her voice was shaky.

Then he was gone. Nina waited until she heard his footsteps fade away down the hall, then, with a howl she launched herself at the bed she'd had such hopes for ten minutes ago. She buried her face in the pillow and pummeled the mattress with both fists.

How *could* she have been so stupid! How *could* she have managed to wreck everything?

As she most certainly had.

CHAPTER SIX

"MURRAY, TAKE SOME of that nice paté and then pass it to Nina. I picked it up especially for her."

Meredith O'Shea smiled at her stepson. He smiled back and promptly passed Nina the cut-glass dish of paté without a word. He had been a vegetarian for nearly twenty years, and his stepmother knew very well that he would not take any of that "nice paté."

"Thank you," Nina murmured with a quick glance at her half brother. Murray was unusually quiet today. Self-preservation? Wise of him, considering the mood their father was in.

It was high noon, but under the umbrellas on the terrace of the Point Grey house and in a scarlet cashmere twin set and tailored charcoal slacks, her mother looked as calm and cool as ever. At nearly seventy, she looked more like a well-preserved fifty-five. Even the weather was on her side; for mid-October, the day was surprisingly warm.

Who would have guessed that the O'Shea-O'Sullivans were in the midst of an annual family squabble?

"*You'll* be at the Halloween bash, Nina," said her mother firmly. It wasn't a question. Murray had just informed her that all three of his ex-wives refused to attend this year's event.

Nina nodded, suppressing a sigh. Would she dare to

stay away? They all hated Meredith's parties, even their father, yet for some reason, Meredith wouldn't hear of canceling even one. Now that she'd retired from her busy law practice, taking on only the occasional consultation, the parties seemed to come more often. The Halloween party was an event Nina particularly disliked.

"And Leo? Will he come this year, d'you think?" her mother asked, eyebrows raised.

"I'll mention it to him," Nina said. She put down her mint green linen napkin and glanced discreetly at her watch. Leo Swain was her partner in Swain and Company, the flourishing textile-design business they ran out of a Granville Street studio. She was meeting him this afternoon to go over her plans for an upcoming research trip to Thailand, and she'd hoped to have time to drive out to Ladner's Landing and back before their three-o'clock appointment. Feeling completely ridiculous each time, she'd checked twice with the village post office since she'd returned from Alberta three weeks before. No letters from McCallum Blake. *Did she really think there would be?*

"Tell him to leave the goddamn boyfriend at home this year," muttered her father, rattling his newspaper violently. Nina ignored him. Jake O'Sullivan had moved away from the table earlier after a brief disagreement with Murray over the way he was raising his—Jake's—only grandson, and had settled in a deck chair in one corner of the terrace overlooking English Bay. A multitude of sailboats dotted the bay as they did most sunny weekends of the year.

"Oh, heavens, darling," his wife returned mildly. "You know very well it's nobody's business what consenting adults do with their willies in this country. And, besides, they'll be in costume. Who would know?''

Murray hurriedly set down his glass, about to burst, Nina could tell. But he contained his laughter and said nothing. Instead, he pushed back his chair and stood.

"Well, Dad?" He glanced at his father, who growled something and shook his newspaper again, not bothering to look up. "I'm off. Meredith?" Murray bent to kiss the cheek she proffered. "Thank you for lunch. Lovely as usual.''

"So soon?" Meredith's clear blue eyes clouded briefly. She really was very fond of Murray, Nina knew, and many times had dampened the fireworks between him and his father.

"I'm picking up Jamie from Sonya's at two. He's having a tryout with that new coach the club brought in from Toronto." Sonya was Murray's first wife. Jamie was twelve, and a terrifically promising figure skater. Naturally Jake preferred that his grandson play hockey.

What a family! Nina thought as she crossed the Oak Street bridge half an hour later. She loved every one of them, but it was tough sometimes to deal with the friction at these family get-togethers. Her mother's final unsettling comment had stayed with her.

"Did you have a good holiday?" she'd asked in the maple-and-marble foyer, arms crossed. Her mother rarely pried, but asking if she'd enjoyed her short vacation was hardly prying.

"Fine, Mother," Nina answered, slipping into her jacket. "Fine," she repeated, then stared at her mother, struck suddenly by something in the older woman's face. "Why do you ask?"

Her mother had hesitated—Nina could still see the indecision on her face—but then she'd gone on. "Because you look sad, dear."

"Sad?" Nina had tried to laugh. "That's crazy! I'm too busy to be sad. You know that." She'd paused for a moment herself, recognizing the truth of her mother's words. "I'm fine, Mother," she'd said. Her voice had felt awkward. "Just fine."

She'd left right afterward, with a quick wave and a bright comment.

Had she fooled her mother? Nina thought not. Meredith O'Shea had not reached the top of the heap defending criminals of every size, shape and form without an acute understanding of human nature.

Had she fooled herself? No.

But it was ridiculous. No one had more going for her than Nina O'Shea O'Sullivan. Money. Youth. Health. A good education. Family who at times seemed downright crazy, but who cared for her. A thriving business situated on one of Vancouver's trendiest streets. A partner who was not only her best friend but a man of complete and total integrity. Male company when she wanted it. Many of Vancouver's best families would welcome an alliance with the O'Shea-O'Sullivans, and Nina wasn't foolish enough not to realize that in her world, that was how things worked. What was that saying her mother had told her long ago—it's as easy to fall in love with a rich man as a poor man? At the time she'd hooted with laughter and derided what she'd felt to be her mother's hopeless naiveté about what really mattered. But now, at nearly thirty, she accepted the truth of that advice. Truly there was no reason to feel sad. There was no reason to feel, as she had to admit she often did lately, that she was missing out on something…real. That some important part of life—she didn't know what— was passing her by.

And the stupid thing was, she hadn't felt *any* of this until she'd ended up stuck in southern Alberta one weekend waiting for a part for her new car.

Nina took the River Road exit off Highway 99 and meandered along the grassy south bank of the Fraser River toward Ladner's Landing.

Funny, she'd barely known this town existed until a couple of weeks ago when she'd driven out to check for letters. She'd heard of it, that was all. She'd had to track down the drugstore that dispensed stamps, rented post-office boxes and handled general-delivery mail. There'd been nothing for her.

At the stop sign, she glanced right. The cluttered masts of fishing boats punctured the sky. Half a dozen were tied up at the wharf across the narrow reach, any one of which could have been the boat that belonged to the father she'd invented. *Sampson's Pride* or *Ruby B.* The first day she'd driven out, she'd taken some time to explore the little town, and now, on her third visit, she felt as though she knew the place.

She turned left, past the ancient wood-frame sec- ondhand store—once a livery stable, she'd learned from a tourist brochure she'd picked up. Past the tiny cottage that had its sandwich board outside informing passersby that "free range eggs are now in!" Past the auto-repair shop and the machine shop, which lined the tidal slough that ran behind the buildings and drained into the river. Ladner's Landing was situated on the vast Fraser River delta and, without dikes and canals, would have been underwater much of the year.

At the drugstore, she parked. She flexed her fingers on the steering wheel. This was absolutely amazingly ridiculous! Why was she here? Even if there was a letter from McCallum Blake, what did it mean? She couldn't keep up a relationship with some Alberta cowboy by mail. Besides, what about all the lies she'd told him?

No, it was impossible.

All right, all right, she bargained with herself. *If there's no letter today, you'll give this up. Be sensible. It's best if there's no letter, really. If there's nothing today, you've got to promise you'll never come out here again. Okay?*

Feeling a little foolish, she got out of the car and walked toward the drugstore.

There was no letter. There was nothing at all for Nina O'Shea, General Delivery.

THE FOLLOWING WEDNESDAY, Nina left for Bangkok. She reveled in the bright orange robes of the young Buddhist monks walking barefoot through the streets at dawn, alms bowls in their hands, to collect their daily food. She smiled at the schoolboys, book bags on their backs, looking like so many moths in their bright white shirts, as they ducked among the crowds. She ate noodles at Ped Tun Jao Thaa and spent an entire day at a shop in the Rajdamri Road examining antique royal *benjarong* ware, dating from King Chulalongkorn's day.

Nina used these frequent trips abroad to absorb the

sights and sounds and textures that she and Leo would draw on later to design unique textiles. In the past year, they'd been on a Thai kick. Seeing and handling beautiful objects of the past, whether ceramics or leather or carved teak furniture, provided the fuel Nina needed to come up with her unusual paintings and drawings. She and Leo would then weave experimental textile samples based on her art. If the samples passed the scrupulous requirements of both partners, they'd be assigned for custom weaving to specialty houses. Some of those houses were right here in Thailand. Swain and Company had contracts with two Bangkok houses to supply them with the silks they were currently selling in Vancouver and New York. Part of the purpose of her trip was to meet with their suppliers.

Each night, though, when she went back to her sumptuous room at the Oriental Hotel, the sights and sounds and smells of Bangkok would fade and she'd think of that sunny afternoon she'd ridden out into the hills with McCallum Blake. She'd see the antelope again, and the smooth variegated brown of the hills. She'd see the blue dome of the September sky and taste the supreme nothingness of the icy clear spring-water Cal had brought her in the battered tin cup.

Nina felt as though she were stuck in a dream from which she couldn't awaken, no matter how hard she tried. She didn't want to be thinking about McCallum Blake. She wanted to forget about the weekend she'd spent in Glory. It was past, gone—she wanted it forgotten.

If he wrote to her, as he'd promised, and if she was foolish enough to write back, she'd just have to tell more lies. Or she'd have to start fresh and tell him the complete truth. And that would surely be the end of that. She wouldn't hear from him again. And who could blame him?

So what was the point?

ON HER LAST DAY in Bangkok, Nina bought a beautiful *pha sin,* a richly embroidered ankle-length sarong traditionally worn by the women of northern Thailand's hill tribes, to wear to her mother's costume party. That, with a mask, would have to do. She arrived in Vancouver early the next morning and, after a brief meeting with Leo, headed home to sleep off her jet lag.

She entered the foyer of the mansion that had been converted to luxury condominiums a decade before and nodded to the concierge.

"Good trip, Miss O'Shea?" he asked, handing her a stack of mail he'd collected for her during the ten days she'd been gone.

"Very good, Earl." She eyed the pile of mail before stuffing it into her bag, resolutely putting all ideas of a letter from Glory out of her mind. "Thanks. Letty back?"

"Not yet, Miss O'Shea." Earl helped bring her bags up. In the elevator, she leaned her head against the bronze faux-painted wall. She was exhausted. The *last* thing she needed was to have to put in an appearance at her mother's party tonight.

The apartment was empty. Letty, her old Filipino nanny and friend who'd lived with her for the past few years, had gone to Seattle to visit a cousin. In the bath, Nina nearly fell asleep. She got out and stumbled, wet and naked, to her bedroom and sank gratefully into the down pillows of her own bed. Her last thought as she pulled up the cool lavender-scented sheets was, *I will not think of that man. Ever again. I most certainly, most definitely, will not.*

At half-past three, Nina sat up in bed, wide-eyed and bewildered. What time was it in Bangkok?

By four-fifteen she was in the Porsche, heading south to the George Massey Tunnel. By a quarter to five she'd reached Ladner's Landing and had pulled up to the post office.

Five minutes later she had two letters from Mc-Callum Blake in her hands.

October 16
Dear Nina,
I apologize for taking so long to write. Just after you left, I got tangled up with some lawyers in Calgary about some business and then it was time for roundup. We lost five yearlings this fall and one of the old cows never showed up. We found her calf. Henry and Jeremiah say it's a grizzly, but I'm not convinced. We didn't see a kill of any kind that would have told the story.

As you can imagine, Henry and my brother are up to all kinds of schemes to go after the grizzly that's doing the damage—if that's the problem. As I say, I'm not convinced, but when some wild animal gets a taste for my beefsteak, it's trouble both ways. Naturally I've got to protect my stock. On the other hand, the grizzlies were here a long time before we were. When you're in bear country, as the Rocking Bar S is, it's a risk you always take. In the spring it's the cougars and coyotes. I've heard other ranchers say a golden eagle will carry off a newborn calf, but I find that tough to believe.

I don't suppose you're too interested in bear stories. Lou is fine and, so far, there's no ring on her finger. George Edward is hanging around an awful lot, though, so I expect it's coming. Henry's favorite bitch just had another litter of pups. Nine, this time, under the toolshed.

I hope you're well and happy, and you didn't lose your job over that business with the car here last month.

The letter was written in an even, masculine hand, black ink on plain white paper. It was signed simply "McCallum." Nina's eyes swam and the words on the page wavered before her. She sniffed loudly and looked around. The Ladner's Landing Harbour Park, where she'd decided to take refuge to read her letters, was deserted. Dry leaves were lifted by the intermittent wind off the river and bumped and bounced along the dirt paths. Most of the picnic tables had been stacked in preparation for winter, and the sandboxes looked shabby and neglected, a few forgotten toys from the summer crowds poking through the rain-caked sand. In the near distance, just across the reach, she could hear faint sounds of "Trick or treat" from small hobgoblins out early, shepherded by cautious parents.

Smiling despite her tears, trembling, Nina refolded

the letter and put it back in its envelope. The other one was postmarked nearly two weeks later. It must have just arrived.

October 27
Dear Nina,
I know I promised I'd write you, especially after what happened in the hotel before you left. We were pretty hot, both of us. I don't know if it's such a good idea now. You've got your life out there on the Coast and I've got mine here. Maybe you thought it was just a bunch of words when I said I'd never felt what I felt for you so fast before, not with any woman. It's the truth. But, on reflection, maybe it's not such a good idea to stay in touch this way. Maybe it's best that you live your life there, and I live mine here. If you don't reply, I'll understand.

                                        McCallum

P.S. If I can ever help you in any way, or if you ever need money or a place to stay, let me know.

Nina wiped away the tears with her sleeve and stood up, jamming the letters back into her bag. She needed to talk to someone about this; she needed to see Leo. He'd be at the party tonight. She could talk to him then. Leo knew her better than anyone, and he never lied to her. He'd advise her on this—she'd tell him everything, how she'd lied, how they'd nearly made love, her and Cal. Everything.
If you don't reply, I'll understand....
But at the party that night, Nina didn't tell Leo. In the hours between receiving Cal's letters and arriving

at her mother's house, Nina had made some decisions on her own. She'd decided she wanted to hear his bear stories, all of them. Cal's letters had given her a glimpse into his life—arrow-straight, simple, strong. He stood for things, he believed in things. He *felt* things.

We were pretty hot, both of us.

The following week, Nina drove out to Ladner's Landing, signed a sublease on a small apartment overlooking the harbor, sent Cal a change-of-address card and started living another life.

She didn't tell a soul.

CHAPTER SEVEN

November 3

Dear Cal,

I was so happy to receive your letters and realize that you really did mean to write to me. I want to thank you again for the wonderful day at your ranch in September.

I've been very busy lately or I would have answered sooner. I've just moved into a new apartment here in Ladner's Landing and right now that's taking up a lot of my time. There's not much furniture in it, so I'm painting the walls a lovely cranberry color. With the walls and the view—overlooking the river—that should be furniture enough. What do you think?

Nina drew up one knee and leaned forward, frowning, to stare out the window at the river. It seemed that the only path away from the crazy impulsive story she'd told him led to other lies.

As it turns out, I did end up losing my job. It wasn't because of what happened in Glory, just because my boss's business has fallen off lately and he decided to wind things down for the winter. But I got lucky and found something else. Didn't I tell you I would?

This time it's a job I think I'm going to keep. I've been hired by a textile-design shop here, Swain and Company. I'm learning all kinds of interesting things about textiles and design and the fabric business. The owners travel a lot. I've always had a talent for sketching and drawing and painting, so I hope I'll fit right in.

At least she had herself working in the right business now. She'd have to feel things out as she went along. Anyway, he might not even reply to her letter. Maybe, in the end—she didn't really want to think about this possibility—it would be best. Just like he'd said in his brief second letter.

Please keep writing to me. You're probably right that it doesn't make much sense, but I'd like to stay in touch with you. I've decided I want to hear <u>all</u> your bear stories.

Nine pups! Henry must be a proud papa.

Regards,
Nina

November 10
Dear Nina,
I have to say I was surprised to get your letter. I'd been thinking you might have come to your senses since you went back home, and decided writing to an Alberta rancher wasn't something you wanted.

I'm glad to hear your new job is working out

so well. Jobs are tough to get, so it's good news
to hear you finally found something you like. I
couldn't face going to a job I hated every day.
But then, I couldn't imagine a nine-to-five job,
anyway. Now that roundup's over, I've got to
turn my attention to all the work that needs doing
during the winter, maintenance mostly. Winter's
a slow time for most farmers around here, but not
for ranchers. The cows still need feed and water
every day, no matter what the weather's like.

Henry's pups are doing fine, growing like
weeds, as Lou says. He's moved them into the
barn and my paint gelding has taken a fancy to
one of them. I think my suspicions about my
brother were right, after all. A couple of rumors
have come my way about him and one of the
Galloway girls, the oldest daughter of a farming
family east of Glory.

Ever since you were here, I've given quite a
lot of thought to the idea of marriage myself and
have decided it's time I took the plunge. I'll let
you know how that goes.

                                        McCallum

November 15
Dear Cal,
I got your letter this afternoon and could hardly
wait to write back. I haven't corresponded with
anyone like this since I had a pen pal in Illinois
in fourth grade.

The winter rains have set in, and it's been
gloomy for a week now. Luckily, my apartment

has a gas fireplace and I've had that on quite a bit. Not as romantic as wood, but better than nothing! The red walls make it look cozy.

Cal stopped reading. He gradually became aware of Myra Schultz's interest focused on his left shoulder, where she could just about peer over and see what he'd been in such a hurry to read. *Hell,* Cal thought. You couldn't get away with a damn thing in a town as small as Glory.

Come right down to it, though, he didn't really care what the postmistress thought. He'd recognized Nina's stationery the minute he'd opened his mailbox. He'd been thinking about her ever since he'd written that last letter, and he couldn't wait to get out of Myra's line of vision before ripping open her reply. Plus, it was warm in the post office and damn cold outside. He wanted to know what Nina thought about his plans for marriage. He didn't know why it mattered what she thought, but somehow it did. He also wanted to wish himself into that cranberry-colored apartment of hers and show her that a gas fire could be just as romantic as a wood one. But there was no point in thinking those thoughts....

"Morning, Myra," he said, and casually tipped his hat, ignoring the glint in her eye. Luckily another customer came into the post office and he quickly shuffled the pages of Nina's letter into the rest of his mail and left. He'd finish reading it in the truck.

I was interested to hear about all the things you have to do in the winter. I'm ashamed to say I know nothing about how my beef gets into the supermarket and really had no idea about all the work involved.

So Jeremiah has a girlfriend. That's interesting. What's she like? Have you met her?

I was pretty shocked at your statement that you'd decided to get married—just like that. I didn't think that was how a person went about something so important. Have you got someone in mind?

Give my regards to everyone, especially Lou.

All my best,
Nina

November 24
Dear Nina,
We had quite a snowstorm the past few days, so it looks like winter's really here. Lou's been home, busy with the knitting and crocheting she does every year for her church group. They have their big Christmas bazaar next week. I usually get roped into taking her and buying all kinds of stuff I don't need. Maybe this year she'll get George Edward to take her.

You asked about my matrimonial prospects. I got quite a chuckle out of that. Henry and Jeremiah have been busy, set me up with a couple of women since you left. I have to admit, neither of them seemed too impressed by either my grazing leases or my cows.

On the other hand, I do believe that my family has finally realized this is something I can figure out on my own. I've got you to thank for that, going along with my little joke. The way we're writing to each other now, back and forth, has put a gleam in Lou's eye. Every time she hands me a letter, she looks about to pop with curiosity. She figures there's more to this than I'm letting on.

Henry has a short holiday planned, now that the weather's set in and there isn't so much repair work to do on the ranch. He's visiting his sister over in Maple Creek for a week the beginning of December. She's a widow and he visits her twice a year, like clockwork. Can't stay more than a week because they fight like cats and dogs. Did I tell you? Henry and Jeremiah found tracks up on one of our back ranges. I talked to the Mounties. Seems we were losing our stock to a two-legged predator and not a bear, after all.

Not much else going on here. I think of you often.

McCallum

He thought of her often. Impulsively Nina held Cal's letter to her face and breathed deeply. Paper and glue, not even a hint of the leather and horses and snowy cold air she thought the paper should hold.

It was Saturday morning and Nina had come over to the apartment the evening before, determined to spend the entire weekend in Ladner's Landing. She treasured the quiet times she spent in her hideaway. There was no fax, no message machine, no Letty in the kitchen chattering about this or that. The phone never rang. No one knew she was there. The tiny apartment held the peace Nina craved, an escape from her hectic social and professional life. Lately, she'd had more attention than she wanted from a man she'd dated off and on over the past two years. Douglas Waterman. She'd turned down his last two invitations—a gallery opening and a fund-raising ball—but he didn't seem to get the hint. The apartment was becoming an oasis from more than work pressures.

Besides, this was where she wrote to Cal. It had become almost a ritual. Somehow she could only write to him in this apartment, with real paper and real ink. She'd even bought a fountain pen. Then she'd press a real stamp on the envelope, kiss it twice for luck and speedy delivery, and walk to the corner to drop it in the red Canada Post box.

There were days when she felt her weekends on this side of the river were more real than the rest of the week she lived on the other side. Sometimes Nina worried about the overlapping of her two lives; most times she didn't. The relationship she'd developed over the past couple of months with Cal had become more precious than she'd ever dreamed it could be. Through the magic of letters, he knew her in a way she didn't think anyone else in her life did. Not even Leo.

Cal had asked about her plans for Christmas. She couldn't say she'd probably go up to Whistler to ski, as she did most years, returning to a catered turkey dinner at her parents' house on Boxing Day. As for the "family" she'd told Cal about, it was high time she got them out of the picture any way she could. There was no need to tell the whole truth about her real family, but she didn't want to maintain the fiction about her made-up one, either.

December 14
Dear Cal,
No, I won't be going anywhere special for Christmas. My two brothers both work up north somewhere, I'm not sure exactly where. They hardly ever get down here to Vancouver. One of my sisters is away right now. She went to Australia with a friend and they're planning to stay a year or so. She's a nurse, so she can work just about anywhere. I might spend Christmas with my other sister.

Nina realized she could hardly dispose of the entire family at once. Nor did she want Cal to feel sorry for her, thinking she'd be all alone for the holidays.

We haven't made any plans yet.
I've pretty well finished decorating my apartment. You should see it. I filled every window with candles in cans and pots and bottles, which I light in the evening. They're beeswax and give off the loveliest smell. I like to think the fishing boats out there on the river will see them, kind of like a beacon bringing them home although it isn't fishing season now.
And I've sewn some big floor cushions in every possible shade of red, pink and purple. They look great on the Chinese rug I found in the local secondhand store. I've lived in a lot of different places, but I think this little apartment feels just right for me. I've never been happier than I am here.
Have a wonderful Christmas, Cal. Kiss the puppies for me.

Love,
Nina

December 24

Dear Nina,

It's late. I couldn't sleep so I got up and then—
I don't know what got into me—I just had to
write you. I always feel a little down at this time
of year. That's when I think I should have gotten
around to getting married and having a family
long ago. Lou always puts up a tree, but it seems
pretty depressing having a tree and a couple of
lumpy-looking presents around it, just me and
Lou and Jeremiah and Henry. Socks, gloves, a
new toaster. Not the stuff of kids' dreams, is it?
At least nobody ever gives me a tie.

Christmas is for kids. And when there are no
kids around, what's the point? Sometimes I wish
Lou wouldn't even bother with the tree.

Sorry for sounding so gloomy. Maybe it's because I turned thirty-six this month. I didn't tell
you, because I hate fuss about that sort of thing
and I figure you're just the type to make a lot of
fuss about birthdays. Am I right? Anyway, it was
the 17th.

Merry Christmas, Nina. I get the feeling that
the new year is going to be a lucky one, for us
both. Do you have any mistletoe in that fancy
apartment of yours?

                                                    Cal

Cal read over what he'd written and nearly tore the
pages in two. He didn't want to sound so depressing.
After all, at least he had his family around, such as it
was. Things could be worse.

It wasn't just the season that was getting him down this year. Since he'd made up his mind to get married, he'd done his best to put the plan into action. Trouble was, he just couldn't seem to get all that interested in the women he was taking out. He'd kiss them and it'd be, well, okay—but he kept thinking of the fireworks that had gone off when he'd kissed Nina. Sometimes it was clear that his dates wouldn't mind going farther than a few kisses, but he just couldn't bring himself to do it.

What kind of fool was he? Jeremiah would laugh himself silly if he knew. Cal shook his head and sealed the envelope. Then he got up and stood at the darkened window. The crescent moon was reflected on the fresh snow outside. He could see the distant hulk of the barn, the sheds, the corral posts, topped with snowy mounds. It took a special woman to appreciate all this. So far, he wasn't having much luck finding that woman. Maybe he ought to start thinking seriously about revising his expectations and making a big play for second best.

January 12
Dear Cal,
I just got your letter of last week. What news! Does this mean you're off the hook as far as Lou is concerned? I guess if Jeremiah's engaged, your aunt's dream has finally come true, for one of you, anyway. What's Jeremiah's fiancée like? When do they plan to get married?

I have to admit I'm a little relieved to hear it. The way you've been talking about marriage lately, it sounded like you were about to go off

and ask absolutely anyone to marry you just to
get it over with. I don't like that idea. In fact, I
don't like the idea of you marrying <u>anyone</u>—not
without my approval!

I'm just joking of course. But it seems as
though we've become such good friends over the
months we've been writing back and forth that I
would really feel hurt if you didn't confide in me.
Does that seem crazy? When we've actually
spent less than a day together in real time?

I'm going on a business trip to Japan next
week with my boss.

Nina chewed the end of her pen, frowning. Leo was
hardly her boss. If only she could tell the whole truth
and be done with it. What if Cal got angry, though,
and broke off writing to her? Nina could no longer
bear the thought of that happening. She knew she
could never see him again, but was it selfish to want
to keep writing to him? Wasn't their correspondence
completely harmless?

I'm so excited. I'll be taking photographs and
doing some sketching and keeping notes. I'll
write to you from there if I have a chance, but
I'll probably be back before my letter arrives. Until then—

                                            Love,
                                            Nina

January 31
Dear Nina,
I guess you'll be back from Japan by now. I can't
tell you what it felt like when I got your letter

saying you were flying across the Pacific Ocean. It's crazy. It's not as though it should make a bit of difference whether you're in Vancouver or Tokyo. But somehow it did.

What's your boss like? Is he married? You never mention anyone else, except that one time when I asked you what you were doing for Christmas. What do you do with your spare time? Do you go out a lot? Tell me to mind my own business if you want.

He could hardly write and tell her the truth—that the moment he'd heard about her flying off to Japan with her boss he'd been miserable. But he *could* ask her what this boss of hers was like. Somehow he knew it was too much to hope that he'd be old and bald and happily married.

It's been damn cold here lately, 35 below for the past three nights. You can think of me freezing my butt tending my cows while you're sitting there watching the fishing boats go by. Saddle leather's stiff, crankcase oil's stiff, stock's not happy, things break.

Henry sold three of last spring's pups. Only half-trained but the new owners don't seem to care. He got a good price, too. Guess I ought to give the old man more credit for what he calls his breeding-for-excellence program.

Better go for now. I'm heading to town right after lunch to pick up the mail and order some feed and get some groceries for Lou. Maybe

there'll be a letter from you. The lady in the post
office is giving me some awful suspicious looks
lately. This is a small town. No secrets here.

                                                  Cal

P.S. Lou got her ring last Sunday. Guess this
means it's serious. No mention yet of setting a
date. Jeremiah's owly as hell lately. Hope everything's going fine there. I've met a woman I think
I could settle down with, all things considered.
Donna's her name. She used to live here, then
went off to Calgary to get married. She's divorced now and moved back to town a few
months ago.

February 14
Dear Cal,
Imagine you thinking of me on Valentine's Day.
When I got home from work today, there they
were! Thank you for the chocolates and all the
nice words in your letter. I had a little sniffle
when I read it. You are the sweetest man! I hope
I can be as good a friend to you as you seem to
think I am. Also, I certainly hope you're not just
practicing up your sweet words so you can use
them on somebody else!

   Tell me more about this Donna you mentioned
you were dating. Is this someone you met on your
own? Do you think you're really serious about
her? What's she like? Does SHE know you're
sending chocolates to a mystery lady in B.C.?

   Give my best wishes and congratulations to
Lou. I often think of her. By the way, did I tell

you? My other sister's gone to Australia, too. I have no idea when they'll be back. Maybe they'll meet a couple of handsome Aussie men and never come back.

Love,
Nina

February 15
Dear Nina,
Bad news. Jeremiah's fiancée broke it off with him yesterday. He's pretty ticked, since she waited to do it until after they'd been to a fancy Valentine's party at some big-shot friend of hers up in Calgary.

Lou's mad—says it's all Jeremiah's fault. I don't know what to think, except I'm sorry it happened. Jeremiah's on the wild side, as I'm sure you've figured out, and I'd hoped marriage would settle him down some. He's plenty old enough, twenty-seven in March. Maybe Carol Jean thought he was a little wild, too. I don't know.

Henry isn't saying much.

I'll write next week with more news. Maybe this'll blow over.

Cal

February 20
Dear Nina,
Jeremiah took off yesterday. I tend to think he'll be back once he's got some of this worked out of his system, but Lou doesn't. She wants me to hire a housekeeper and a hand to replace Jeremiah, so I told her I'd put an ad in the paper. But I don't plan to replace Jeremiah just yet. He may

be back any day. Besides, the real hard work doesn't start until calving season, and that's still a good month away.

I told Lou to stick to her plans, no matter what. She and George Edward set the date on Valentine's Day. Did I mention that? Probably not, what with all the news about Jeremiah and Carol Jean breaking up. Anyway, Lou and George Edward are going to tie the knot the end of April—the 27th to be exact. Just a small family wedding, Lou says. Don't see how that can be called small—George Edward's got seven kids by two different wives and all of them are grown up and have good-size families of their own.

I'm feeling kind of twisted up over this thing with Jeremiah. Not that Carol Jean would have been happy moving in here with me and Henry. Maybe that was part of the problem, I don't know. Nobody ever tells me anything.

I'm half tempted to go ahead and put the question to Donna, but I can't quite work up my nerve. She's got a gift store in town and probably doesn't see herself giving all that up and living out here on a ranch with me. Not that I'd expect her to give up her work, but I'd always thought I'd want children, that sort of thing. We get along well enough. I'm pretty sure it would work out. But something's holding me back, and I don't know what it is, Nina. No spark there. Something like that. Anyway, my mind's made up. One way or another, hell or high water, I'm figuring to get married this year.

Cal

Cal settled a little farther down in his seat. The seats in the new theater attached to the high school were big enough and soft enough, but somehow he just couldn't get comfortable. Or maybe it was this new tweed jacket and tie he was wearing.

He reached up and stealthily loosened his tie a notch, then glanced sideways at the woman beside him.

Donna was entranced by the play. She leaned forward, lips moving slightly. Well, Jenny, her eldest, was playing the part of Johnny Appleseed's mother; no doubt Donna had heard the words a million times. James, her son, was sitting somewhere behind them with his father, who was taking both kids to Calgary after the play. Donna and her ex got along well enough to share the kids on weekends. Cal supposed it could be a whole lot worse.

His mind wandered…first to Donna's kids. They were keen, enthusiastic, good-looking children, redheads both, like their dad. Donna and her ex had done a fine job with them. Ever since he'd first thought of popping the question, he'd mulled over all the ramifications, including the idea of being part of an instant family. On the one hand, he'd be proud to be stepfather to her kids; on the other, he'd always thought he'd like children of his own. And Jenny and James had their dad, whom they idolized. Their mother was close to his—Cal's—age. Would she want to start all over with babies?

He liked Donna well enough. Very well, in fact. But ever since Nina's letter had come last week, the words practically leaping off the page with outrage that he'd have the nerve to think of asking a woman he didn't love to marry him, he'd been having second thoughts.

Of course, in one way, Nina was right. Sure, he'd prefer falling in love first. Who wouldn't? But he was thirty-six years old, and it didn't look like that was going to happen anytime soon. And he'd made up his mind he wanted to get married. Nina was a lot younger; it was natural that she wouldn't see it quite the same way he did. Besides, he didn't rule out loving a woman like Donna in the end. That could happen *after* they got married, as well as before.

He allowed his mind to drift back to the half hour he'd spent in Nina's room at the Wild Goose Inn last fall. He'd come *that* close to making love with her. More than once, during this long lonely winter, he wished he had—at least he'd have the memory. But for all the letters back and forth on every possible topic this past winter, both of them had steered well clear of that particular subject. They'd had to; what possible good could come of it? They lived in separate worlds.

Now she was off on another trip with that damned fellow she worked with. Probably some handsome slick guy in a navy three-piece—she'd never said. Meanwhile, he sat here in a high-school auditorium wearing an itchy tweed jacket, wondering if he'd have the nerve to ask the woman beside him if she'd consider marrying him.

"Oh, Cal! Isn't she wonderful?" Donna suddenly whispered proudly. Her face glowed with love and pride in her daughter. Cal could only envy her.

"Yeah, she's great." He squeezed Donna's hand and she returned the pressure, moving closer to him.

Cal tried to block out the intermittent laughter of the audience around them and concentrate on the feel of Donna's hand in his. He tried to imagine, with all his might, that they were a couple already, that they were married, that they were proud parents attending a school theatrical production.

It didn't work. Something inside him just wouldn't let go and make it work.

Later, when Cal drove Donna home, listening to her chatter about this scene and that scene and how wonderful Jenny had been, he felt whatever was inside him build and build until all he wanted was to be gone. To be back on the dark winter road, heading home.

Just inside her door, he made no move to take off his coat. Donna was surprised.

"You'll come in for coffee?" It wasn't really a question. Ever since they'd started dating shortly after Christmas, he'd come in for coffee after their dates, and if the kids were at their father's for the weekend, more often than not he'd stayed. Coffee usually meant bed.

"Not tonight, Donna," he said, putting his hands on her shoulders. Her face clouded slightly. She was too experienced not to read the signs. Too self-assured, too confident, far too mature to ask him why.

He hesitated, aware of her unspoken questions. "Lou's home alone." He hated using Lou as an excuse. He just plain didn't feel like making love tonight. In fact, he knew from the way he'd been feeling all evening that he was probably never going to wake up in Donna's bed again. Nor was he going to be taking her to high-school plays and movies anymore. It wasn't right, not when his intentions were all wrong.

He bent and kissed her and felt regret sweep through his body as he held her close. She felt warm and inviting, and he wished he could accept that invitation, and then, maybe tomorrow morning when they woke up together, he could ask her to marry him.

But it wasn't going to be that way. Cal pulled back, looking down into her face for a long moment. She didn't say anything, and her dark eyes searched his for answers he didn't have. "Bye, darlin'," he said softly. "Sweet dreams."

"Goodbye, Cal." She smiled and closed the door behind him. He stepped out of the porch into the bitter wind. Damn weather! Still felt like winter and it was coming up to the middle of March.

Cal got back in his truck and started the engine. If he was going to jump slam-bang, feetfirst, eyes closed, into the middle of this marriage business without being in love, he might as well ask someone he really wanted in his life. Someone for whom he *did* feel some kind of spark. Someone who didn't have a whole lot going for her, not even any family around to help her out. Someone who just might need him the way he needed her.

Donna didn't need him. In fact, she might turn him down flat. Probably would. She had a nice arrangement with her ex as far as the kids went, child support on time, a good business of her own in town. She was on the school board; she was an attractive divorced woman who could probably get any man she wanted. Hell, what had made him think she might want *him?*

Cal laughed out loud in the cab. The irony struck him. Here he'd been all primed to ask her to marry him and hadn't given even a moment's thought to what he could offer a woman like her. *You're crazy, Blake, plumb crazy! No wonder Henry and Jeremiah think you're such a hopeless case with women.*

Snow began to pelt the windshield as he drove into the Horsethief Valley. He wondered if Henry'd been able to handle feeding the stock by himself that evening. He shouldn't have gone off to the school play with Donna. That was the trouble with courting—it cut too deep into your regular life, the part that paid the bills. He turned on the radio. Rollicking country music filled the cab. All of a sudden he felt better, a whole lot better.

Of course. He'd tackle this whole marriage question from the other end. Why hadn't he thought of that before? He'd *start* by asking someone he really wanted to spend his life with, love or no love. He'd start there, and if she turned him down, why, then he'd maybe move on to Donna or someone else.

I know you've never considered something like this before, but I thought I'd ask, anyway. If you want to try it and then if it doesn't work out, or if you find you can't stand living out here in such rough country and as remote as it is, you can change your mind. I wouldn't hold you back.

Cal grinned and applied the brakes gently to the grade before the bridge. The road was slippery with new snow, and the rear of the pickup whipped sideways. He automatically steered the truck back into the center of the road.

It isn't as though either one of us expects something that isn't there. I like you a lot—you know that. We've had a chance to get to know each other better over the past few months than a lot of couples. And, well, maybe there's a chance we can work out a pretty good life together.

By the time Cal drove into the ranch yard, he had it all thought out. All he needed was to find a piece of paper and a stamp.

CHAPTER EIGHT

SPRING RAIN. It had rained cats and dogs all the way from the condo to Ladner's Landing this evening, and Nina's navy gabardine jacket was drenched.

She fumbled for her key, repeating under her breath the nonsense verse a long-ago nanny had taught her as a substitute for swearing. The nanny was Irish, as she recalled, a replacement when Letty had gone home to the Philippines for a visit.

The imitation gaslight outside the door to her apartment had burned out, and she couldn't see into her bag with only the light from the neighbor's fixture. These apartments had access from an open corridor that ran along the outside of the building, a feature she'd liked when she took over the lease. The brass mail slot to one side of the door fed directly onto the slate tiles of her foyer, an advantage when she didn't actually live here and wasn't around regularly to collect the mail, not to mention the flyers that built up.

She'd been away. Eight days. Eight long days, she reminded herself. Hong Kong. She used to adore her trips to Hong Kong. But now she couldn't wait to get home. She was getting to be like a kid with candy; she just couldn't go for more than a week without a letter from Cal. Even the thought that there might be one waiting for her in Ladner's Landing was enough to draw her out here tonight, rain or no rain. She had the trip down perfectly—twenty-three minutes after rush hour.

Letty thought she was crazy. Letty, the Filipino woman who'd mostly raised her, had moved in with Nina when Meredith retired. The two older women had never gotten along well, and Nina was glad of the company. Nina hadn't told Letty that she'd rented an apartment, or that she was carrying on a secret correspondence with an Alberta rancher, or that she was living a secret second life on the south shore of the Fraser River as an orphaned fisherman's daughter deserted by her family. She'd just told her something vague about a friend in Ladner's Landing. Letty was no dummy; she probably thought the "friend" was a man Nina was seeing.

Well, Nina thought, triumphantly pulling her keys from the bottom of her bag, it *was* a man. Except that she wasn't seeing him.

Letters! Nina flicked on the hall light and carefully closed the door behind her. She fastened the safety catch out of habit. Big-city habit. Did Ladner's Landing have crime? Well, she supposed they had their share of vandalism and traveling too fast in a school zone, just like any village.

Even before she took off her coat, Nina hurried to the wide window in the living room that overlooked the river. She lit the assortment of candles on the sill. It was a ritual with her whenever she visited the apartment after dark. The honey-soft glow of the candles winking off the bright dark glass brought life to the room.

She hung her coat in the tiny bathroom to dry and

turned on several lamps in the living room. Then she sank into the press-back rocker she'd picked up at the secondhand store on a weekend trip and kicked off her shoes. She examined the letters—two of them today.

This was always an indescribable moment. Two letters. She'd usually study the postmarks to make sure she read them in the proper sequence. Sometimes the second letter was fatter than the first, which always made her scan the first one quickly, anxious to get on to the other. Then at leisure, she'd reread them both over and over, sometimes going back and rereading the last five or six letters she'd received from him, most of which she kept in a small black lacquered Chinese chest in the apartment. These moments gave Nina such intense pleasure that, lately, she'd almost felt frightened by the sensation. It wasn't good—it couldn't be!—to feel so strongly about her part in this old-fashioned dialogue between two virtual strangers. Except she didn't feel that she and Cal were strangers; she felt closer to him than to anyone in her own family, closer than to Letty, who'd been a second mother to her, or to Leo, whom she'd always regarded as her dearest friend.

The first letter, this time, was the thicker. Nina read it, aware of her rising indignation. It was mostly about this…this *woman* Cal kept talking about wanting to marry. This Donna somebody or other. Then Nina reminded herself that she had no right to feel outraged. Cal deserved happiness; as his friend, if she considered herself that, she should *want* happiness for him. If marriage to this divorcée with two kids, love or no love, was the key to his happiness, well…

When she finished the letter, she let her hand fall to

her lap, still holding the pages. She stared out the darkened window at the lights of the fishing-boat masts.
She felt herself trembling. It was crazy. *Crazy!* Why
should she get so worked up over the love life of some
rancher on the other side of the mountains? Somebody
she could never even see again because of all the lies
she'd told him. Someone she called her friend. She'd
write to Cal this very evening. She'd wish him well
in his new life with Donna. She'd tell him it would
be best if they stop writing; she knew she'd feel
that way if she were in Donna's place. She'd tell
him…well, other things. Polite and proper things. Not
that her blood ran cold at the very prospect of him
married to some other woman.

For a few seconds, Nina thought about telling him
everything. All her lies, everything. Then she realized
that to do so would be more than foolish; it would be
selfish. She'd just be getting the whole guilty business
off her chest at the expense of his feelings. He'd be
shocked. And now that he was probably going to get
married, they'd stop writing to each other, at her insistence. He'd have no chance even to express what
he felt about her miserable deception. And there was
another reason not to confess at this late date. She had
to be honest—she didn't want Cal to think badly of
her. *Not Cal.* Not after everything. All the letters. The
hopes and dreams they'd confided in each other….

Still, why did it hurt so much to face the end of
what had been so foolish—and hopeless—right from
the start?

She let the letter in her hand drop to the floor and
picked up the other envelope, slitting the end carefully

with her thumbnail. There were only two pages in it, the writing scrawled.

Nina began to read slowly, then gasped and sat straight, her eyes wildly scanning the lines. *"Oh, no,"* she wailed. *"Oh, no!"* Then the pages fluttered from her nerveless fingers and she began to sob.

McCallum Blake wanted to get married, all right. He wanted to marry her!

"Is MR. SWAIN THERE? Yes, Leo Swain," Nina spoke forcefully into the telephone to mask the tremor in her voice. She'd finally tracked Leo down at one of his favorite restaurants. "Please ask him to come to the phone. He is? Thank you. I'll wait."

Oh, please, Leo, be there, she prayed silently. The maître d' had told her that Leo was just leaving. Nina sniffed loudly. After the initial shock, relieved by a rush of tears, she realized she had to talk to someone. She should have confessed long ago.

Oh, why had she made up that stupid story when she'd first met him? Why hadn't she told Cal everything right away when they'd nearly made love in that hotel room? When it was still a fairly small transgression? The next day she could have phoned him before she left Glory. She could have told him the truth when she started to write to him, apologized for being so childish. Instead of making up more stories, as she'd done. Finding an apartment, inventing an elaborate life here in Ladner's Landing—

"Hello?"

"Oh, Leo, I'm so glad you're still there!"

"Nina? You sound kind of upset."

"I need to see you, Leo. Now. I need to talk to you. Can you come over right away?"

Leo paused for a few long seconds. That was one of the things Nina loved about him. He was so calm, so orderly, so unflappable. "Yes. I think I can. I'll have to make a phone call first and then I'll be there in, oh—" she could almost see him consulting his beloved antique Rolex "—say, twenty minutes?"

"Leo…" The truth was going to hurt; she could feel it already.

"Yes?"

"I'm not at the condo."

"Where are you?"

"I'm at another place. An apartment I rented a few months ago. In Ladner's Landing, south of the river. Do you know how to get here?"

Leo paused again, and when he spoke he asked no questions, although he must have had a million. "Give me the address."

Leo arrived in under half an hour, bringing the night with him. He was dressed in black, as was his habit. No leather, though. Exquisitely tailored trousers, a collarless shirt and beautiful cashmere jacket—all in black. Nina was struck by just how handsome her business partner was. They were the same age exactly. Nina had met Leo Swain in art school ten years earlier when they'd discovered they had the same birthday. They'd been friends ever since and become partners when Nina invested a small legacy she'd received in the design business Leo had begun. Between them, complementary in every way, they'd built Swain and Company into a very successful enterprise.

Her father's dour predictions that a partnership was a sinking ship had been wrong.

"Nice little place you've got here," he said dryly after a quick survey of the apartment. "Love nest?"

Nina laughed and then, when the laughter threatened to turn to tears, made an exaggerated face at him. "*No-o-o.* Do you see any sign of a man around?" Since her frantic phone call, she'd had a chance to pull herself together.

"No." Leo tossed his jacket onto one of the quilt-covered upholstered chairs Nina had rescued from the secondhand shop. He walked around the small space, studying everything with interest, the St. Jean–Port Joli *habitant* scenes on the wall, the tattered hand-pieced antique British flag. Nina knew he was allowing her to begin the story in her own time.

There wasn't an object in the apartment that was new. Everything was old and loved, something she'd brought from home or had brought back from a trip—or had been loved by someone else before ending up at auction or discarded in the secondhand store. Even the kitchen table-and-chair set she'd bought at a garage sale—a tubular steel affair dating from the fifties, with aqua-colored vinyl seats and backs—looked as though it had seen its share of birthday parties and cereal bowls.

"So." Leo finally turned his back to the wide curtainless window and put his hands in his pockets. "What's going on?"

Nina told him. Through the occasional weepy moment, she told him everything, right from the beginning, from meeting Cal and writing to him and subletting the apartment last fall, until the moment she'd received the marriage proposal. Leo listened, his face thoughtful. Once in a while he asked a question to clarify parts of her story—she was so mixed-up that sometimes she wasn't sure what was truth and what was fiction. When she was finished, he stood looking at her. Finally Nina couldn't stand it anymore.

"For heaven's sake, Leo, say something!"

"What do you want me to say?"

Nina stared at him in disbelief. "I want to know what to do. What should I do?"

"That depends."

"Depends?" Nina couldn't believe he could be so calm. This was just about the most momentous thing that had ever happened in her life, and he seemed completely unmoved. "Depends on what?"

Leo continued to watch her. "You could do nothing. Simply refuse his proposal—that part seems clear enough. And definitely stop writing to him."

Refuse his proposal… Something struck Nina with the force of a runaway locomotive. She didn't want to refuse his proposal. Leo had seen clear through her. He'd cut right to the essential point. She felt the blood drain from her face.

"Hey." Leo frowned. "You all right?"

"Leo," she began slowly, her voice hoarse, "I don't…I don't think it's quite as simple as that."

He regarded her for a very long moment. "Does that mean what I think it means? You want to *marry* this guy?"

Did she? Nina realized she'd never faced anything so…so preposterous in her life. How could it be? She didn't even know McCallum Blake, not really. You couldn't count two dozen letters and a couple of hot kisses in a hotel room. Who could base a marriage on that? Her family would go ballistic. If Jake O'Sullivan had been disappointed that his only son had dropped out of law school, what was he going to think when his only daughter left Vancouver to marry some back-woods rancher from Alberta?

They wouldn't have to know, said a little voice inside her. *Not right away.* Nina shuddered. No! No more lies.

"I don't know," she said in a small voice. Then she looked up at Leo, her eyes swimming suddenly, her voice breaking. "It...it seems kind of crazy, doesn't it?"

"Oh, honey." Leo came over to her and put his arms around her. She leaned against him and let the tears soak into his shirt. "Look, it can't be that bad, can it? Maybe you could just talk to him. Tell him everything."

Nina shook her head. "I couldn't, Leo. Not after all this time. And...and if I really do want to marry him..." She laughed shakily. "I can't believe I'm saying this! But if I really do want to marry him, it'd just wreck everything if I told him now."

"What do you mean—now?" He held her away from him and looked down into her face. "You mean you'd tell him later—after you were married?"

"I'd have to, wouldn't I? I mean, eventually." Nina gazed deep into Leo's calm green eyes, looking for answers. "But maybe by then...well, maybe by then it wouldn't be so bad. Something would work out. We'd, well, maybe we'd be in love or whatever, or we'd have had a chance to live together, get to know each other..."

"What about Jake and Meredith?" Leo asked bluntly. He stepped back and handed her his handkerchief. Nina smiled through the tears. Who but Leo in this day and age carried a fine Belgian linen handkerchief embroidered with his initial? God, how she loved this guy! Then she blew her nose. She felt better, a lot better.

"What about them?" she repeated.

"Nina! Listen to me. You can't just take off and marry this...this cowboy. Sell your condo, move to Alberta... You've got to tell your family, don't you think?" Leo's lips thinned. "Jake's not going to like it." Nina knew her father was not Leo's favorite person. And her father had made no secret of the fact that the feeling was mutual.

"I'm not afraid of Dad," Nina said, "and Mother wouldn't really be against it. Not in the long run. She'd be shocked at first, but mostly she'd be worried how Dad would take it." She paused, wild new thoughts filling her head. "I *could* just not tell them—"

"You're serious, aren't you?" Leo interrupted flatly. "You really want to marry this...this rancher."

Nina closed her eyes for a moment, examining her feelings. Yes. Yes, she did. It was true. She wanted to marry McCallum Blake, even though it was the single most ridiculous, irrational, impulsive thing she'd ever done. Her mind drifted to that lazy Indian-summer afternoon she'd spent with him. She recalled the peace, the feeling of being with a man who understood the important things about her without saying a word. He'd accepted her completely as she was. No trappings, no society name, nothing. Simply Nina. Then, in the hotel…

She still felt her cheeks warm when she thought of the way he'd turned at the top of the stairs, the rough urgent way he'd said her name, the way he'd pulled her into his arms. *The way he'd kissed her.* Nothing as romantic had ever happened to her before or since. And then her letters, the soul-baring letters. Even though she'd lied about her circumstances, it had been the real Nina who'd written those letters. She'd been honest about herself, her feelings, her thoughts. Yes, they had something they could base a marriage on.

Still, she valued Leo's opinion. "What would you do, Leo? If you were in my situation."

Leo didn't speak for a moment. He settled back on the heels of his Italian loafers and then rocked forward onto the balls of his feet. When he finally spoke, frowning, Nina realized he was on her side. Come hell or high water, Leo Swain was behind her on this. "The orphan story means he wouldn't question no family at the wedding," he began slowly.

She nodded.

"And Jake and Meredith probably wouldn't even notice you were gone at first, not for a while. You're always traveling, and I know you're not the closest of families." Leo smiled grimly.

Nina nodded again.

"You wouldn't have to give up the condo. Letty can stay there. In fact, you probably should keep it just in case things don't work out. I gather he's given you the option." Leo regarded her with one raised eyebrow.

Nina nodded. "Yes. He specifically said that if it

didn't work out or I didn't like living there, I could go. Don't forget,'' she went on, ''it's sort of a marriage of convenience for him, too. He wants to get married. He's made up his mind about this. If he doesn't marry me, he'll ask someone else.''

''What about the business?''

That was the big question. How could Leo support her on this when she had obligations to him and to their business?

''I could keep up with my designs. I could send you stuff regularly. Maybe even develop a new line based on the colors and textures there. You should see the hills, Leo! Winding and brown and sinewy, just like a lion's pelt—'' Nina stopped abruptly. Her enthusiasm for an unknown new life as a rancher's bride was rising unstoppably. She *could* pull this off. She knew she could.

Still...there were other people who depended on her. ''Look, Leo. If you think this is absolutely mad and totally impossible, please say so.''

''Do you love him?''

''I...I know it's crazy,'' Nina whispered, ''but I think I do. I...I could. So easily. I can't explain it.''

Leo turned to look out the window. He traced the shape of one of the Indian brass pots Nina used for candleholders with a long elegant finger. Then he put his hands back in his pockets. He straightened his shoulders but didn't look at her as he spoke. ''You know something of what my life has been like, Nina.'' He paused, and Nina felt her eyes swim again.

''I spent too many years trying to be someone I wasn't back in Golden when I was growing up. Then I came here when I was nineteen and started to breathe oxygen for the first time in my life. There are still people I haven't told. My mother said it would kill my grandmother to know her grandson was gay. I don't think my mother's right, but I respect her wishes. What *has* happened, though, is that I've lost my grandmother. She's living, but dead to me. That's just one of the people I've lost. Do you understand my meaning?''

Nina nodded.

''I regret I had to live a lie for so long. You have no idea how cruel a small town can be. I couldn't face it.'' Leo shrugged and met her eyes. ''On the other hand, I wouldn't have been able to go to art school or pursue my career in Golden. So maybe it all amounts to the same thing. Works out in the end.''

Leo turned back to the window. ''I've seen a lot of friends die, Nina, with nobody around them. No mothers or fathers, no brothers or sisters. They kept too many secrets.'' He shook his head and sighed heavily.

Then he swung to face her. ''Go where your heart takes you, Nina. Don't do what you think somebody else wants—me, your parents. When fortune comes knocking, for God's sake get up and answer the door. If you happen to think it's this rancher—'' Leo carelessly lifted one shoulder ''—go for it. If it doesn't work out, take the consequences. Do what you have to do. But don't play it safe. Playing it safe isn't all it's cracked up to be.''

He smiled wryly and Nina jumped up and threw her arms around him and burst into tears.

She knew exactly what she was going to do. Her fantasy was about to become her reality. How many people ever got that chance?

CHAPTER NINE

"Blake?"

Cal turned. He had hoped he wouldn't meet anyone he knew at the airport.

"Well, I'll be damned—Cal Blake!"

"Ray." Cal held out his hand and the other man shook it vigorously. "How are you?"

"Fine, just fine. Picking up the wife. She's come back from a little trip to Winnipeg to visit our daughter, y'know. You remember Melissa?" He winked at Cal; Cal wasn't exactly sure why. "I'm a granddaddy now. Lissy just had her first. A boy."

"That's great news, Ray."

Cal wished the other man would move off. He didn't mean to be rude, but the last thing he wanted right now was to talk cows and grandkids with Ray Wallenstein. He glanced up at the monitor that showed arrivals and departures. Nina's plane was late, and each minute that went by made him feel worse. More than once since he'd started for Calgary early this morning he'd wondered just what kind of prime fool he was. If he could've called the whole thing off, he thought he would've done it.

Now to run into Ray Wallenstein, of all people. He was with the Calgary law firm Cal had hired last fall to pursue grass and water leases for the expansion Cal planned over the next two years if the market for grass-fed beef stayed strong.

Unfortunately Ray showed no sign of moving on.

"So what're you doing here, Cal? Goin' somewhere?"

"Nope." Cal took a deep breath. No sense pretending. After today, the whole world would know, anyway. "I'm meeting my fiancée." The unfamiliar word almost stuck in his throat. "She's coming in from Vancouver—"

"Fiancée! Why, you sly old dog, you. I never knew you were fixing to get married. Congratulations!" Ray wrung Cal's hand again, then gave him a broad wink and a one-man-to-another leer. Cal hated that sort of thing. "Bachelor days over, eh?"

"Looks like it," Cal replied tersely. He looked nervously over the heads of the crowd that surged into the passenger-arrivals area. Was this lot from Nina's flight? No, the monitor light had just started to wink, indicating her plane had only now landed. The passengers would be in the terminal any moment.

"Who is she? Anybody I know?"

Jeez... "Don't think so, Ray. Nina's her name, Nina O'Shea. From Vancouver." Wallenstein just wouldn't let up.

The other man frowned. "Name rings a bell. 'Course I suppose there're a lot of O'Sheas in the phone book out there. Oops, there's Millie now!" Ray waved. "Yo, over here, darlin'." Millie saw her husband and smiled and to Cal's huge relief, Ray hurried off to meet her.

Cal searched the crowd again, jaw set. Would he even recognize Nina? What was she wearing? All he could see her in were jeans and a big yellow shirt, the way she'd been dressed when she came out to the ranch last September.

Then his heart slammed into his ribs. She hadn't noticed him yet. She was talking earnestly with an older woman who'd come down the escalator with her, then moved off toward the baggage carousel when they reached the main level. Nina looked around expectantly.

She still hadn't seen him. *Damn, she was gorgeous.*

Cal let out his breath on a ragged rush. He felt like a teenager before his first big date. She wore some sort of pale green swirly thing. A skirt and jacket. Her hair was loose and she carried a big shoulder bag, like the one she'd had in September, only leather, instead of canvas. He drank in every detail, glad of the few seconds he had to compose himself. He'd suspected that he'd know, one way or another, exactly what kind of fool he was the instant he saw her. And fool he might be, but the truth was clear to him: no matter what, he wanted this particular plan to work out. He wanted this woman for his wife.

She saw him then, and he knew immediately that she felt the same way. Her eyes lit up and she waved. He strode toward her.

"Nina." His voice didn't sound right. He took both her hands in his. God, he couldn't believe it. She was here. *And she was his.* "It's good to see you."

"Hello, Cal." Her cheeks were deliciously pink. She seemed flustered. "I...I was hoping you'd be here."

He couldn't stop smiling. "I was hoping you'd

come," he said. What else could he say? What else *was* there to say? It was a miracle.

The crowd faded away. He pulled her into his arms and buried his face in her hair.

"Hey, you two lovebirds!"

Cal groaned inwardly. *Damn.* He released Nina and kept one arm protectively around her shoulders as he turned with her to face the Wallensteins.

"I was just telling the wife you were here, Cal, and we didn't want to miss the chance to meet your young lady, did we, Millie?"

Millie shook her head, eyes bright with curiosity. Cal knew there was no way out of it.

"Millie and Ray Wallenstein, I'd like you to meet Nina O'Shea." He paused. "My fiancée."

Nina shot him a glance—did the word surprise her, too?—before she smiled and stepped forward.

"Our firm's doing some work for McCallum," Ray explained, pumping her hand. "Say." He paused and regarded her closely. "You wouldn't be related to Meredith O'Shea, would you? The famous lawyer? Why we've even heard of her out here in Alberta." Ray beamed at Cal.

But Cal wasn't looking at him. He'd seen Nina go white and he drew her close and tightened his arm around her. "You okay?" he murmured.

She seemed paralyzed for a second or two, then she recovered. "I'm fine, Cal," she said in a low tone, glancing up. "No, Mr. Wallenstein, I...I can't say as I've ever heard of her."

"Well, well. Just thought there might be a chance, what with the names and all. Well, good to see you, Cal. Give me a yell anytime you come up to town.

Come on, Millie, let's go get your suitcase.'' The Wallensteins moved off toward the slowly revolving baggage carousel.

Nina looked after them for a few seconds. Cal had the feeling she didn't want him to see her face. He didn't like the way she'd gone pale. "Look, Nina, you sure you're okay?''

She nodded, her eyes dark, though she managed a faint smile. "I'm fine, Cal. I…I guess I'm just a little hungry. I was too excited to eat before I left.''

"Well, we can soon fix that.'' He tucked her arm under his. "Let's get your stuff and then we'll go to the hotel and get something to eat.''

"When are we getting married?'' she asked with a flash of her usual sunny smile, the one he remembered. Cal felt immeasurably better.

"How does this afternoon sound?''

"YOU STILL WANT to go through with this?''

They were driving south on the Barlow Trail toward the office high-rises and spinelike Husky Tower of Calgary's city center, jagged against the brilliant backdrop of the Rockies to the west. Spring had broken early on the northern range. Trees shone with soft green leaves, and city boulevards had been freshly mowed. Farther south, toward Glory and the Rocking Bar S, the Horsethief and the Highwood still ran floodhigh with meltwater but, on the hillsides, the brown of winter had given way to the first green growth. The previous morning Cal and Henry and Lewis, the new hand, had moved 150 cows and their newborn calves onto the bottomland along the Horsethief. It had been no trouble, even shorthanded; the cows were bawling

and eager to get to the grass. His calf crop was out-
standing this year, better than he'd expected, which
made him feel good about the future. He'd heard from
Jeremiah finally and figured he'd turn up at the Rocking Bar S any day. And now...

Cal glanced sideways at the woman sitting silently
beside him, staring out the passenger window. *Marriage?* Sometimes he felt like pinching himself to
prove this was all happening.

"You know, you don't have to go through with it
if you don't want to," he continued when she remained silent. "We can call it off right now, no problem. Whatever you want."

Her eyes were very blue and serious. "Is that what
you want? To call it off?"

He studied the road in front of him. "No. I want to
marry you." He turned to her again. "But I can sure
understand it if you've changed your mind. Any way
you look at it, this whole thing is kind of crazy."

"Yes." She glanced down, rolled the hem of her
jacket between her fingers once or twice. "It is," she
agreed, raising her eyes to his. "But I've given it a
lot of thought. It's what I want to do."

Cal couldn't believe the relief that flooded through
him. He wanted to stop right there in the middle of
the traffic on the Barlow Trail and haul her into his
arms and kiss her until she couldn't breathe, until they
both couldn't breathe.

He'd meant it—she could change her mind right
now. Hell, she could change it any time she wanted
out, even after they were married. He'd told her that
in his letter and the last time they'd spoken on the
phone. Still, when push came to shove, he hoped she

wouldn't change her mind. He wanted her—in his arms, in his bed, in his life. He'd do whatever it took to keep her there. To make her *want* to stay.

He didn't stop the Suburban; he didn't even slow down. But damned if he could wipe the silly grin off his face. Neither spoke for a few moments.

They were coming down the hill now, about to turn onto Memorial Drive and then cross the Bow River into downtown Calgary. He'd taken a room at the exclusive Palliser Hotel for the weekend. They weren't planning much of a wedding, but that didn't mean they had to cut corners on the honeymoon.

Honeymoon. Even the thought of the word and all it meant made his throat go dry and his hands sweat.

Then they were at the hotel, and a college student in white gloves and top hat stepped forward to open the door.

Cal tossed him the keys, handed him a couple of bills and told him he'd need the Suburban back in two hours. They had an appointment at the city clerk's office at four. He hadn't told Nina yet. By five o'clock on this sunny April afternoon, they'd be husband and wife.

Cal slung his bag over his shoulder, picked up Nina's case in one hand and walked up the red-carpeted steps with her. One of her suitcases had gone missing—the airline promised to deliver it to the hotel as soon as it appeared—and the rest of her stuff was being shipped later directly to the ranch, she said. The preparations she'd made, the fact that several trunks were arriving addressed to her as his wife, brought home just how final this step was.

Inside, the past-world grandeur of the old railway

hotel never failed to impress him, no matter how many times he stayed here. He could see immediately that Nina was impressed, too, with the grand lobby and the elaborate fittings and the many fine paintings on the walls. That pleased him in some elusive way. Of course, he knew her life hadn't been filled with a lot of the pleasures money could buy, but at the same time he felt proud that he'd been the one to bring her here. The Palliser, named for an early Alberta explorer, went back to the earliest ranching days, long before Turner Valley oil had been discovered, back to the last century when the country had been stitched together from sea to sea by the construction of the Canadian Pacific Railway. Prime ministers and crown princes and movie stars had found temporary comfort under the twenty-foot ceilings. Many deals had been made here and, no doubt, as many promises broken.

It only took a few minutes to register and then they were in the elevator, headed for the ninth floor. Cal wondered if she felt as nervous as he did. She didn't *seem* nervous, just quietly interested in everything.

"Did I tell you we have to go down to City Hall at half-past three?" he asked as they left the elevator. "Fill out some papers?"

She looked startled for a moment. "That's when we're getting married?"

Cal nodded, not taking his eyes from her face. "Four o'clock." She flushed slightly. "I figured you might want to change first? Rest? Whatever."

He paused and set down their bags at the door to their suite. No going back now. Cal took a deep breath and inserted the coded key. The heavy wooden door swung open.

"This is nice!" Nina said, and he was glad that she immediately started fussing—adjusting the window so that a breath of air brushed into the room, pushing back a chair that stood too close to the coffee table.

Cal glanced around. They had a suite, with a sitting room, into which the outer door opened, and a separate bedroom that led to the bathroom, or so he presumed. He held her suitcase in a death grip.

The bed. He didn't even want to look at it right now, although he knew it was in the next room, where he was going to take these bags. He didn't want her to see it, either. He just felt so damn embarrassed all of a sudden, as though he'd been guilty of cooking up some complicated underhanded plan to trick a woman he hardly knew into sleeping with him on a first date.

While Nina blithely inspected the whole suite, commenting on everything, including the old-fashioned porcelain bathtub she'd discovered, he willed himself to quit being such an idiot. She came back into the sitting room and he met her gaze.

"Well?"

She laughed, that delightful sound he remembered so clearly. "Well, what?"

"Is it all right?"

"Fine. Here, give me that." She took her suitcase from him. "I've got a dress in here I thought I'd wear. I want to see if it's wrinkled. I suppose there's an iron somewhere—" she looked vaguely around the room "—or I could get one from housekeeping...."

"Nina." He moved toward her and put his hands lightly on her shoulders. His voice sounded rough, rougher than he'd thought it would sound. He realized suddenly that she, too, was nervous, maybe even as nervous as he was. This was a big thing for them both.

She held his gaze, her eyes dark and questioning.

"Look, Nina," he began again, his voice not much more than a whisper. "Are you *sure* this is what you want? Really sure?"

She nodded, her eyes still on his. He brought one hand around to the back of her neck, under her hair, massaged the warm smooth flesh of her nape for a few seconds, then bent quickly and kissed her. He felt her breath ease from her, felt the tension ease from him, felt her yield a tiny sigh. He didn't deepen the kiss or pull her close. Now was not the time.

He kept his hands on her shoulders for a few more moments, gazing deep into her eyes. "Okay?"

She nodded. "Okay," she said tremulously with a crooked smile.

He reached into his pocket and pulled out a velvet jeweler's case. He opened it, then carefully removed the ring that rested there, winking and blue. He took her left hand and raised it between them and slid the ring onto her third finger.

"Sapphire. I thought it matched your eyes," he said. "If you'd rather have a diamond, we can trade it."

"No, I like this," she said so faintly he barely heard her. She looked up then from inspecting the ring on her hand. Her eyes were swimming. "Thank you, Cal."

"I'll, uh, go downstairs until you have a chance to get changed or do whatever you want to do. Order something from room service if you're hungry."

"What about you?"

"I'll change my shirt when I come back up," he said, and felt a warmth rise in his chest as she smiled. "After all, it isn't every day a guy gets married. Right?"

"Right."

"I'll come up in an hour or so."

Alone in the long thickly carpeted crystal-lit hall, he took a couple of deep breaths, then set off for the elevator. He could use a drink. A stiff one.

And McCallum Blake wasn't a drinking man.

WHEN THE DOOR CLOSED behind Cal, Nina stood for a few moments, frozen, her emotions whirling. Then, as she started to move slowly toward the suitcase she'd set down at the doorway to the bedroom, she saw her face in the mirror over the writing desk.

"How can you do this?" she whispered to her image. *"To him?"* "How could you even dream of involving him in a...a *charade* like this?"

She looked down at her hand. The ring he'd given her was a bit big, but that could be adjusted. It was beautiful—limpid and blue and deep as a mountain lake. *He'd said it reminded him of her eyes.*

How could she tell him the truth now? Yet how could she *not* tell him? It was already too late to spare him the embarrassment of the whole world knowing, either way. That man—Ray Wallenstein. She had no doubt he'd spread the news of their marriage to everyone he met.

Moaning, Nina sank down onto the low chair in front of the mirror. She'd already missed her chance to come clean. She'd denied—publicly—knowing her own mother. How could she say to Cal now, "Oh, by the way, that lawyer your friend asked me about at the airport? She's actually my mother. And I'm not who I've said I am, either.''

The fact was, she couldn't do it. Meeting him today, seeing him after so many months...she just knew in her bones she'd made the right decision. She hadn't had a doubt, not a real one, since she'd talked it over with Leo. The only question that had arisen was how to carry it though. Somehow she'd do it; she'd been sure of that. Somehow she'd make it all work out in the end. *Then...to meet someone who'd heard of her mother!*

Nina remembered her joy when she'd spotted Cal at the airport, standing back, leaning slightly against a steel girder, behind the crowd. Tall, serious-looking. Watching her. He'd smiled then, that gorgeous smile that went straight to her heart. And she'd known, known *absolutely,* that she wanted him. She would let nothing stop her now. Certainly not a dumb story she'd told him months ago, the kind of story most people told a stranger at one time or another. Or were tempted to tell.

No. She wanted to share her life, her days, all her conversations with McCallum Blake. Love? Maybe love, too. Someday. It just might happen. Stranger things had happened in people's lives. He was taking a big chance; so was she.

As for *falling* in love, what was that kind of love, anyway? Sometimes Nina thought the whole concept overrated, a notion that belonged in novels and movies and songs. Obviously he didn't care, either; he'd been perfectly prepared to ask that Donna person to marry him. The thought galvanized Nina.

She picked up the phone and asked for a sandwich to be sent up. Then she opened her suitcase and shook out her dress. It wasn't too badly wrinkled and, with its soft floral pattern, the wrinkles wouldn't show. It would do. Would her husband-to-be recognize shantung silk and the artfully simple cut of this dress, her wedding dress, that spelled high fashion? Or the wickedly expensive Renée LaRue matching hat? She didn't think so. And there was no way she was spending her entire new life in jeans and T-shirts. She'd done enough pretending.

She went into the bathroom and turned the faucets on full blast, reveling in the clouds of steam that filled the white-tiled room. She tied up her hair and carefully fitted a shower cap over it. No time to redo her hair; no time to worry about her nails, either. She grinned at herself in the rapidly fogging mirror and patted her plastic cap jauntily. Who cared about perfect nails and great hair now?

She was getting married!

CHAPTER TEN

A FEW PAPERS to sign, a brief ceremony with the sun beating down through the high windows and the muted murmur of City Hall business being transacted elsewhere—and it was over. She was married. Less than twenty minutes to join yourself to a man, in sickness and in health, in good times and in bad—how could it be possible?

But this smiling man beside her was no illusion. He stood there, accepting the congratulations of the official who'd married them and the two clerks who'd scrawled their names as witnesses. He was flesh and blood, one-hundred-percent rugged handsome Western man, sexy as hell in his jacket and tie and polished dress boots. The broad-brimmed hat was missing naturally, but no doubt he'd put it back on when they left the building. Nina reached up to check the position of her own hat.

The look in Cal's eyes when he'd returned to their room an hour earlier had been one Nina knew she'd treasure forever. Absolute undisguised admiration—what woman could resist? She'd glimpsed desire, too, a smoldering look that told her everything she wanted to know. The attraction they'd both felt back in September was still there. Simmering, hidden...explosive. By the time Cal had emerged from his own shower ten minutes later, hair brushed down but still damp, tying his tie in front of the mirror where she'd glimpsed so many of her own doubts, Nina's cheeks were pink. He'd caught her eye in the glass and smiled, and her cheeks had grown even hotter.

Now they were married. Cal turned as one of the clerks started to gather up the various documents. "Well, ma'am?" He grinned at Nina. "Ready to ride?"

"Anytime you are, cowboy," she retorted, unable to stop smiling. She felt so good, so happy, so incredibly pleased with herself and with him, with the world. If only Jake and Meredith had been here—if only she could have shared such an important moment with her parents and Letty. With Murray and her nephew and all of Murray's ex-wives. With Leo.

The two clerks sighed. Nina could see they were nearly as taken with her new husband as she was. "Hey—what are you doing?" she gasped as Cal suddenly stepped forward and pulled her into his arms. "Careful, you'll crush my hat," she warned.

"To hell with your hat," he growled.

And there, before the delighted clerks and the crusty old justice of the peace—now smiling as broadly as the clerks—Cal kissed her. Properly. He wrapped his arms around her and held her solidly against him, bending down until the light from the windows behind them disappeared and all she could see was him. This wasn't the brief ceremonial kiss they'd shared earlier. This was new and different. Possession—definitely possession—tempered with hope, with eagerness, with the promise of more to come. *Later.* He took his time, exploring her mouth slowly and thoroughly. Finally, when she thought she'd burst with pleasure and dizziness, when the world had melted entirely away, he released her and grinned. The clerks sent up a ragged cheer. She knew her face was bright red, her dress was mussed, her darling hat was crushed—she'd even dropped her purse. But she didn't care. She was legally married to the only man she'd ever wanted to marry.

The deed was done.

And now—very soon—she had to tell her new husband the truth. And pray that he'd forgive her.

WHY WAS IT you could drive to the big city on business and find nobody around? Then you could come to town with no interest in company, only to discover you couldn't cross the street without running into people you knew.

On the way to the parking lot, Cal passed one of his neighbors, Ed Baines, rancher and onetime contender for his aunt's hand—or so Cal had always suspected. Naturally Cal introduced Nina and had to suffer while the old rancher's eyes lit up and he looked her over about as skeptically and carefully as he might check out a saddle horse someone was trying to sell him. Cal groaned inwardly. What kind of luck was this to run into one of the valley's major eccentrics before Nina'd even been married to him for five minutes? Before she'd had a chance to realize what she'd gotten into? Well, at least Ed was in a hell of a hurry to get to City Hall before it closed and couldn't stop to gossip. Small mercies.

Nina would find out soon enough that being a rancher's wife was nothing like going to a nine-to-five job at a fancy decorator studio, or whatever that place was where she worked in Vancouver.

At the Palliser, they'd barely walked into the lobby when he ran into Gus Lidgate, another rancher he knew well from down Claresholm way. Gus owned the old Triple Dot ranch and was known for his tender heart—he'd hire three extra hands at top wages before he'd pitch in and help with his own branding—and for never being without a wad of chewing tobacco. There he was, sweating mightily in a tuxedo, no sign of the telltale tobacco bulge in his cheek, heading determinedly across the lobby to the Oak Room.

"Blake!" The older rancher spotted him. "Son of a gun, am I glad to see you." He shook Cal's hand heartily. "Wife's got me all decked out in this here monkey suit and made me swear on a stack of Bibles I'd stay away from the whiskey and the Copenhagen." He ran a beefy finger around his starched collar and winked. "Beer ain't whiskey, now, is it? Just heading for the bar— Say, this your little lady friend?" He beamed at Nina. "Why don't the two of you join me?"

"My wife," Cal said quietly with pride. "Nina O'Shea." He smiled down at Nina and she smiled back. He resisted the overwhelming urge to kiss her again.

"Well, I'll be damned. I never heard you were hitched."

"Just this afternoon, Gus." Cal pulled Nina closer. "At City Hall."

"Now, ain't that a coincidence? My, oh my, congratulations." Gus reached up as though to tip a non-existent hat, then made Nina an awkward little bow, instead. "We just had us a weddin' too. Wendy—that's our second youngest—she got married in the Leduc Room up there, not an hour ago. One of those bean-counter fellas from Lethbridge, insurance or something. Not what I woulda handpicked for one of my girls, McCallum. I don't believe he knows the business end of a branding iron from a garden rake." Gus leaned confidentially toward them, his bright blue eyes taking a quick survey of the lobby, perhaps on the lookout for his better half. "The wife's real pleased, though. And Wendy don't seem all that interested in her old dad's opinion—"

"Thanks, Gus," Cal interrupted, and caught Nina's eye. She was smiling, apparently charmed by the old rancher's palaver. "But I think we'll pass on your offer. Maybe another time. Fact is, we got married less than an hour ago ourselves."

"Where's Lou? Where's Jeremiah? Henry in town?" Gus seemed to rouse himself. He looked around wildly. "By God, Henry's never turned down a free drink—where's he staying?"

"Nobody's in town. We just up and got married. They don't even know about it yet." Cal was beginning to realize that maybe he should have told a few people. It would've made this part easier, for Nina, at least. Dealing with the surprise and shock when his friends and neighbors—people who'd always taken him for a lifelong bachelor—found out he was a married man was going to get tedious fast, he could tell. And not just married, but married to a stranger. From away. That was big news in a small close-knit ranching community.

"Well, you listen here, McCallum." Gus rested a

huge paw on Cal's shoulder and included Nina in his earnest glance. "You two want a little dancin' and celebratin', you don't think nothin' of joinin' the party down here in the ballroom this evening. You'd be more than welcome, you know that. The wife'd be proud to see you, Cal. You know she always thought an awful lot of your mama."

Making no promises, Cal and Nina walked toward the elevators, leaving the parched rancher to make his way to the hotel's main watering hole, the Oak Room.

Now what? Cal felt his hands begin to sweat.

What were they supposed to do now, except go to their room and take up where they'd left off last September? Cal felt his heart pound at the prospect. Damn. What kind of notion was that for a mature, supposedly sensible man? And who was going to broach the idea—him?

"Well, what do you think, Nina?" he began awkwardly. "Did you want to go have a drink with Gus?"

"He's kind of a neat old guy, isn't he?" she said, looking up at Cal with those big blue eyes. Something inside him was melting fast.

Neat old guy? "That's not exactly how I would've described him," he said. For some reason, he was pleased that she liked Gus Lidgate.

"Well, I thought so," she said, squeezing his arm. "I'm looking forward to meeting more of your friends. And seeing Lou again. And everybody else. And seeing all those puppies you've been writing to me about."

He felt his heart catch. "So, uh, what would you like to do now? Do you want to go up to the room? I made a reservation for dinner at seven o'clock." He glanced at his watch and frowned. "It's not quite five—"

"Let's go upstairs and make love," she said softly.

He stared at her, surprise giving way to delight. Just then the elevator doors opened in front of them. No one got out, and they were the only people to get on.

"All right," he said, nodding as he pulled her into his arms. "I could go for that."

THEY FORGOT to punch the button for their floor, and the elevator didn't move from the main floor while Cal kissed her the way he'd wanted to since he'd met her at the plane. The warm sweet taste of her mouth blended with the warm soft feel of her in his arms, and he didn't even notice when the elevator's doors snapped open, then shut. The second time the doors snapped open, he realized they had an audience as he heard a faint twitter and raised his head, startled to see two giggling Japanese girls, hands over their mouths, just as the doors closed again. He leaned forward, careful not to overbalance Nina, and pushed the button for the ninth floor.

"Damn!" he said faintly, grinning down at her. Her mouth looked soft and damp with his kisses and she didn't say anything. "Maybe if I keep at this long enough, I'll get it right."

"Mmm," she said, reaching for him. "I hope so." The trip to the ninth floor wasn't long enough to satisfy either of them. Two elderly couples were waiting for the elevator there, and when the doors opened and one matron cleared her throat loudly, Cal and Nina suddenly came to their senses and sprang guiltily apart. Cal felt foolish.

"Just married," he said sheepishly as he held the
door for the matrons. "Sorry." He couldn't stop grinning and Nina giggled. As one of the ancient gentle-
men got on the elevator, he gave Cal a very solemn
wink.

"A word of advice, young man," he said before the
door closed. "Never apologize."

Nina burst out laughing and Cal put his arm around
her. Then they were at the door to their room and he
had to search through his pockets for the key. Finally
he found it and the door swung open.

"Oh, Cal! They're gorgeous—" Nina rushed forward to bury her nose in the two dozen long-stemmed
red roses he'd ordered when he reserved the room last
week. A silver ice bucket held a magnum of Mumm's.
Cal shrugged off his jacket, pleased that he'd had the
foresight to arrange for the flowers and a bottle of
champagne. He thought fleetingly of the gibes he'd
had to take from Jeremiah and Henry over the years—
was this romantic or what?

He reached up to loosen his tie, stopping short of
removing it entirely. He could hardly wait to take off
his clothes, and hers, but maybe he should crack the
champagne first?

"Oh, Cal, you're so thoughtful." She was in front
of him, her hands flat on his shirtfront, her eyes earnest. "You're such a caring sexy man and I'm so glad
you asked me to marry you. I know it was crazy the
way it happened, but I think this is going to work out,
I really do. I want it to, so much." The blue of the
sapphire paired with the plain gold-and-platinum wedding band glittered on her hand.

"Hell, Nina." His throat felt tight; he didn't know

what to say. "I'm just glad I took a notion to ask you. I don't know what I'd have done if you'd turned me down. It wouldn't have been the same if I'd ended up married to someone else. I meant everything I said today at City Hall. I'll do my damnedest to be the husband you deserve. I don't want to ever give you cause to be sorry you married me."

She placed her lips on his and he took a deep quick breath and wrapped his arms around her, running his palms along the smooth warm planes of her back. Whatever this dress was made of, it was almost as though she had nothing on, so distinctly could he feel the silky texture of her skin. Then the thought of her having nothing on pushed his heart into triple time, and he shifted, pulling her hips against his, hard. She gasped.

"I want you, Nina," he whispered against the smooth skin of her throat. "You know I do. I've wanted you for so long. I've thought of making love with you since the moment I met you. I never thought it'd happen." He covered her face with kisses. "Not like this."

"Oh, Cal," she whispered brokenly. He discovered the catch at the top of her dress and fumbled to unfasten it with one hand, then grasped the tab and slowly, ever so slowly, pulled down the long zipper that fastened the back. How had she ever done this up by herself?

He ran his fingers lightly down her bare spine. His fingertips plucked at the narrow band of her bra and she shuddered. His blood surged. The idea that she wanted him as much as he wanted her was beginning to penetrate his brain. How in hell had he ever gotten so lucky to meet and marry this woman—this fabulous, beautiful, warm, good-natured, high-spirited woman? It was the kind of thing that never happened to him. He'd worked for everything he'd ever gotten in his life, worked hard. Good fortune didn't just fall into his lap, the way Nina had that September afternoon.

One side of her dress slipped away, and he kissed the smooth roundness of her shoulder, drawing the sweetness of her skin, strange and yet oddly familiar, deep into his lungs. She threw her head back and he kissed her throat and all the little pulsing hollows at the base of her throat. Again and again and then lower, until he'd reached the small soft mounds of her breasts, white as winter snow spilling over the fragile lace of her bra. Navy blue lace.

Cal felt a wave of pure male sensation flood through him, and every action suddenly took on new meaning. He held her tightly against him, measured the frantic pace of her breathing against his, then boldly slipped the other shoulder free. The dress slithered to a heap on the carpet.

"*Nina.*" His voice sounded as ragged as he felt. He stepped back, daring to look at her fully. "You're so beautiful. So perfect." She stood, proud before him, in only that tiny lace bra and brief matching half-slip. She still had on her high-heeled shoes. As he watched, she stepped away from the puddle of her dress and kicked off her shoes, her eyes not leaving his for a second.

She stepped toward him again and wound her arms around his neck and pressed her breasts hard against his chest, her mouth open and eager against his. Her message was unmistakable. *She wanted him.* He kissed her roughly, greedily, as though he might never have another chance. He felt her hands on his shirtfront, fumbling at his buttons, and, impatient, he tore off his shirt. Then he swept her up in his arms and carried her into the bedroom.

The bed was very large, king-size, with a thick spread, palest blue. He set her down on it. Her cheeks were pink, and her eyes were very bright. Cal began to unbuckle his belt, then remembered his boots and sat down on the bed to pull them off. He felt Nina's hand, feather-light, on his bare back,and the sensation shot into every nerve. He caught his breath, then turned to her. He didn't dare breathe. She looked so beautiful. She was his wife, ''from this day forward...''

She wanted him.

She held out her arms and he lay beside her, holding her close for a moment. He began to kiss her again, each kiss growing deeper and more urgent. She trembled and whispered his name over and over and arched her body against his.

He tore his mouth from hers, not trusting himself, and kissed her everywhere. He unfastened her bra and tossed it away and slid the rest of her clothing, her panties and slip and stockings, from her and tossed them over the side. Then he stood and quickly stripped and joined her, naked on the bed, hungry for her warmth and her satin skin against his. He felt the coolness of her thighs and her hands setting him on fire, and then, amazingly, he was inside her and she cried out and clung to him and cried out again. She was smooth and hot and more wonderful than he'd ever dreamed. The heat and shudder of her climax and her sharp cries of completion brought him instantly to his own. He felt himself dissolve and felt the endless pulse of hot blood, emptiness and fullness all at once.

He dragged oxygen into his aching lungs. Her face was flushed and her eyes glowed, and she kept whispering tiny things he couldn't hear for the thunder in his head. He felt her take a deep breath and hold it for a few seconds, and then he realized she was crying.

"What's the matter, sweetheart? Did I hurt you? What's wrong?" Cal examined her face with urgent fingers, wiping clumsily at the tears. *If he'd hurt her— in any way—he'd never forgive himself.* What about birth control? Goddamn it, he'd totally forgotten about that. Was she using anything? She'd written and told him she'd take care of it.

"No," she whispered through the tears. "It's just… just so *wonderful.*" She stopped, held her breath, then he heard a sob escape. "Everything." She sniffed loudly and tried to smile, and he smiled, too, feeling foolish and proud as hell at the same time.

"I know, sweetheart. I know." He kissed the tears from her cheeks, then holding her close, he rolled to one side, letting the mattress take his weight.

For a few moments he said nothing. They were well and truly joined. Husband and wife. This was the deepest, most ancient commitment two people could make: to share, to face the future together. To trust each other. This was when he really *felt* married—not when he'd signed the papers at City Hall.

He stroked her hot cheek, pushed damp tendrils of hair from her face. He kissed her gently, over and over. He loved kissing her. He loved the softness of her skin and the warm womanly scent of her flesh.

After a while he felt Nina relax, and when he looked at her, he saw she was smiling again. "So," he said, holding her a little tighter, "I take it you wouldn't mind trying that again."

She grinned and sniffed noisily, the last of her tears. For good, he hoped. "I sure would," she said, and her eyes shone wickedly in the late-afternoon sunlight that streamed through the tall bedroom window. "I think you should know this is the first time I've had to marry a man before he'd make love with me."

Cal heard the roar of his laughter echo from the plaster ceiling. That was when he knew—*really knew*—that everything would be all right. That marrying Nina O'Shea was the best and luckiest and smartest thing he'd ever done.

CHAPTER ELEVEN

THEY MADE LOVE and then they drank champagne in bed and made love again. They were late for their dinner reservation. Neither cared. Soft music and wonderful food—prime rib for him and linguine with wild mushrooms for her—lingering glances, the glow of candlelight and wine. The air was dense and fragrant, scented with flowers on the table and crowded with vivid, achingly new memories of physical intimacy. The promise of more...so soon.

That night they danced at the Lidgate wedding, but the band played for them alone. In the morning Cal got up early and showered and ordered breakfast from room service, while Nina tried to block out both the sun and Cal's cheerful comments with two down pillows over her head. She needed her sleep, and the truth was, she'd barely slept all night. Nor had he—not that he seemed to mind. Finally, grumbling, she emerged, to be fed tea and bits of toast with marmalade by her new husband and then soundly made love to all over again. This time, they showered together, and it was a miracle they managed to be dressed by the time the bellhop knocked discreetly on their door to announce that her errant suitcase had arrived from the airport.

That was a relief. Nina had been worried because they'd taken no precautions, but quickly calculating, had decided the risk of pregnancy was very small. She'd accepted the responsibility for birth control when she'd accepted Cal's proposal and had been fitted for a diaphragm by her Vancouver doctor. That diaphragm had been safely stowed in the suitcase that had gone missing.

Someday—soon, she hoped—she'd like to start a family with Cal. She knew he wanted children; that was partly why he'd made up his mind to get married in the first place. But before that, they had to establish a real marriage. They had to learn to know each other better and she had to confess the truth about her background. Very soon. Eventually he'd have to meet her mother and father and her brother.

Nina shuddered at the thought of what lay ahead. It was too easy, these magical few days of their honeymoon, to forget that her marriage was founded on a lie. A story she'd accidentally, even innocently, begun and then not so innocently maintained. The apartment, the made-up brothers and sisters, the succession of dead-end jobs—how could she have been so stupid!

Once or twice during the weekend she'd gone over the words she'd need to begin. "Cal, there's something I think you should know about me—I lied to you when we first met." Or, "You have to believe me when I say that I never meant anything like this to happen, I never dreamed I'd see you again...". Or, "You know that car I was driving last September? That Porsche? Well, actually it's mine..."

But she never found the right time to say the words. She couldn't bring herself to prick the glorious bubble they were living in. She'd find the right time later, she promised herself. At the Rocking Bar S. As soon as they'd settled down. Once her things had arrived, her trunks. Once they'd established some pattern to their life together. Once he realized how important he was to her, and how much she'd really, truly wanted to marry him.

After lunch on Sunday they started for Glory. Nina's bags were piled in the back of the Suburban, her new sunglasses perched firmly on her nose and a relaxed and smiling Cal at the wheel.

In a way, wonderful as these past two days had been, she was glad they were leaving. She'd been terrified that she'd run into someone she knew or who knew her parents. She hadn't spent much time in Calgary and had never stayed at that particular hotel, but her mother was well-known throughout Western Canada and her father had certainly been to Calgary many times either politicking or doing business. Worst would have been meeting someone who actually knew her. After all she'd gone through, the last thing she needed was to have the whole situation upset by sheer chance. Once she'd told Cal everything herself, she didn't care how many people she met who might know her or her family.

"What are you thinking about?" In his open-neck white cotton shirt and black jeans and sunglasses, his dark hair ruffled by the wind from the open window, Cal looked devastatingly attractive. It always amazed her when she remembered what a low opinion his own family had of Cal's success with women. She couldn't imagine a woman who wouldn't be impressed by such a man.

But maybe she was biased. "Just thinking about the

way things happened. How lucky it was I met you when I did.''

Although she couldn't see his eyes behind the dark lenses, she could see his slow smile. The bone-tickling one. The smile that turned her inside out every time. ''Maybe we should thank Walter.''

She frowned. ''Walter? The old guy who fixed my car?''

''Yeah.'' He grinned and turned his attention to the road. ''If Walter's hearing aid worked better, he might've answered his phone and then Jeremiah and I never would have stopped to offer you a ride.''

''And…?''

''If I hadn't met you that afternoon, I don't think I would've had the nerve to walk up and invite myself to sit down at your table the way I did.''

Nina laughed. *If only he knew all the ifs!* ''Remind me to send him a box of chocolates.''

''I think a bottle of Captain Morgan might be more his style.''

''All right. Rum it is.''

They were traveling south on Highway 22. Cal had told her it was faster to take Highway 2 past High River, double lane all the way, but it wasn't as scenic. Nina was enthralled with the view revealed each time the Suburban crested one of the many hills, hills that rose and fell in a regular rhythm. The country was so open here she could see the undulations of the range-land clear to the forested foothills and the mountains beyond. The Rockies stood snowcapped and magnificent, shoulder to shoulder as far south as she could see. All the way to the American border, she knew, and past into Idaho and Montana and Wyoming and

Colorado and beyond. Still, nothing compared with the magnificence of the Canadian Rockies—prairies, rolling foothills and rugged mountains, all in one broad vista.

The fenced pastures that edged the roads held glossy red-brown cows with white-faced calves romping stiffly at their sides. From time to time they'd pass a field of mares and foals, the mares of every hue, the foals frisking and racing in the sunshine while their dams tended to the serious business of grazing. As they approached Turner Valley, Nina was struck by the sight of huge spare grasshopperlike constructions nodding in the fields—oil-well pumpers, Cal informed her. Turner Valley had been the scene of the first Alberta oil strike back in 1914.

Then they were in the dusty little village of Longview, where Cal stopped briefly for gas. Nina looked around. There was the combination post office and library, the feed store across the street and the nononsense Longview Hotel, a drinking establishment with perhaps the best view in the entire country. The dirt parking area in front of the hotel was deserted; it was Sunday, after all. The aging clapboard community hall beside it was in need of paint.

While Cal paid for his gas and stopped to speak to a leathery old man in jeans and a vest who was buying gas, she felt a strange prickle start in her shoulders and send cold fingers into the happiness she'd been feeling.

This was her home now, this vast and lonely place. This was the road she'd chosen. This was a village she'd see many times; she'd come here with Cal and perhaps they'd have dinner at this very restaurant. She eyed the handwritten notice tacked up on the restaurant door, tattered and fluttering in the wind: Open Thursday Through Sunday Only.

She shivered. The openness, the emptiness, the silence...the wind. She'd married McCallum Blake despite all the strong sensible reasons against it. Telling him the truth was one thing. But even when that was behind her—behind them—the fact remained that this was her home now.

She'd chosen to carve out a new life for herself with a stranger. She'd chosen this desolate empty landscape when she'd chosen the man. Nothing could have contrasted more sharply with the busy streets of Vancouver, the noise, the color, the excitement, the chattering lineups in front of movie theaters. Or the hurry and bustle of the many cities of the world she'd traveled to and grown to love—Bangkok, Hong Kong, Paris.

Nina felt a small pang of foreboding skitter down her spine as Cal got back into the vehicle. Then he smiled and the feeling was gone. Cal was so warm, so strong, so full of good humor and vitality. So understanding. He was the lover of her dreams, the husband of her choice, the companion of her spirit, as she'd discovered through the old-fashioned method of writing letters. He was a man who would never let her down. He leaned forward suddenly and kissed her. "Ready to head for home?"

"Couldn't be readier," she said. And it was true.

On the way to the Rocking Bar S, several miles west of the highway, Nina tried to prepare herself for their arrival. He'd confessed that he hadn't told anyone he was going to Calgary to get married. His reason, he said—and she believed him—was that he hadn't been one hundred percent sure she might not change her mind, and he didn't want to have to explain coming home without a wife. She appreciated his concern. At the same time, she wished she wasn't walking into her new role at the ranch completely cold.

Funny how she noticed things now that she hadn't noticed in September. She hadn't realized how many miles there seemed to be between ranches, for instance. She had no idea how large the average spread was out here, but they appeared to be very large. She hadn't noticed the small windblown white-painted church or the iron-fenced cemetery at the crest of a hill. Nor had she noticed the ramshackle house surrounded by the hulks of vehicles, discarded household appliances and other debris a mile or so beyond the church. A couple of dogs charged out from the rutted driveway to bark hopefully at the Suburban's wheels until they were left far behind. She hadn't realized what a large stream the Horsethief was, either. When they'd crossed the bridge that led to the ranch last fall, it had been only a narrow trickle. Now it ran high on its banks with milky-blue fast-flowing water.

The Rocking Bar S seemed different, too. Cal drove slowly as they crossed the cattle-guard under the tall peeled-pole gates. Several dogs ran out to greet them, tails wagging. The ranch buildings seemed more spread out, and the grass, of course, was greener. The house seemed larger than she remembered, with its white-painted veranda and shutters crisp against the warm russet glow of the brick. She held her breath a little, taking everything in as though in a slow-motion movie. *This was her home now; she was coming home.*

Cal smiled and reached over to squeeze her hand.

She returned the pressure. Then he brought the Suburban to a halt in the driveway by the house. Lou hurried out.

"Boy, oh boy, am I glad to see you."

"Something wrong?" Cal frowned out the open window. Nina knew Lou hadn't spotted her yet. She leaned forward.

"Jeremiah's home," Cal's aunt announced. "This morning. Am I happy to see him in one piece back here where he belongs! But you're going to have to talk to him, McCallum, talk some horse sense into him."

"What do you mean, talk some sense?"

"Well, he's talking wild. Says he's going to leave here and hire on with the Diamond Eight. You know Tom Leavitt quit a while back?"

Cal nodded and shot Nina an amused glance. "I knew that. Look, Lou. Why don't you let me get out?" He opened his door an inch or two. "Fact is, I've got some news for you, too."

"*You* do?" Lou stepped back, a look of faint alarm settling on her plump features. She fanned her face with her apron. "Hoo-boy. And George Edward wantin' to go to Vegas now for the honeymoon and that darn goose Henry brought home from the auction last week gettin' into my strawberries already with 'em barely through the ground and—" Suddenly she leaned forward and peered through the windshield. "*Nina!* For heaven's sake!"

Cal took the opportunity to get out of the vehicle. He hugged his aunt and bent to kiss her cheek. She beamed. "Is that really Nina in there, McCallum? Well, let me see you, child!" She bustled around to the passenger side of the truck. Nina climbed out and Cal moved forward to drape his arm around her shoulders and pull her close.

"We-ell, I...I..." Lou was momentarily speechless, looking from one to the other, her mouth agape. "Gosh, I don't know what to say."

"There's good news, Lou, and then there's more good news." Cal grinned, taking his time. Nina wished he'd put his aunt out of her misery.

"Yes, Nina's here. That's the good news." He grinned again and Nina felt like pinching him. "And the even better news is, she's staying. We're married."

"What?"

"Yes, married. On Friday. In Calgary." He put on a mock-injured look. "Now, come on, Lou. Haven't you been after me to go out and find myself a wife? Well...I did."

To Nina's amazement—and Cal's, she realized when she glanced at him—Lou burst into tears. She promptly sat down on the steps to the veranda and covered her face with her apron and wailed.

Nina dropped Cal's arm and hurried over to the older woman. She bent awkwardly and patted her shoulder. "Oh, dear, Lou, don't worry—everything's okay." She looked at Cal helplessly. "Everything's fine. Isn't it?"

"For crying out loud, Lou," Cal said, brow furrowed. "I thought this'd be *good* news."

"It is," Lou sobbed, mopping her face with her apron. "It's wonderful news."

"Well?" Cal seemed so completely flummoxed at his aunt's reaction that Nina felt like laughing.

"It's just that...I've had too *much* good news

lately,'' she moaned, mopping her eyes with a corner of her apron. "Jeremiah's come home at last and…and my own wedding's not ten days away and…and now you've finally found somebody to love a-and brought home a bride just when we'd all given up hope—'' She began to wail again.

Cal shook his head. "Damn it all,'' he said to Nina with a pained look. "I told you I was no good with women.'' He strode up to his aunt and squatted down in front of her. "Here.'' He took one of her hands and cradled it in both of his. He spoke to her sternly. "Now, listen here, Lou.''

His aunt peeked at him over the apron.

"You just quit that. Right now.''

Lou started to smile, her laughter mixed with tears. "Fine way to welcome home your new bride, Mc-Callum, ain't it?'' She wiped both eyes and then rummaged in the pocket of her apron, pulling out a tissue with which she proceeded to blow her nose vigorously. "There.'' She tucked the tissue in her sleeve. "I'm okay now.'' She patted Cal's hand. "I'm an old fool, I know. I just wish your dear mama had lived to see one of her boys married, that's all.''

Cal stood and helped his aunt to her feet. Nina felt her own eyes fill as the older woman turned to her, smile as wide as the arms she held out. "Welcome home, Nina, dear. Welcome home!'' Nina hugged her tightly, not daring to trust her own voice. Lou felt pillowy soft and smelled of cinnamon.

Cal cleared his throat. "All right. You go on into the house with Nina. I'll bring in our stuff.'' He went back to the Suburban, causing several dogs who'd been avidly inspecting the Suburban's wheels to look up and wag shaggy tails.

Nina walked up the veranda steps with her arm on Lou's shoulder. She'd been deeply touched by the older woman's reaction to her arrival. She felt an elemental affinity with Cal's aunt; she could not have said why. No one could've been more different from her own mother, whom she loved deeply, than this short plump plainspoken country woman, whom she knew she'd come to love just as much.

The kitchen was cool and tidy, with sun streaming in the many-paned windows. The reason for the cinnamon aroma was on the counter: several pans of cooling cinnamon buns.

"Mmm, don't those look good?" Nina smiled.

"Jeremiah's favorite," Lou explained, bustling forward. "I don't usually bake on a Sunday, oh, no." She wagged one finger at Nina. "My mother always said if you couldn't get your work done in six days, you couldn't get it done in seven."

The brief spate of tears had left Lou cheerful and, apparently, full of energy. She quickly ran the teakettle under the faucet and put it on the stove to boil. Nina knew she wouldn't be able to turn down a cup of tea. And maybe even one of those cinnamon buns....

A dog that had been lying under the table got up with a baleful glance at Nina and padded stiffly to the screen door where it waited patiently to be let out. Nina obliged, receiving a disdainful glance for her trouble.

"But I think the Lord would forgive me, don't you?" Lou said with a twinkle in her eye. "After all, my baby's been gone over two months. Near scared me to death, Jeremiah did, taking off like that, not a word to anybody. Oh, he's an aggravatin' boy, that one.'' She shook her head, lips pressed firmly together. ''Always has been!'' Jeremiah had to be close to thirty—hardly a ''boy'' any longer, although it was clear he'd always be a boy to the aunt who'd raised him.

Nina felt as comfortable and as welcome in the big ranch-house kitchen as if she'd just stopped in for tea on her way to town. As if she was a neighbor Lou saw regularly, not a near stranger who'd only been here once many months before. A stranger who'd just married one of her beloved nephews.

The door banged open and Cal entered, hands and arms full of suitcases and bags. He put the luggage down and straightened, reaching up to take off his sunglasses, which he set on the windowsill nearest the door. ''Could that possibly be fresh cinnamon buns I smell?'' He grinned wickedly and walked toward the counter.

''Don't you dare touch 'em—they just came out of the oven. You'll burn your fingers and give yourself a bellyache.''

''Okay, okay.'' Cal backed away, hands raised in surrender. He obviously enjoyed teasing his aunt. And she seemed to like it as much as he did. A faint shadow of the feeling she'd had in Longview rippled through Nina. She was stepping into the lives of these people; they weren't stepping into hers. This could be the set of a play she'd walked onto the moment she'd come through that screen door. This was Lou's kitchen, and this was her nephew. Whoever *she* was— the newlywed Nina O'Shea Blake, wife of this tall dark smiling man—was someone she'd have to discover.

Cal came toward her and put both his hands on her shoulders, tilting her face to his. "Lou show you around the place yet?"

She shook her head.

"Want me to?"

His eyes warmed until she couldn't mistake his intentions. "Yes. I'd like that."

Cal dropped a quick kiss on her mouth, his eyes full of promise, then bent to pick up the bags again. Nina took her leather carryall and one of her suitcases. "I'll show Nina around, and maybe when we come back that tea'll be ready," he said to his aunt.

"Take your time. Maybe those buns'll be cooled down by then," Lou said, and Nina was shocked to see that the older woman's eyes were twinkling. "I'll wait to brew the tea."

Nina felt herself blush. She caught Cal's eye and saw that he was close to laughter. Mortified, she walked behind him into the hall, feeling like a fool. She might as well get used to it—their newly married status was going to be the source of plenty of jokes and sidelong glances over the next month or so. Lou was probably mild compared to what they'd get from Henry and Jeremiah.

Nina followed Cal through the interior hallway to the stairs that began just inside the front door. They paused on a landing with a small square window that looked out onto the Rockies in the near distance, then continued up to a central upstairs gallery. There were several doors off the gallery. Cal led her to one on the west.

"This is my room," he said simply, pushing open the door with his knee. "We can move in here or we can take over one of the other bedrooms if you want."

Nina briefly surveyed the room. A big bed covered in a patterned cotton duvet stood centered on one wall. A long low table against the same wall held books and newspapers and magazines and a lamp. A dark wood chest with several drawers occupied part of the adjacent wall, along with a tall mirror and another chest. There were two large multipaned windows, one facing west with a glorious view of the mountains, the other facing north toward the barn a few hundred yards away and some corrals. Outside the window a poplar sighed in the wind, a few of its pale green leaves scraping gently against the glass.

Cal came up behind her. She felt the warmth of his body as he bent forward to brush the side of her neck with his mouth. "I like this room," she whispered dreamily, leaning against him. He put his arms around her. "I don't want to change to another one."

"You can paint it or paper it or do whatever you want with it," he said quietly, moving his lips over her skin. "You can do what you want with this whole house. It's yours now." She held her breath, feeling her breasts tighten almost painfully, her skin contract to gooseflesh under her jeans and cotton sweater. Remembered pleasure, so new, so wonderful, rushed in on her, and she turned and wrapped her arms around his neck and pressed herself against him. "Oh, Cal—"

"Nina!" His voice was harsh with feeling as he took her mouth. He kissed her slowly and perfectly, until she collapsed against him, wanting more, so much more. Wanting all the pleasure she knew he could bring her.

"Do you want to make love? Now?" he whispered hoarsely in her ear, making her shiver convulsively to the ends of her toes.

She nodded. "I do," she whispered back, "but I can wait. If you can," she added slyly.

"I don't know if I can, damn it," he growled, kissing her throat. "Why later?"

"I don't want to give your aunt the satisfaction of being right. What she hinted at downstairs."

He laughed softly. "Who cares whether she's right or not?" He pulled back a little to look down at her. He still held her close. His eyes searched hers. "Okay. I want to go find Jeremiah, anyway."

"Now?"

"Yeah." Cal frowned and stroked the length of her back soothingly. Nina liked that almost as much as his kisses—almost. "I want to talk to him before he finds out about us from someone else."

"Why's that?" Nina wasn't sure what he meant.

"Well, he was pretty torn up when Carol Jean dumped him." Cal's eyes sought hers, pleaded for understanding. "I just want him to hear the news from me, that's all. Plus, I want to find out what Lou was talking about, about him going over to the Diamond Eight." Nina nodded, not understanding much of the meaning behind Cal's words. But she understood the feeling: he cared deeply for his younger brother.

"Is that bad?"

"No." Cal seemed to pause to think something through. "It could be good. Depends on what he has in mind."

"Okay," Nina said, smiling. She hated to be parted from him for even a few hours, but it had to happen. He had a life here and others he cared about. Things to do. A ranch to run. People who depended on him. It was up to her to fit into his life, not the other way around. And after all, neither of them had pretended that theirs was anything more than a marriage of convenience, anyway, despite the excitement—natural excitement between two healthy adults—of discovering each other physically and sexually. *A marriage built on lies,* shrieked a tiny voice inside her. *All built on lies.* "Go ahead. I'll unpack my stuff and talk to Lou for a while. I'd like that."

"Good." He smiled and Nina felt her knees go weak all over again. She reached up and kissed him full on the mouth.

"Hey...careful," he warned.

"Maybe I'll even get your room redecorated by the time you get back," she teased.

"*Our* room," he said firmly.

"Yes. Our room."

CHAPTER TWELVE

CAL FOUND JEREMIAH playing cards in the Diamond Eight bunkhouse, pretty much where he'd expected to find him. On the way there, comfortable again wearing old clothes and driving his pickup over the pitted gravel back roads, he marveled at his incredible good fortune. Damn. He could hardly believe he was actually married—to Nina. The past weekend was like some kind of fabulous dream. *Nina*. Even her name was wild and sweet and exotic to his ears. Nina O'Shea Blake. He spoke her name aloud in the cab of the truck. "Nina O'Shea Blake. My wife." He repeated it, just because he liked the sound.

Last week he hadn't believed it could happen. The whole scheme was just too good to be true. Letters! He was no writer. Yet, somehow, they'd kept scribbling letters back and forth to each other, and by the time winter was over, he'd worked up the nerve to ask her to marry him. How many men would have been as bold? Cal smiled to himself, squinting into the glare of the lowering sun. Not many.

The idea that he'd planned to marry Donna not so long ago amazed him. He liked Donna all right—he liked her and her kids and still believed he could have made a marriage with her work—but never once had he felt even a shred of what he felt with Nina. Nina was strong, smart, sexy…funny. She knew what she wanted. She made him laugh. She was the woman he thought he'd never find in Glory.

Now he just had a few more things to iron out and organize, and life could get back to where he wanted it: running smoothly. He'd see what Jeremiah was up to, get Lou married off, start thinking about cutting his first hay crop. Hire a few more hands for the summer—he'd heard John Baines, Ed's boy, was looking for work. Get ready for branding, maybe ride a few lines himself if he had the time and try to figure out what was happening to his steers, at least to the five he'd lost last fall. Get the Mounties back on it. Maybe the rustlers would make another play this summer and they could catch them.

And now, after all these years on his own, he had a woman to come home to. *A wife.* Maybe even a family in the not-too-distant future. Maybe. If things worked out. If she stayed. Kids, birthdays, anniversaries. Life just didn't get much better. *Knock on wood.* An image of his aunt's quick phrase and habitual gesture flashed into his mind, and he quickly scanned the cab. Fake wood, even on the dash. Wouldn't you know it? But then, he was not a superstitious man.

Jeremiah was cleaning up at five-card stud in the bunkhouse, judging by the pile of wooden matchsticks on his side of the table. He pushed back his chair when Cal stepped through the door.

"Well, well." Jeremiah stood, his smile wide. "Cal—how you doin', man?" Cal noticed that his brother's hair was a lot longer, black and glossy, tied at the nape. His handshake was strong, the skin callused. His face was tanned. Cal put his other arm around his brother's shoulders as they shook hands, as close to a hug as either of them would permit.

"You're looking good, Jeremiah," he said quietly. "Damn good. What've you been up to?"

"New Mexico," Jeremiah said, sliding back into his chair. "Well, boys? Ready to cash in?" The three Diamond Eight cowpunchers nodded and threw their cards into the center of the table. Jeremiah gathered them up, grinning, accepting the rumpled bills the others tossed him. "Better luck next time, fellas."

"If you ride herd like you play stud, the bosses oughtta be happy," one of them grumbled. He and another puncher headed for the door, nodding briefly to Cal. Cal had met all three of them before. The third man stretched out on his bunk, crossed his wool-clad feet at the ankles and leisurely rolled a cigarette. Then he lit it, picked up a paperback novel and started to read, eyes narrowed against the smoke.

Cal wanted to talk to Jeremiah alone, but he could hardly ask the cowboy to leave his own bunkhouse. He gestured briefly and moved out onto the worn wooden stoop. Jeremiah pocketed the deck of cards and followed him.

The Diamond Eight was four miles north and a little east of the Rocking Bar S, on the Elk River. The home ranch was nestled under a crook in the foothills, protected from winter winds, yet open to any chinook that happened to blow through. It was a company-owned ranch, as many were in this part of southern Alberta, and Cal knew the Eastern owners were looking for a new manager. According to what Lou had hinted, Jeremiah was after the job.

"New Mexico, huh?" Cal rested his shoulder

against one of the peeled-pole uprights that supported the bunkhouse porch.

"The TS. Wes McKenna's running the show there." Jeremiah threw Cal a questioning glance and Cal nodded. He knew Wes, had met him quite a few years ago in Wyoming. "I helped out for a month while he was laid up."

"Bad?"

"Not too bad. One of those diseases he picked up out there in Asia years ago. Malaria or something." Jeremiah met Cal's gaze. His expression was as serious as Cal had ever seen him. "I want this Diamond Eight job, Cal," he said, and Cal heard the steel in his voice. "I know I can do it and, besides, I've got something to prove."

Cal didn't say anything. He'd hoped Jeremiah was feeling as calm and self-assured as he looked. Maybe he'd been wrong. "To Carol Jean?"

Jeremiah's face hardened. "To her and to all those goddamn farmers she's related to. And to myself, Cal. I'm ready to settle down. Get together a stake, maybe buy my own place someday. I'm finished living crazy like I've been doing the last few years."

Cal allowed himself a glimmer of a smile. Jeremiah? Settle down? He glanced at the worn deck of cards in the pocket of his brother's red plaid shirt. "We'll see. I'll do what I can. Put in a word with the owners. I know old Gunnarsen pretty well." Gunnarsen was one of the original partners in the Diamond Eight.

He smiled at his brother and Jeremiah grinned back. The devilment was still there, no matter what Jeremiah said about wanting to settle down. Damn it, any way you looked at it, Jeremiah was just a kid to him. Cal had always been the big brother, the one who took on the responsibilities. But, after all, Jeremiah was getting close to thirty. Cal could see that his brother had changed since he'd left. Something was different. There was a new maturity on Jeremiah's face he hadn't seen before. Maybe it was just that he'd never noticed.

"I got some news, too, Jeremiah. I'm married."

His brother's shock was impossible to miss. "*Married? You're joshin' me, man.*"

"Nope." Cal threw back his head for a moment and gazed up at the sky. Clear and blue as far as he could see. Looked like the good weather was set to last. "You remember that girl we met on the road to Glory last fall? Nina O'Shea?"

"Not her!"

"Yeah. Her." Truth was, Cal was enjoying this a little. He didn't want to remind his brother of his own unhappiness two months ago when Carol Jean had dumped him. But on the other hand, he enjoyed putting the final kibosh—but good—to any notion Jeremiah might still harbor that his older brother was a washout as far as women went.

"I don't believe it!" Jeremiah thumped him on the shoulder and started to laugh. "When?"

"Friday."

"Henry heard?"

Cal grinned. "Haven't run into Henry yet. Come on home and see her."

Jeremiah let out a bloodcurdling whoop and leaped one-handed over the porch railing. He headed straight for his pickup.

"Last one there's gotta milk the cow!" he yelled out the open window as he gunned the engine. Then he took off in a spray of gravel, sending the dozen or so Diamond Eight horses grazing on the other side of the fence wheeling away.

Laughing, Cal got into his own pickup. That was how they'd egged each other on when they got close to home after a day of riding fences or looking for strays. Nobody wanted to milk the Jersey cow Lou had kept for fresh milk and cream when they were younger. If Jeremiah lost, he'd usually wheedle Henry into doing the job for him. Cal never could, so mostly he'd milked the cow himself. After a while, he'd found, you just got used to it.

"SO WHY DON'T YOU WANT to go to Las Vegas for your honeymoon?" Nina watched as Lou drizzled frosting over the racks of cinnamon buns. "It might be fun."

Nina had come down half an hour ago after she'd unpacked and explored a little. She was amazed at what the older woman managed to get done in such a short time, talking the whole while. Already she'd whipped up frosting—cream cheese, a little vanilla, lemon juice and icing sugar—peeled a huge pot of potatoes with Nina's help, which she'd set on the back of the stove in plenty of cold water, and then proceeded to tear up lettuce for a green salad, which she covered neatly with a damp tea towel and placed back in the refrigerator.

"Fun!" Lou made an impatient gesture with one hand. "Maybe for some. George Edward went down there once with his brother-in-law—that'd be from his first wife, Gladys McPherson—and they won a hundred dollars and saw Wayne Newton and now he thinks I'd like it, too. Just 'cause I go to the occasional bingo game down at the Catholic hall. It's only to support a good cause, I tell him, but he don't listen. Men don't, you know." She paused and gave Nina a direct look.

Nina played with her teaspoon, drawing it across the oilcloth table cover.

"What am I saying? You're just married and hardly had a chance to find out!" Lou cried. "Heavens, child, don't pay me no attention. Besides, McCallum's different. McCallum ain't like most men. Him and Jeremiah's night and day, though they're brothers. I always figured it'd be a lucky woman who managed to snag my McCallum."

Nina looked up and caught Lou's eye. "I feel pretty lucky," she said softly.

"'Course you do, dear. Everyone around here'll be pretty pleased, I can tell you!" Lou snorted. She finished up with the frosting and carried the bowl to the sink. "We've been after him for years to pick a good woman and settle down. It's a darn shame, you know—" she gave Nina another direct glance and turned on the faucet "—a man like him not being married." She shook her head energetically. "He's rock steady and wonderful smart and he loves kids and they love him. He's a careful rancher, looks after his stock good. Folks around here think the world of him. And he's going to make a fine father someday, you mark my words. The sooner the better, in my opinion."

"So why didn't he get married before?" Nina

wanted to steer the conversation away from children. All talk of the future unnerved her. She had to tell Cal the truth. That she hadn't done it yet was hanging on her conscience like the beginning of a big headache.

"Darned if I know." Lou shrugged, her face rueful. "Every woman he's ever dated thinks he's just terrific, but next thing you know, McCallum's gone off 'em for one reason or another." Lou opened the refrigerator and, to Nina's dismay, hauled out a huge prime-rib roast, which she set on the counter. "Just never seems to stay all that interested somehow."

"*That's* for dinner tonight?" Nina was stunned at the food preparations Lou had under way. Uneasily she remembered that soon she'd be responsible for putting these kinds of meals on the table.

"Supper," corrected Lou. "Well, let's see. Jeremiah's gonna be here. First night home. And Henry's somewheres around the place. There's you two now. And George Edward said he might stop by." Lou laughed, her cheeks pink. "It's your wedding supper, for heaven's sake. We'll call it that, since none of us got a chance to go to the wedding."

She studied Nina thoughtfully. "For a while this winter I thought for sure he was going to take up with— Oops!" Lou seemed to catch herself and gave Nina a quick glance, looking a little embarrassed.

"It's okay. Cal's told me about Donna," Nina said bravely. She didn't feel a bit brave. She didn't want to hear how much Cal thought of Donna or how much Lou thought of her or what a wonderful pair they'd have made or…or anything.

"Donna Beaton's a very nice woman, no doubt about that," Lou said, but she smiled mischievously as she caught Nina's eye. "A fine woman. But you're the one for him. No question. I had a feeling about it way back last September, the minute I met you."

"You did?"

"Yessirree. I told George Edward—you can ask him if you don't believe me—I told him McCallum's finally found someone who suits him. I don't know how I knew, I just did. I could tell 'cause of how he looked at you. Although I have to say I had quite a shock when I found out you were from way out on the Coast. I had the notion at first that you lived in Calgary or somewhere fairly close. Maybe Edmonton."

Lou bent to slide the roast into the oven. When she straightened, she wiped her glistening brow with her apron. "Then when I saw those letters start a-comin', I knew something was up." She beamed. "Love always finds a way, they say."

Nina smiled back shyly. Well, not love, perhaps…but there was no doubt that Cal's aunt was absolutely thrilled with this turn of events. That made her feel a little better. If it wasn't for the big web of lies she'd built around herself, everything would've been perfect. The solution to that, she knew, was to tear down those lies as quickly as possible.

"Whew! It's gettin' darn hot in here," Lou said, untying her apron and hanging it on a wooden peg by the stove. "Why don't we go out for a bit? I'll show you around the yard and we'll see if the peonies are up yet."

As IT HAPPENED, George Edward arrived in time for supper. Nina was glad. If anything, it took some of the pressure off her. But perhaps she was imagining pressure where there wasn't any; certainly Cal didn't seem affected one way or another.

When he'd arrived with Jeremiah, she felt the pride in his voice when he introduced her as his wife. Jeremiah kissed her—with perhaps more enthusiasm than a brother-in-law should—but she was pretty sure it was all show for his brother. Henry shook Cal's hand, then her hand, then Cal's again. His pale blue eyes sparkled and he didn't stop smiling once throughout the meal. He talked cows and fences and the price of barbed wire and NAFTA with the rest of the men, but his eyes kept straying back to her. And he just kept smiling. Nina had the feeling that every one of the people Cal cared most about in this world was very pleased with his marriage, sudden or not.

George Edward Robison turned out to be short and wiry, dark-eyed and gray-haired. When he took off his hat, the telltale line of white around his forehead attested to his many years in the saddle, the creases on his sunburned face to his good humor. He was clearly devoted to Louisa Twist and she to him. They traded the kinds of lazy farfetched insults that seemed to pass for compliments in this cowboy culture, and every once in a while Nina would see George Edward's dark eyes soften as he smiled at his intended, and then Lou would go all pink and giggly. Nina was delighted at this evidence of the older couple's happiness. The preparations for their upcoming wedding, too, with all the talk of who was making the wedding cake and whether or not George Edward's oldest daughter was going to have her dress sewn on time, was all foreign and fascinating to Nina.

She could imagine her mother's preparations for her wedding if she'd had one to plan. Hours spent on the telephone and at fittings in some couturier's studio. Solemn consultations about wedding china and silver and whether to have the string quartet play Mozart or Liszt. The exact choice of coffee blend to serve at the reception and the brand of champagne and whether camellias were too artificial-looking or gardenias too highly scented. Interminable discussions about menus and whether the newly restored Hotel Vancouver was a suitable venue—after all, it *was* a hotel—or whether the Point Grey Golf and Country Club was a better choice.

Nina shuddered slightly. Thank goodness she'd avoided all that nonsense!

"Cold?" Cal leaned solicitously toward her.

"No, not cold," Nina said, smiling up at him. "Just excited, I guess."

"Why's that?" His eyes were warm. Nina felt a shiver of an entirely different nature run from her toes to the top of her head.

"Oh, I don't know," she said breathlessly. "Everything seems so different. Interesting."

"Lou and George Edward are going to a movie after supper," he said in a low voice, his eyes alight.

"They are?"

"Uh-huh. And Jeremiah's going to town." His smile widened, and Nina realized he was flirting with her.

"What about Henry? I suppose he'll stick around to do the dishes," she teased.

Cal laughed softly. "I don't think so. Henry's idea of doing the dishes might run to setting them out on the porch for the dogs to lick off. I don't think Lou would allow it.''

"Maybe you could take me out and show me the puppies."

"I could," he murmured. But his eyes told her something different.

As it turned out, Nina and Cal washed the supper dishes. Nina insisted, and finally Lou reluctantly agreed, tsk-tsking about a bride doing the dishes on her first day in her new home. But George Edward encouraged her and after Lou hurried away to change, the two of them went arm in arm out the door, smiling. Jeremiah vanished upstairs, then came down ten minutes later showered and dressed for town.

He settled his black Stetson over his long hair and left with a wink and the enigmatic parting words that they weren't to wait up for him. Cal grinned at Nina and, despite her embarrassment, she grinned back.

Henry was the last to leave. He walked over to the counter and opened the cookie jar and stuffed several in his pocket before slapping on his beat-up hat and heading out the door, mumbling something Nina couldn't hear.

Clearly everyone thought she and Cal ought to have the house to themselves. The knowledge that they were making themselves scarce, and exactly why, made Nina blush furiously.

Finally the last plate was wiped and put away. Nina hung up the damp tea towel and took a deep breath. "Now what?" she asked, turning to her new husband.

"Now we go see the puppies," he said innocently, one eyebrow raised.

CHAPTER THIRTEEN

THAT FINE SUNDAY in April was the day that made all the difference. Until then, every choice taken had opened new doors, for better or for worse. After that Sunday, Nina had the horrible feeling that her future was no longer her own.

If she'd been asked earlier, she might have said the most important day had been the day she'd married McCallum Blake—or perhaps the day she'd agreed to marry him. But she'd have been wrong. It was *that* Sunday that mattered, the Sunday after her wedding. She should have confessed everything and thrown herself on her husband's better nature. Yes, he'd have been hurt, even angry. But surely he'd have forgiven her. They had so much going for them—surely in the end he'd have kissed her and forgiven her and they would have gone on and built a life together.

Or Lou. If only she'd said something to Lou. Maybe as she'd sat at the table watching Lou work. Or later, when they walked around the yard before supper. Perhaps Lou might've had some suggestion that would have made it easier for Nina to tell Cal. But Lou was in the midst of preparations for her own wedding. Did she want to ruin Lou's big day by telling her she'd married her beloved nephew under false pretenses? Lou wasn't the type to stand back and give cool rational advice, the way Leo did. She'd be in there like a terrier, worrying the problem to death.

No, Nina's secret was too great a burden to share with Cal's aunt.

There was no one else. Henry and Jeremiah were strangers. *She was surrounded by strangers.*

After they'd admired the litter of puppies in the barn that Sunday afternoon, after Cal had shown her around the ranch, proudly pointing out this building and that and relating incidents about life on the Rocking Bar S when he and Jeremiah were boys…she could have told him somehow. After he'd taken her back to the house and paused at the green-painted front door and swept her up in his arms saying it was time he did things properly…

After he'd carried her upstairs and brought her into their bedroom and made love to her, so ardently, with such tenderness and passion… She knew it had mattered a great deal, the fact that they'd made love under his roof.

When she'd lain in his arms, smiling, completely happy—why hadn't she confessed then? He was a reasonable man. A considerate understanding man. Weren't the first heady days of marriage the perfect time to cast off the past, *all* of the past? She should have trusted his feelings for her. Should have believed—*known*—that he would want to make it work between them. Didn't this marriage matter as much to him as it did to her—maybe more in his view?

But she said nothing. And each day that went by made it more difficult. By the time Lou and George Edward were married ten days later, Nina realized that her confession might soon be impossible.

The day threatened rain, which threw the bride into a panic. But the clouds burned off by noon and the wedding was scheduled in the Glory United Church for three o'clock. The town was packed. Saturday was a big shopping day in Glory, Cal had told her. The church lot was full and very few parking spots remained on the dusty main street. So much for a small family ceremony, Nina thought with a smile. She had on the dress she'd been married in—Cal's request. Her trunks had arrived the previous week, and she now had some choice in her wardrobe, but that morning Cal had asked her to wear her wedding dress, and how could she have refused him? Even the hat, which she'd patted and coaxed back into shape—Madame LaRue would have fainted!—was wearable.

Cal said she looked wonderful. She thought she looked pretty good; she hoped she wouldn't disappoint all the Glory townsfolk who'd no doubt be after a glimpse of the Blake bride as much as the Robison bride.

She wasn't wrong about the interest. More than once she was grateful for Cal's presence as he stepped forward to make introductions and answer questions in his straightforward tactful style. He only left her once—to walk his aunt down the aisle to present her to a brushed and beaming, very dapper George Edward. The groom's grown sons and daughters made up the bridesmaids and groomsmen—much to Nina's relief when Lou had promptly, the day after she'd arrived, suggested it was only fitting that Cal's new wife be part of the wedding party.

But they couldn't escape notoriety altogether. Cal was too well-known in the community, his sudden marriage to a stranger too recent. The custom of spoons clanking against wineglasses at the reception, which Nina had always found particularly loathsome, hadn't missed the town of Glory. Several times during the evening there were cries of "Cal! Nina!" and Cal and Nina were obliged to stand and kiss for the benefit of the assembled guests.

The third time, Nina knew her face was bright red and she was on the point of bursting into tears. Cal sized up the situation, and next time it happened, he stood alone and said a few words that put the focus back on the newlyweds.

"Okay?" he murmured as he sat back down next to her.

"Thanks, Cal," she said. "I don't know what's wrong with me. I just hate standing up there in front of everyone and…and…"

"And kissing me?" he filled in, eyes alight.

"You know I like kissing you," she said as he gave her a knowing look, "just not in front of strangers like that."

He'd eyed her curiously. "They're not strangers to me," he said quietly. His words hurt. They reminded her, as though she needed reminding, how foreign she still was in this new life she'd chosen.

The truth was, the interest and curiosity of the wedding guests, while understandable, considering Cal's longtime status and respect in the community, was unnerving. She remembered Leo's caution about the inability to keep secrets in a small town. Hadn't Cal acknowledged the truth of that in a letter? The one where he mentioned the postmistress? Knowing she had her own desperate secret to hide didn't help.

Luckily no one seemed too curious about her on a personal level. The main focus seemed to be on the fact that she'd married McCallum Blake. Nina could only hope that after Lou and George Edward's wedding, Cal's friends and neighbors would lose interest.

There was another person Nina dreaded meeting at the wedding. Donna Beaton. She couldn't help but wonder how the other woman would regard her—the usurper. Cal had not mentioned Donna.

When they were dancing, she finally got up her nerve to ask him. She put on her brightest smile and took a deep breath. "So. Are you going to introduce me to Donna?"

"Donna?" Cal frowned. "She here?"

"I have no idea," Nina said, feeling vast relief. "I thought she might be."

"Lou told me she had another wedding to go to up in Edmonton," Cal said. He didn't seem the slightest bit discomfited by her question. "Why?"

"Oh, I don't know," Nina said airily. "I just thought I should meet the woman you were thinking of marrying…"

"Jealous?" He grinned broadly and Nina knew he was teasing her.

"Maybe," she said with a tiny smile of her own.

She gasped as he held her tighter. He ducked his head to whisper in her ear, and she was glad of the dim lights. *Sweet words. Promises.*

Pleasure turned to sudden fear. All of this—*everything*—could vanish. Just like that. The instant he discovered her lies. She had to tell him. Today. Tonight. *She had to!* If he found out from someone else… She shuddered. Already, in ten short days, he'd become everything to her.

She couldn't bear to think of being without him anymore. Was this love? It wasn't supposed to happen like this!

"Cold?" He held her closer.

She shook her head and said nothing, her face buried against his shoulder, but when he stood back from her, a question in his eyes, she knew she had to say something. "A goose walking on my grave, I guess," she said lightly. Still, the silly expression made her shudder again.

The next day he took her riding. They rode far back into the hills to where Cal said he'd been losing stock to rustlers. She'd packed a lunch while Cal got the horses ready and strapped her box of painting supplies securely behind her saddle. It was a glorious day, a cool breeze wafting down from the hills, with the promise of heat in the air. Nina didn't think she'd ever seen country so beautiful.

As they rode, she noticed a golden eagle that wheeled silently overhead and seemed to follow them. Once, Nina's mare shied when a jackrabbit leaped from behind a log. She stopped and watched until the animal vanished, zigging and zagging madly across the landscape until it popped down a burrow somewhere. She glanced back at Cal, who'd pulled up behind her, and saw him smiling. She recalled that first day they'd spent together—when they'd seen the antelopes. The recollection was as fresh as the afternoon it happened, and one of her most precious memories.

Nina was determined to enjoy the day. She wanted to block out the terrible thought that she must tell Cal the truth soon or jeopardize her entire future. *It may already be too late,* a little voice inside her nagged, but she ignored it.

"Why don't I go on up and look around that area I was telling you about, and you can set your stuff up here," Cal said, bringing his horse alongside hers. "I'll be an hour or so."

"Don't you want me to come with you?"

"Sure, come if you want. I just thought this would give you a chance to unpack your paints and do… whatever it is you do with them." He pulled his hat lower to shade his eyes and looked up toward the hills above them. "No sense you riding up there with me. I'll be covering some rough territory."

"What about bears?"

"What about them?"

"I suppose I can holler if I see one."

"Uh-huh. Just make sure you holler real loud," he said, grinning. He dismounted and held the mare's reins while she dismounted.

"Ooh!" Her knees felt wobbly. "Guess I'm not used to this anymore."

He steadied her with a hand at her waist, then dropped the reins and turned to pull her into his arms. "Better get used to it, ma'am. Get yourself toughened up and maybe you can go on roundup this year." He kissed her, and Nina leaned against him. "On second thought," he added, frowning, "maybe not."

"Why not?"

"Too distracting. I'll have work to do."

Nina loved the easy banter. It wasn't something she'd been used to in her relationships with men. To her, it was a symptom of how perfectly suited they were, she and Cal. The sex was just part of it. A wonderful part, no question, but what she really loved was the balance they'd struck between that physical part of their lives and the easy camaraderie and mutual respect that seemed to grow from one day to the next. The compatibility they both must have instinctively felt during their many months of correspondence had begun to turn into flesh-and-bones reality.

Cal helped Nina set up her things, then, with a wave, mounted Blackjack and rode off at a business-like lope. Nina watched until they'd disappeared from sight. She shivered. The wind was chilly on this small promontory where she'd chosen to sketch, and she dug through one of her saddlebags for the jacket she'd tucked in. Then she settled down with her sketchbook and was soon absorbed in transferring to paper the lines, textures and colors of the landscape before her. She'd meant what she'd told Leo; the contours and colors of the land reminded her of a scarred old lion dozing in the sun. That image sustained her, and she knew she'd be able to draw on it to develop the colors and concepts she and Leo looked for when they began the process of designing a new textile.

The hour Cal had said he'd be gone sped by. Nina barely noticed. Once, when she studied the hills behind her looking for a starting point for a new painting, she saw something dark moving and thought it must be Cal returning. But when she picked up the field glasses to see why he wasn't getting any closer, she drew in her breath in surprise—a bear! It was a small black one, completely oblivious to her presence. He had to be half a mile away, maybe farther. The mare hadn't even noticed, but was quietly grazing a short distance off.

Nina studied the animal through the glasses, marveling at the easy ambling gait as the animal stopped to swipe at an old stump, pausing to sniff and lick at its base, then moved on, snapping the seed heads off long grasses as it wandered. The bear's hide seemed loose on its frame, and Nina realized that the animal must have just emerged from hibernation and would be beginning its summer-long search for food.

Better stay away from Rocking Bar S calves, Mr. Bear, Nina thought, watching the animal's progress. Eventually it wandered out of sight. She released her breath slowly.

Half an hour later, Cal appeared. She told him about the bear.

He frowned. "I know there's a few up on this back range. So far, we haven't been bothered. It's the two-legged predators that worry me more."

He took the cup of lemonade she poured, and Nina admired him as he drank thirstily, aware of the tiny spirals of strong simple desire she so often felt when she was with him. He looked so uncompromisingly male in his faded jeans and plaid work shirt, his leather vest, his dusty hat and scuffed boots. So handsome... so utterly desirable.

"Thanks." He handed the cup to her and wiped his mouth with his sleeve. Nina noticed a scratch on the back of his hand, fresh and bloody.

"What's this?"

Cal glanced at his hand. "Blackjack took me though a shortcut that was a little rougher than I'd expected." He stepped close to the gelding and ran his hand carefully over the animal's chest and forelegs. "He's fine." Cal straightened. "Ready for lunch?"

"Sure." Now that he mentioned lunch, she realized how hungry she was. "I'll just pack up my stuff—"

"This what you've been busy at?" Cal stepped up to her easel and examined the small watercolor she'd just finished with interest. It was still a little damp. Nina felt shy watching him look at her work.

"That and a bit of sketching," she said.

He turned to her and smiled. "You're very good. I like it."

Joy flooded her heart. "Do you?" she asked breathlessly, not really wanting an answer. She began to gather up her gear, flustered. "Shall we eat here?"

Cal came over and touched her arm lightly. When she looked up at him, her heart did another little tumble. "You're a wonderfully talented person, Nina, I can see that. I never want you to think that you can't continue on exactly as you were before you married me. I married who you *are*, not someone you might *think* I want you to be," he said in a low voice. "Do you understand that?"

"Yes," she managed. Her throat felt tight and thick with emotion. *But who was she? A liar and a cheat? If he only knew…*

"Good."

He pulled her gently into his arms and kissed her and she shut her eyes, treasuring the moment. "Now," he continued, "I have somewhere else in mind for lunch. Remember that spring I took you to the first day you spent here?"

She nodded, barely daring to breathe. "Uh-huh."

He grinned. "Well, I never told you this. But when

we were there, I spent quite a bit of time thinking how much I'd like to make love with you beside that spring. Bad, huh?"

"Very bad," she agreed, smiling.

"I imagined taking all your clothes off and lying down beside you in the moss up there and kissing you until I got tired of kissing you." His eyes burned into hers. "Except I don't think I'll ever get tired of kissing you," he added in a soft voice.

"Oh, Cal..." she said helplessly. She reached up and wound her arms around his neck and kissed him.

"I still kind of like that idea," he murmured after a while. "Sound good to you?"

"Sounds perfect."

CHAPTER FOURTEEN

NINA THREW HERSELF into a fury of activity at the Rocking Bar S. It was as though she felt her happiness, so huge and new and wonderful, was at the same time so very fragile. She was greedy for more—and terrified that any moment she'd lose everything.

Two weeks into May she planted the garden behind the house with Lou's help. The two of them drove to the gardening center in Glory and spent a morning picking out seeds. Lou was amazed that she wanted to try growing squash and watercress.

"Melons, maybe," Lou said doubtfully, busy picking out her own packets of seeds for the Robison garden. "Cantaloupes. Muskmelons, my mother used to call 'em. If you get a good hot year, you can't beat 'em. But watercress? Hmph!" She examined the picture on the packet Nina held. "Looks more like a weed to me."

Nina happily tossed the watercress into her basket. She also tossed in packets of everything else that caught her interest. She'd never planted a garden before. Henry had promised to till the garden plot, and Cal had agreed to help her dig holes for the potatoes she planned to put in. Yukon gold. The man at the gardening center said they were very popular. Henry was aghast—yellow spuds?—but Cal advised him to wait and see. He just might like them.

Nina spent an entire weekend planting, and she was thrilled with the neatly laid-out results. Sticks pushed into the soil at the ends of rows sported empty illustrated packets so she would know what came up. It looked just like something out of Mr. Macgregor's garden, from what she could remember of the Beatrix Potter books she'd loved as a child.

Lou came over one afternoon at the end of May to show her how to make rhubarb pie. Lou flatly didn't believe her when she said she'd never had rhubarb pie before.

"For heaven's sake, girl, where've you been?" Lou snorted. The question shook Nina a little, considering what kind of answer she might have given.

"They used to call this pie plant out here on the prairies in the old days." Lou fingered the broad leathery leaves, then gave an expert tug and brought up a two-foot-long thick red stalk with the leaf at one end and a pink glistening bulb at the other. "I suppose it was the only fruit some of those poor pioneers ever saw, although I've heard it's not rightly called a fruit, being a stem and all. Just like tomatoes being a fruit, instead of a vegetable. Hmph. Whoever pays any attention to that foolishness? It makes good pie and sauce, and some make a kind of a chutney with dates or raisins, although I'm not overly fond of it," she finished. "Don't forget to cut off all the leaves. They're poison. Although who'd ever try to eat one would have to be nine-tenths fool, I'd say...."

So Nina baked a rhubarb pie. Two pies, in fact. And when Henry and Cal and Lewis and John, the new hand, came in that afternoon for coffee—Jeremiah was in town—they polished off one of them. One-quarter each, served up with vanilla ice cream and many compliments to the cook. Next time, Nina vowed, there'd be three pies in the oven. Maybe even four.

All this time, she refused to think about what she'd left behind. Leo, her family, Letty… She couldn't bear to think about them when she still hadn't figured out how to put her two worlds together.

In early June, when most of the garden was up, Nina decided to tackle some redecorating in the ranch house. She spent hours with paint swatches and sketches and consulted Henry and Cal, but when Cal said he preferred to leave it entirely up to her and Henry said he'd always been partial to a kind of hospital green in the way of paint color, she decided to take Cal's suggestion.

She painted the walls of their bedroom the butternut color she'd been thinking about since she'd bought the seed packet the month before. She painted the woodwork throughout the house a beautiful rich cream. The living-room fireplace, with its rather undistinguished dirty-yellow brick, got a coat of paint, and the walls ended up green—but not Henry's green. She decided that she'd call the color she'd chosen artichoke, in honor of her first garden, and was very pleased with the elegant gray-green effect.

By the third week of June, the wild strawberries were ripe, and Nina went out one afternoon with Lou and her stepdaughters and their daughters. Only one boy was along, Cindy's two-year-old, Tommy. All the cousins wanted to baby-sit, so the girls followed Baby

Tommy in a chattering clump, threading daisy-chains while the women picked berries.

Nina had plenty of time to think, waiting for the bottom of her bucket to disappear under the tiny sweet berries; it seemed to take forever. She swatted at the occasional mosquito—luckily there was a breeze so they weren't too bad—and listened to the desultory gossip of the others. They discussed people and places she didn't know. Affairs they suspected were going on in the community. Being overcharged at the hardware store. Whether it was better to transplant raspberry canes in the spring or fall. The credentials or otherwise of one of the new high-school teachers. Whether Mexico or Hawaii would be a better holiday *if* they could ever get away from the kids....

It was the kind of rambling hither-and-thither womantalk Nina loved. She felt a flash of grief. *Meredith.* What was she doing now? Could she imagine her mother out here picking berries? Hardly. But then... Meredith had always surprised her.

Her mother was turning sixty-nine in ten days. Suddenly, with a strength of feeling she'd forgotten existed, she wanted her mother. She didn't want to send a birthday card; she wanted to talk to Meredith the way they'd talked when Nina was a child. She ached for that undivided attention, that gentle guidance, that tenderness that made no demands.

Nina stood straight up, nearly overturning her bucket. *My God,* she thought. *Here I am standing in a railway right-of-way picking wild strawberries somewhere west of some piddly little town nobody's ever heard of called Glory. I'm married to a man I'm crazy about who doesn't have a clue who I really am because I've lied to him from the day we met. I haven't seen my mother in months or Letty or my father or Murray or…or anybody! Nobody I love even knows where I am, except Leo. I could be living on another planet.*

Maybe I am.

She felt like one of those insects caught in tree sap millions of years ago. Frozen in amber. Suspended in time. She had to make a start; she couldn't continue to block out what she must face sooner or later—she had to tell Cal everything. She had to tell him the whole story and simply accept the consequences if he never wanted to see her again. *She had to risk what she feared most in the world.*

She'd start by calling her mother on her birthday.

Ten days later Nina went to Calgary to look at fabric samples for slipcovers she planned to have made for some of the living-room furniture. One of Lou's talented daughters-in-law had said she'd take on the project. Nina spent several hours shopping, had lunch at a small bistro on Ninth Avenue to compose herself and plan what she wanted to say, then found a fairly private telephone booth on the main floor of the Calgary Convention Centre and phoned her mother.

Thank goodness Meredith answered on the second ring. "Happy birthday, Mother."

"Nina! For heaven's sake, darling. Where are you? We haven't seen you in weeks. Letty's been very mysterious."

"I'm in Alberta…" *On a research trip,* had been on the tip of her tongue. *No more lies.* "I'm married, Mother. I'm living in Alberta now."

There was a very long full silence at the other end

of the line. Then, "Married. I see. Well, this *is* a surprise. I must tell you I'm very pleased for you—"

"Oh, Mother! I've been so stupid, I can't begin to tell you. For heaven's sake, don't tell Dad. Not yet."

"What do you mean, dear? Of course, your father will want to know. This is such lovely news, and coming on my birthday, too. When do we get to meet your husband?"

"That's just it, Mother. You can't meet him. Not yet. You see—" Nina bit her lip to prevent it from trembling "—I haven't told him who I am, really. He doesn't know anything about my family. Mother—" her voice broke a little "—I've been so stupid. Oh, it's so complicated now. I don't know what to do, where to start. I've made a mess of everything."

"Surely you're not ashamed of your family, Nina?" Nina could hear the hurt in her mother's voice, although she knew Meredith was trying hard to mask it.

"No, no—it's not that, Mother. You see, I met m-my husband last September when I came out here on holiday...."

"Ah, yes. When you came home sad, I thought. I might have known you'd met a man."

"Yes. Well, what happened is I'd met him and I liked him and I really got the feeling he liked me and...and I just lied, Mother. It was just an impulse and I'm so sorry now, but it's too late. I never dreamed I'd ever see him again. I told him this crazy story, that I was an orphan and we were poor and...and that I had two brothers and two sisters and—"

"I—I can't believe what I'm hearing," her mother said quietly.

"I know." Nina blinked back tears. Her mother

wasn't really offended. She was grateful for that. "I know." She bit her bottom lip. "I thought I was just passing through. You know what it's like—sometimes you're tempted to tell a stranger a crazy story. I…I just wanted him to take me seriously as…well, as who *I* am. I didn't want him to know I was rich and from a well-known family and related to such…such… Well, you've got to admit, Mother, you and Dad are pretty notorious."

Her mother's clear sweet laugh lightened Nina's spirits considerably. It was such a relief to talk to her. Oh, why hadn't she done this long ago? Before things had gotten so out of control?

"Well, you'll simply have to tell him the truth now, that's all. He'll have to know eventually that he's related to two of the most outrageous off-the-wall—what did you call us, darling?—*notorious* creatures this side of the Rockies. Three, if you count Murray."

Nina smiled. Her mother made it sound so easy. "I know, Mother, I know," she said softly. "I'll call and tell you what happens when I do—"

"Nina, what do you mean by 'what happens'? This man loves you, presumably, or why did he marry you? Of course he'll be angry that you lied, but surely he'll understand. If he loves you, he'll forgive you. Your father would never hold something like that against me," she finished stoutly. "Now, just go ahead and tell him, and let me know when we can come to visit you."

That's just it, Mother. He didn't marry me because he loved me. He married me because he wanted a wife and children and he thought it was time he got mar-

*ried. I married him because…well, I thought I could
love him. And now—now I think I do.*

The numbers on the telephone in front of her blurred
suddenly, and Nina straightened her shoulders. ''Well,
Mother,'' she said briskly, ''I must go. I'm in Calgary
doing some shopping and I've got to get home.''

''Where's home, dear?''

''A ranch south of here. It's called the Rocking
Bar S,'' Nina said, then realized maybe she shouldn't
have told her mother the name of the ranch. The last
thing she needed was to have her and Jake driving up
unexpectedly, full of best wishes and bearing belated
wedding gifts, before she'd spoken to Cal. ''Please
don't tell Dad. I want to…well, I just want to wait
until everything's straightened out. Promise?''

Meredith promised, reluctantly, Nina thought, but
she knew her mother would keep her word. She left
the phone booth, not caring if passersby saw tears
streaking her face. She felt better, a lot better.

Now—all she had to do was break the news to her
husband.

JULY WAS A BUSY MONTH. The garden started to pro-
duce, and Nina picked beans until she thought she
never wanted to see another one. Part of the problem,
in Lou's opinion, was she'd planted too many kinds.
Pole beans, bush beans, romano beans, even something called gourmet snap beans. Lou said it served
her right. But she often dropped by and helped pick
and showed Nina the proper way to blanch and freeze
the vegetables.

Then there were weeds to hoe. The raspberry canes
started to bear, and there was jam and jelly to make.

Nina was enthralled with all the provisioning work that seemed to be part of a ranch woman's life and delighted that Lou was so willing to teach her. But she had to admit it was darn hard work, and many nights she fell into bed and was asleep even before Cal arrived at the ranch house from wherever he'd been working. Sometimes he'd let her sleep, and sometimes she'd wake up and they'd make slow sleepy love in the endless hot summer night. He told her she was crazy to work so hard.

They'd finished branding in late June; Nina had shuddered to see the dear little calves separated from their bawling mamas, then vaccinated, castrated, dehorned and branded before being turned out, disoriented and trembling, to find their mamas again. Cal said it had to be done, that was all there was to it. Then there were fences to fix and machinery to repair and animals that needed doctoring. Cal had told her summers were busy; she'd had no idea how busy.

Somehow she found the time to paint, too. And every ten days or so, she'd bundle up some of her paintings and sketches and send them off to Leo. Cal never commented on what she did with her work. The few times he came into her studio—she'd fixed up one of the north bedrooms as a working space—she could tell by the look in his eyes that he liked what he saw. Cal's approval felt better to her than any money she'd ever received for one of her paintings, many of which Leo sold in their shop. At Cal's request, she'd framed a few of her smaller sketches and hung them in his office on the main floor of the house.

She thought constantly about confessing everything to Cal. Often she'd awake in the night and go over one scenario after another. Still, the time never seemed exactly right. More than once, she'd begun in a round-about manner, but as soon as she'd seen how absolutely unsuspecting Cal was, how incredibly proud he was of her in the community, how much pleasure it gave him to please her in bed, she just couldn't do it. She'd made a pact with the devil: for happiness now she was trading unhappiness down the road. *Maybe forever.*

Then, in mid-August, something happened that forced her to act. She discovered she was pregnant.

CHAPTER FIFTEEN

*S*HE WASN'T GOING to stay.

Cal pushed hard along the top of the hill, then pulled the gelding up, sides heaving, snorting and blowing at flies that materialized out of nowhere.

He hunched over the saddle and gazed down into the valley where Henry and the haying crew had started to cut near the river. They missed Jeremiah now that he'd gone over to the Diamond Eight, especially when it came to some machine breakdown or other. But Lewis Hardin, the new fellow they'd hired back in February when Jeremiah had left the first time, had worked out well. He'd turned out to be a hard worker and quiet, which Henry liked. Cal was thinking he might keep him on over the winter. Henry had hired half-a-dozen extra hands back in early June before branding, but they were mostly seasonal and would be gone after roundup.

Nina.

Each week that had gone by this summer made it clearer and clearer what was happening—he couldn't hold her. And it ate him up inside not to know why.

Their physical relationship wasn't the problem; if anything, it had sweetened and deepened in the short time they'd been together. Nina always welcomed his kisses; she met him halfway when he touched her, as

ready as he to make love anytime, anywhere. He knew
her body so intimately now, her needs, her moods—
as she knew his. *Her joy, his joy.*

He'd never met a woman like her. He'd never made
love with a woman who pleased him more. Yet, many
times, especially in the last few weeks, he'd awakened
to hear her weeping softly into her pillow. He'd lain
there, paralyzed with fear, knowing that somewhere
deep inside, somewhere he couldn't touch her, she was
desperately unhappy. Something had gone wrong and
he didn't know what.

He'd seen the shadows gradually grow to darken
her eyes. He'd seen her fearful look when visitors arrived unexpectedly or when the telephone rang late at
night. He'd seen her shut herself in her studio for
hours, painting furiously. He'd seen the finished work
and had known how good it was. Then he'd seen her
pack the paintings up, wrap the package in brown paper and take it to the post office to send to that company in Vancouver where she used to work. They still
wanted her work, she said, although he'd never seen
any checks.

He didn't care about that; he wanted her to have her
own life. He was old-fashioned enough to want to support his wife, but he wasn't fool enough to try to stop
her from earning money her own way if that was what
she wanted. He'd never stop her from being who she
was—she had to know *that* about him, if she didn't
know anything else. He knew she was different. He
appreciated that. He didn't need to be reminded that
she wasn't a local girl, someone who'd been raised to
take over as a rancher's wife someday or a farmer's
wife, content to feed chickens and slop pigs and hang

out clothes and raise a series of grimy-knuckled, rough-haired, sunburned kids.

Many times he'd worked up his nerve to ask her why she wept, but in the end he was afraid—afraid of the answer he might get.

Whatever the reason behind her sadness, deep down she didn't want to be here on the Rocking Bar S with him. He could no longer believe anything else. He didn't know what she *did* want, but he was beginning to realize it wasn't him. He couldn't make her happy. He couldn't stop those silent tears at night. It hurt even to think about it. He'd had a feeling all along that hooking up with a woman like her was just too good to be true.

Maybe it was too lonely out here in the Horsethief Valley, although she didn't seem eager to go to town or to invite visitors out to the ranch. Lou stopped in from time to time, but she was busy with her new life over at the Robison place. Jeremiah had moved to the Diamond Eight when he got the manager's job, and Henry had moved into the bunkhouse shortly after their marriage. Maybe life was too boring and ordinary. He'd hired a cook for the summer crew and had temporarily opened up the old cookhouse, but she still cooked meals for him. She did her painting and weeded the garden, and maybe with him gone from dawn to dusk most days, it wasn't enough. Maybe she'd just made a big mistake agreeing to marry someone she barely knew. Maybe she thought he'd expect her to make the best of it.

Cal didn't want that. *He wanted her to be happy; he wanted her to laugh.* He tightened his jaw as he touched his heels to Blackjack's side and the gelding broke into an easy trot, following the crest of the ridge. He'd let her go with as much grace as he could muster, that was what he'd do. He'd have a talk with her, try his damnedest to figure out what was wrong and then, if it didn't work, if he couldn't fix whatever seemed to be broken in their lives, well…he'd let her go and wish her luck. He didn't give a damn what the rest of them—Jeremiah or Henry or Lou or anybody else— would think about her leaving him.

He was tired and hot after a long morning riding fences. He'd left the house just after dawn. Nina had been asleep, her honey blond hair tangled on the pillow, the taffy-colored spread she'd bought to replace his old duvet covering her bare back. He'd carried that image with him all day long. *His wife, asleep. Safe.*

Safe from what? Damn. Irritated, Cal spurred his horse into a gallop, deliberately shutting Nina from his mind. He had to; if he got sidetracked by his domestic problems, he'd never be able to run the ranch.

He was pretty sure now where the rustlers were loading up his steers, and he intended to call the Mounties when he got back. He felt good about his morning's work. Someone had been using a box coulee that bordered the Diamond Eight range, up in the high country. There were tire tracks down into it. The bottom was dry and hard enough to take a good-size truck and trailer, at least until the fall rains started. Not a quarter of a mile from a hard-packed dirt road, either. He'd seen where the fence had been cut and repaired. The steers could have been chased into that box coulee and a brush fence thrown up to keep them there until the truck came, probably at night. It wouldn't have stopped wild horses, but it would be enough to keep back a few steers that had been handled before. Or maybe the rustlers had put a trailer down there, with a truck coming in to pick it up, loaded, after dark.

Cal knew it was all speculation, but the point was, it could be done. The Diamond Eight had lost eight head last year; Adam Garrick's ranch was almost five miles away, and Cal had heard he'd lost a few. So had the Winslow boys. Clearly some sort of ring was operating, not taking too many from any one ranch. Picking them off here and there, a few at a time. Probably holding them somewhere in these hills, then trucking them across the Montana border and getting rid of them where the buyers weren't always particular about the brands.

An inside job. The thought had occurred to Cal, but he couldn't see how that could work. Why would steers be disappearing from all over the summer range? The rustlers couldn't have an inside man on three or four different outfits. Didn't make sense.

Cal topped the last rise before heading down to the home ranch. He loved this view. He loved seeing the saddle ponies grazing in the fields, the broodmares, glossy and fat, a few with long-legged foals at their sides. He loved the square simple way the log corrals and chutes were laid out, solid and gray in the August sun. Everything made sense to him; everything had its place. He loved the way the garden stretched out behind the house, the lilac hedge on one side, the raspberries Lou had planted years ago on the other. The old crab apple tree. He liked the way the windows shone and winked in the sun, beckoning him home.

This was his world. His home. He liked to think of it that way—and with his wife waiting for him.

They needed to talk.

Cal frowned and started down toward the barn. He pulled off the saddle and bridle and brushed down the gelding quickly before turning him out. For a long moment he hesitated, looking toward the house. Should he go up? He felt hot and sticky; a cool shower right about now and a cold beer from the fridge was a powerful draw.

And Nina. He longed, suddenly, to see her.

Then, not yet ready to trust himself with the decisions he'd come to that morning, the knowledge that he had to take some action to try to repair what had gone wrong between them, he turned, instead, toward the small office he kept just off the tack room. He dialed the RCMP detachment in Glory, spoke to a new constable and told him what he'd found and where. He called the Diamond Eight and left a similar message for Jeremiah. Then he got into his pickup and drove up the back road toward the place Henry and his crew were cutting hay.

He couldn't face her. Not now. Not yet.

NINA WATCHED CAL ride into the yard. She saw him glance toward the house and resisted the crazy impulse to wave frantically, to rush out onto the porch and call him.

She scrubbed angrily at the tears that suddenly spilled. God, her emotions were a wreck! *She must be crazy, leaving a man like this.* But how could she stay? This whole situation was her fault, completely and totally her fault. She'd made a mess of everything.

She had to think. She had to get away from him and the Rocking Bar S and all his well-meaning relatives and neighbors. She'd carried her secret too long; what had started out as a fairly innocent pretense had turned into a nightmare that threatened to consume her and everything she treasured. *Her husband. And now their baby.*

She had to step back and breathe and figure out what to do. She hadn't known what a tightrope she'd been on until she found out about the baby. She'd nearly cracked. She'd burst into hysterical tears in the doctor's office and then had to spend ten minutes putting his fears to rest. Yes, she was thrilled about her pregnancy, it was just…just that she was overtired and stressed out and…

If only he knew the half of it!

A few weeks in Vancouver with Letty to take care of her and coddle her as she always had would be heaven—no lies, no secrets.

She needed time. Time to come to terms with the presence of this new being, Cal's baby, growing inside her. Time to decide what to do next. To figure out *how* she could tell him.

Her mind was spinning. She was inches from the edge—she knew it. It was going to kill her to leave Cal for a month, maybe two, or however long it took to rest and figure things out and turn herself and her life around. Yet the thought of staying was worse.

It was best this way. She couldn't tell him part of the truth—say, about the baby—without telling him absolutely everything. She knew he'd never let her go if he found out she was pregnant. It was his child; she knew how much he wanted a family. And he'd think she'd tricked him all along, by not telling the truth about her background. He'd hate her for all her lies. How could he not?

If that happened, if he made her stay—then how would she ever be able to sift the truth from the lies? What chance would they ever have to build something strong and loving out of this mess? She'd never know if he'd only wanted her to stay because of the baby....

Then another thought struck her. What if he came up to the house, as he often did when he returned in the middle of the day? She'd packed the two suitcases she intended to take. They were still upstairs. Maybe she should hide them, at least until he'd left again.

There were a dozen flights every day between Calgary and Vancouver. She'd catch one, even if it was standby. That wouldn't be a problem. The main thing was to leave without Cal's suspecting anything. He'd try to stop her; she knew he would. He'd want to talk about it; he'd want to know why. When she got to Glory, she'd call Letty from a pay phone and tell her she was coming back home for a while.

Except this was home now. The Rocking Bar S. The place where she'd done some of the best work of her life, according to Leo. Her baby had been conceived here. This was where they all belonged—she and Cal and their child.

If he came in and asked her questions, or if he seemed at all sympathetic, or if he looked at her the way he did when he wanted to make love—oh, God... She'd tell him everything; she wouldn't be able to help herself. She wasn't made of stone. She'd tell him about the baby. She'd tell him about all the lies. *Everything.*

She couldn't risk it. Telling him the truth now meant the end for sure. She was too desperate, too mixed-up. She'd waited too long. She'd made too many mistakes.

Nina stood at the kitchen window, far enough back that she couldn't be seen. She saw the paint gelding lope out into the pasture from the side door of the barn, kicking and bucking a little before trotting off to join the rest of the horses at the far corner of the pasture. She held her breath and waited. Ten very long minutes ticked by.

Finally she saw Cal emerge from the barn and glance toward the house. Then he pulled his hat down low over his eyes and got into his truck. A moment later all that moved was the column of summer dust hanging in the wake of the pickup.

Silence descended. She heard a dog bark faintly in the distance and the sigh of the cottonwood outside the kitchen door. The buzz of flies on the screen. That was it. That was all.

Nina realized she might never see Cal again.

BY THE TIME Cal came back to the ranch, it was a lot later than he'd planned. He'd helped Henry and his crew cut the hay, and then, feeling aimless and out of sorts, he'd driven over to Adam Garrick's place to tell him about the ruts he'd found in the box coulee. Adam had been out cutting some of his own hay, so they'd sat in Adam's pickup in the field with the doors open to catch the breeze and popped a couple of beers from the cooler Adam kept in the back of the truck.

Cal liked Adam. The one subject they didn't touch on was Cal's marriage. Cal knew Adam was soured on women after his own marriage went bad a few years before. Helen had left him for good back when he was still on the rodeo circuit, and Cal didn't think his friend had ever really put it behind him. Adam listened carefully to Cal's description of the tracks he'd found and suggested, with a grin that reminded Cal of the old hell-on-wheels Adam Garrick, that maybe they ought to lay a trap for the rustlers. Cal was inclined to let the Mounties handle it, but he knew Jeremiah and Henry would be hot to go along with Adam's idea once they found out.

Well, they'd have to see what the Mounties did first.

It was almost nine when he finally got home. He was surprised to see that there were no lights on in the house. Henry's truck was gone, but there were lights down at the bunkhouse. Probably the nightly poker game.

Cal stepped over a couple of dogs snoozing on the porch and opened the kitchen screen door. The inner door was closed. In this heat? The house felt empty, and Cal felt a foreboding crawl down his spine.

"Nina!" he called from the bottom of the stairs, then cursed himself. She was probably sleeping. She'd been complaining about feeling tired these past few weeks. Cal had told her to slow down on all the gardening she was doing and all the pickling and jam-making Lou had started her on. He'd told her she didn't have to break her neck preserving, the way Lou always did; they could buy their pickles and jam this winter. But had she listened to him? No.

Cal paused, his mind continuing to register the profound silence in the old house. Then something cold and ugly grabbed at his vitals and he took the stairs three at a time, not caring how much noise he made. *"Nina!"*

The note lay on the bed they'd shared, the paper brilliant white, caught in a shaft from the last rays of the dying sun. The sunbeam glimmered, shooting honey and gold all around the room she'd painted the butterscotch color he'd had misgivings about, but had to admit was perfect when she was done. The note lay dead center between the two pillows under the taffy-colored spread.

Cal wrenched his gaze from the folded sheet of paper and walked to the window. Every bone ached, every joint felt stiff and sore. His throat hurt. He felt icy cold, and it had to be eighty degrees in the room.

She'd gone. She'd left him—just as he'd known she would.

Feeling like an old man, he turned and walked back and picked up the paper. He opened it, scanned the few lines. He didn't have to read them; he already knew what was there. His heart felt like a stone. He'd been right: she was lonely, she missed her friends…she was sorry for being a coward, leaving like this, but she just had to get away for a while and maybe this way was best….

For a while. *She'd never come back. He knew she wouldn't.*

Cal crushed the paper in his hand. He slammed his fist into the wall with a cry that echoed through the empty house, a sound that, for a moment, he didn't know had come from his own throat. Then, wheeling, stumbling, blindly missing steps, he went back downstairs. He went around to every window and door and locked them. He pulled down blinds and shut curtains.

He shut off the kitchen lights, which he'd flicked on when he'd first come in.

Oh, Cal, I think this is going to work out, I really do, she'd said the day they got married. *I want it to, so much.*

Well, she'd been wrong, hadn't she?

He went to the cabinet where he kept the liquor and took out a bottle of rye. Brand-new. He cranked off the cap as he walked through to the living room and tossed it on the floor.

She'd redone this room, too. There'd been one hell of a flurry of activity that first couple of months after they were married. Only the furniture, most of it old and comfortable, had remained the same, although she'd put slipcovers on several chairs.

Cal chose one she hadn't touched. He leaned back, put his feet up on the matching footstool—he noticed then that he hadn't taken his boots off—and proceeded to raise the bottle to his lips. The whiskey ripped down his parched throat, raw and hot at first, then pleasantly numbing.

That was what he wanted.

Before the night was over, he intended to empty the bottle.

JEREMIAH CAME LOOKING for him before breakfast. Cal saw his pickup slam to a stop in a cloud of dust just outside the back door and remembered how Lou had insisted they park over by the garage in the summertime. Lou was always complaining about the dust. Had Nina complained? He couldn't remember if she had.

"Why don't you answer your goddamn phone?"

Jeremiah stormed into the kitchen. He looked angry. He also looked worried.

Cal glanced at him and set his plate down on the bare wooden table. "Take off your boots." The phone had rung several times during the night, as he recalled. He hadn't checked for messages yet.

Jeremiah kicked off his boots and came into the kitchen. "What in hell's going on around here? Where's Nina?" He half turned toward the door that led to the hall. "What's this I hear about rustlers taking off with that stock last year? You talk to the cops yet?"

Cal sat down. "Pull up a chair," he said to Jeremiah. "There's coffee." He gestured toward the stove. "Help yourself." He stuck a fork into his bacon and eggs. He felt pretty good, considering. The whiskey hadn't done much. He'd finished most of the bottle before sunup, but he hadn't gotten drunk. Instead, he'd ended up feeling something different. New purpose. New focus. It was as though something he'd always believed deep down to be too good to be true had turned out to be exactly that: too good to be true. He'd just been deluding himself. He'd been living in a fool's paradise for a few months, and in a way it was a relief to know that.

He'd dumped the bottle, still a quarter full, into the trash, opened the blinds and curtains—it was a gorgeous day, all blue sky and fresh early-morning breeze. He'd unlocked the doors and then gone upstairs and taken a long hot shower. He'd shaved extra carefully—his hand would start to tremble all of a sudden for no reason—and changed his clothes. After that, he'd come downstairs and made his breakfast.

Boiled coffee, the kind he liked. None of that damn fine-grind gourmet drip stuff.

Jeremiah poured himself a mug and came back to the table. "I gotta talk to Henry. I figure we ought to get busy and set a snare for those rustlers, don't you, Cal? Ha! When I think Henry damn near had me convinced it was a grizzly." Jeremiah caught Cal's eye and grinned sheepishly. "Well, hell, maybe it was my idea in the first place, but Henry sure got up on his pegs and tore off with it." He shook his head and stirred his coffee—two heaping sugars and a big splash of evaporated milk. "You talk to the cops?" He blew on the surface of the hot coffee, then took a quick swallow, eyeing Cal over the edge of his mug.

Cal nodded, methodically working his way through his plate of food. "I talked to some new constable they've got over there. Don't know how much good it'll do, since half those guys they send out from Regina wouldn't know a market steer from a dry cow…" He gave his brother a hard look. "It's up to the cops, Jeremiah. It's their job to go after bad guys."

Jeremiah didn't look convinced. "Anybody else lose stock? Besides Adam?"

"I heard the Winslows lost a few head."

"I think I'll truck on over to the Double O." Jeremiah grinned. "Adam probably likes the idea of catching these bastards himself. Make sure they get the rehab they deserve, if you know what I mean."

Cal nodded again. "He does. I talked to him yesterday. But I don't like the idea. I'm holding off here until we see what the Mounties come up with."

"Fair enough." Jeremiah pushed back his chair and stood. "Thanks for the coffee." He glanced at the kitchen clock. It wasn't quite seven yet. "Where's Nina? Still sleeping?"

Yes, probably still sleeping—on some pillow I'll never share.

Cal frowned. There was no point in avoiding the truth. "She's gone, Jeremiah," he said quietly.

"What do you mean, *gone?*"

"She left." Cal made a vague gesture with his hand. "She took off. Yesterday."

His brother stared at him. "I can't believe that," he said flatly. "You and her were like...*like this!*" Jeremiah held up his first two fingers, joined.

Cal shrugged. "Apparently not."

"She took off? She just—" Jeremiah snapped his fingers and whistled softly "—took off?"

"Yeah."

"Well, damn it, Cal, what are you going to do about it?" he demanded, thumping his hand on the table. "You're going after her, aren't you?"

Cal felt a lot calmer about this than he'd thought he would. Go after her? He shook his head. "I hadn't planned on it. She's an independent woman. She ought to know her own mind. If she wants to leave, she's free to leave."

Jeremiah slammed his hat on his head. "Well, all I can say is, you're nuts. You know that? *Nuts!* Woman like that? Leave you? For no good reason?" He snorted. "Anybody with one good eye in their head could see she was crazy about you."

He shoved his feet into his boots and bent briefly to pull them on. Then he turned to Cal again. "You're not the man I thought you were if you let her go like that. That's where I went wrong with Carol Jean.

Never mind anybody's tender delicate *civilized* feelings. I should have stepped up toe-to-toe with those damn stubble-jumpers she's related to when I had the chance. Kicked some ass. I didn't do it. I don't particularly like playing the fool, and I didn't figure you would, either.''

Cal said nothing. He'd been so focused on his own problems he'd forgotten the pain his brother had gone through. Obviously Jeremiah felt he should have handled things differently with the woman he loved.

But this wasn't the same. He wasn't in love. This was a marriage of convenience. Wasn't it?

Sometimes he had to think hard to remember how it had all started. During their marriage, things had seemed so good most of the time. But Nina had always known—and he'd known—that she could leave if things didn't work out the way she wanted. That had been what they'd decided way back. Back before they'd discovered the secret joy of each other—laughter, smiles shared, great sex.

He cleared his throat. ''I appreciate your concern,'' he said gruffly.

''Listen here, Cal.'' His brother glared at him. ''I'm not going to let on I heard this. You take my advice and keep it to yourself until you decide what you're going to do about it. If you go after her, no sense telling everyone she left, is there? You could always say she's…'' Jeremiah made a wild gesture. ''I don't know, anyone asks, say she's gone back to the Coast to visit her folks. Tell them she's gone to Disneyland. Tell them to mind their own goddamn business. Anything!''

''You think I should?'' Cal couldn't believe he was

discussing this with his brother. It was private, damn it, between him and Nina.

"Damn right you should." Jeremiah held out his hand, palm up. "You had it, man, right there. Most men only dream about that kind of luck. Go after her. Or you'll spend the rest of your life wishing you had."

With that parting shot, Jeremiah flung himself out the door and slammed it.

Cal sat very still at the kitchen table. A few seconds later he heard Jeremiah's pickup leave, tires squealing, gravel flying.

He sighed. Good thing Lou wasn't here.

CHAPTER SIXTEEN

It was not Cal's habit to make up his mind in a hurry. The one time he'd done something impulsive was when he'd asked Nina O'Shea to marry him, and look how that had turned out.

He told himself he had no interest in chasing after her. He believed what he'd told Jeremiah: Nina was her own woman. If she wanted to be with him, she wouldn't have left. She'd no doubt thought this way was easier. A simple note. Quicker, not as messy as explanations and maybe even arguments. In fact, Cal couldn't think of a single argument they'd ever had. Not even over the color she'd painted their bedroom, although he'd expressed his reservations.

Maybe—he frowned as he swerved to avoid a pothole on the road to Glory—that was part of the problem. Wasn't it normal for a man and a woman to disagree once in a while? Establish territory? Hammer things out? Damned if he knew; he'd never had a successful long-term relationship with a woman before. Maybe they'd both been extra-cautious, considering the oddball way they'd decided to get married in the first place. Love could accommodate some hardship, a little give-and-take; a legal agreement picked out in black on white could not.

Of course it hadn't worked out that way with Jeremiah and Carol Jean, had it? So much for philosophizing.

A couple of the Hardin dogs ran out to bark at the truck at Sweetgrass as always. Cal swore and kept his eye on his side mirror. It'd be his damn luck to run over one of those dogs someday. He'd mention it to Lewis, not that it would make any difference. Lewis couldn't work at the Rocking Bar S plus keep track of his crazy mama and sister and their dogs all day long.

Cal had made up his mind to keep him on. Henry was pleased with his work. The kid was young—couldn't be a day over nineteen or twenty—but he had cow sense. A lot of young fellows these days didn't. And he needed the job. Cal didn't know what the family lived on, that weird reclusive mother of his and the eccentric sister who had to be twenty years older than Lewis if she was a day, but it couldn't be much more than his salary. Cal sighed and made a mental note to ask Henry what he was paying him. Maybe he could move the kid up a notch if his work warranted it. At least he stuck around, made sure there was food on the table for his mother and sister. A lot of young fellows wouldn't have put up with the home life he had.

Cal slowed for the speed zone that marked the approach to Glory. It was hot and the dust lay in thick sheets on the country roads. Real August dog days. Here in town, lower down, closer to the river, the giant cottonwoods and elms planted at the turn of the century threw shade onto the streets and sheltered the white-painted picket fences and open verandas on the big houses. Most of these older places were brick. Cal supposed lumber wasn't that easy to come by in this wide-open country back then. And many of the pioneers had come from the East and knew how to build with bricks.

Cal drove slowly along Macleod Avenue. A couple of kids in shorts and sneakers, no shirts, played road hockey with a tennis ball. He stopped while they cleared their game, then drove on through with a wave to the kids. He thought he recognized Donna's boy in a blue baseball cap, which froze his smile for a few seconds.

Donna. What was happening with her these days? His mind jumped from the fleeting vision he'd suddenly had of the two of them last winter. He was a married man, he had no right to be thinking like that. Yet he'd damn near asked her to marry him! He couldn't imagine that now, not since Nina'd come into his life. Cal felt guilty down to his boot heels. He hadn't even seen Donna since his marriage. Was that fair? Or honest?

Maybe he'd stop in at the store and say hello before he left town.

He pulled up in front of the Sheep Creek Saddle Company and got out of the pickup. Henry had brought in a couple of bridles last week to be repaired. Cal frowned as he opened the door to the harness shop, cool and dark and heavy with the rich other-world smells of sawdust and leather and neat's-foot oil. He put Donna Beaton out of his head. Nina, too. *Women.* He had a lot to get done in town before he headed back to the ranch. Last thing he needed on his mind was women.

As it happened, he ended up having lunch with

Donna. He stopped in to say hello just as she was giving a few parting instructions to the high-school girl behind the counter of her gift shop. He could hardly say no when she suggested they walk down the street to the new deli and grab a sandwich. He was glad she'd suggested the deli, instead of the old-style café in the Glory Hotel, where he usually ate when he was in town, and then kicked himself for being glad. It wasn't as though he was doing anything wrong in having lunch with Donna. Everyone knew everyone else in this town.

But with the deli's blackboard menu featuring squash soup, samosas and veggie burgers with sprouts and tofu mayonnaise, he didn't think it all that likely he'd run into any of his neighbors over lunch, which suited him. The fewer explanations, the better.

"So?" Donna smiled. They sat down at one of the small cast-iron tables near a window and waited for their order to be called. "I hear you're married."

"Yeah," he said. "Last April."

She looked at him curiously, a small smile on her lips. "That was sudden, wasn't it?"

"You could say that." Cal hunched forward. "Look, Donna. I don't want you to think it was anything to do with you and me. I thought things were going pretty well between us. It's just that—"

"You met someone you liked better," she said with a smile, her eyes dancing. "I can understand that. You don't owe me any explanations, Cal. I think things were over between us, anyway. I wish you every happiness. In fact, I'm looking forward to meeting your wife one of these days."

"I met her last fall," he said gruffly. He was immeasurably relieved to find that Donna didn't harbor any hard feelings. "We'd been writing back and forth."

"I hear she's from Vancouver."

Word sure traveled. "Yeah. Matter of fact, that's where she is now, visiting for a few weeks." Cal couldn't believe it—he'd just lied. Bold-faced and bareheaded. Stunned, he looked out the window to gather his feelings together.

Why had he lied? No one had asked about Nina in the two weeks she'd been gone, not even Lou. So far, he hadn't had to say anything. And now he'd lied about where she was and why. Did that mean he was about to take Jeremiah's advice?

"Number nine!"

Cal jumped up to get their orders, and in the subsequent juggling to transfer their meal onto the small table and return the tray to the counter, the subject was dropped. They talked about Donna's kids and how business was going at her gift store and some of the issues that the school board was debating in these days of province-wide cutbacks.

As they got up to leave, Donna put her hand on his arm. "I want you to know I don't have any hard feelings about us, Cal. None at all. You're a wonderful man and I'm glad you found someone you want to settle down and share your life with. I hope she knows how lucky she is."

Cal's throat felt tight. "Thanks, Donna. I appreciate that." He patted her hand awkwardly. "You know, at one time I was thinking pretty seriously about, well…" He cleared his throat and took a deep breath. "Well, about asking you to marry me."

"You were?" Her dark eyes were soft. "That's so sweet of you, Cal. I'm glad you didn't, because I probably would've turned you down."

"Well, damn!" He laughed. "How d'you like that? And here I was thinking you might consider the offer," he teased.

"I like my life just the way it is, Cal. I do. Can you understand that?" Her gaze met his as he held the door for her. The heat on the sidewalk was like walking into an oven. "I love my store and my customers. I make a good living. My kids keep me busy. I don't need a man in my life. Not marriage, anyway. I date. In fact, I'm seeing someone I like quite a lot right now—that new lawyer. Lucas Yellowfly? He took over when old Pete Horsfall finally retired?"

Cal nodded. "I heard Lucas was back in town."

"Back?"

"Yeah. I know him from years ago, out at the Sweetgrass School. He's a few years younger than me."

"Well, anyway. He's a nice man. And guess what?"

"What?" Cal grinned down at Donna. She was full of surprises today.

"I wouldn't marry him, either, if he asked me," she said with a merry laugh.

Cal was smiling as he got back into his truck for the trip home. He waved to Donna as she stood outside her store looking cool and competent in a loose white dress, her dark hair pulled up into a casual knot. She waved back and smiled, then strolled into her shop.

He was going home to an empty house. Just being with Donna today, laughing, having a little fun with her, reminded him of everything he was missing. Somehow he'd hardened his mind toward Nina; somehow he'd hoped she'd disappear out of his brain, along with all the memories. It wasn't working. He knew now it wasn't going to work.

Maybe Jeremiah was right. Maybe he should go after her. Find out just why she left and see if there was any chance, any chance at all, they could work it out between them. She'd said "for a while." Had she meant it? Damn. He wanted her back. He wanted her back in his arms. He wanted her back in his bed.

Jeremiah had said any fool with one good eye could see she was crazy about him. Was that true? It couldn't be—or why would she have left like that?

As though he'd finally given himself permission to think about her, memory rushed through him. He recalled the way her skin smelled at the back of her neck and the grumpy look on her face when he asked her too many questions in the morning. He saw and felt her delight when they uncovered yet another litter of Henry's hounds, this batch in an earthen den by the garage. He saw the shine of her hair, a bright haze against the sky, and remembered how it would curl around her face, in damp tendrils, in the heat. He heard her throaty cry when they made love, felt her fingers dig into his shoulders, her legs twine tight with his.

Just thinking about her made him hard. He wanted her back. He had to find her first.

NO WAY, THOUGH, was she going to mess up his ranching year. If he was going to take the time to find her and bring her back, he was going to do it right.

That meant he had to get the rest of his hay in. All

of it. And his feed grain. It also meant he had to do what he could to cooperate with the Mounties' investigation. He didn't have much hope of their success, considering how cold the trail was now. Nor would he know if any steers had been stolen this year until they brought the cattle down from the summer range, probably toward the end of October. Adam Garrick and the Winslows and the rest of the ranchers in the area would start roundup about the same time. Then there was the work of separating the two-year-olds and the yearlings, the dry cows from the heifers, sending the market steers off to the feedlot and the auction barn. Bringing in the bulls for the winter.

He'd go for her in September, he decided. Maybe close to the end of September. Between harvest and roundup. He wouldn't tell anyone. He'd give himself a week to track her down and talk her into coming back with him. If it didn't work out, well, at least the ranch would be on schedule.

CAL LEFT on the twenty-seventh of September, a year to the day since he'd met her. He hadn't planned it that way. In fact, he'd forgotten that it had been exactly a year since he and Jeremiah had seen Nina standing there at the side of the road with the hood up on the Porsche. He didn't think of it until he was past Blairmore and heading for Fernie. He had the windows down in the Suburban and an empty stock trailer rattling behind. He'd decided to take the Suburban, instead of the pickup, mainly because he thought it might be more comfortable for Nina if she came back with him. Besides, he planned to stop off in Cranbrook and see Martin Basaraba about some Maine Anjou bulls. If they could come to an agreement, he'd leave the trailer there and pick up trailer and bulls on the way back from Vancouver. The Suburban could easily handle a loaded stock trailer over the Crow's Nest Pass. No sense wasting the trip completely if Nina decided to stay where she was.

You're avoiding the truth, Blake, a voice inside him said. *You're pretending this doesn't matter, that if you bring back a couple of goddamn bulls, the trip will have been worthwhile.*

That was true. Cal knew it. And knowing it made him feel bad. Why couldn't he just plain admit to himself that he wanted his wife back any way he could get her? That he'd promise anything, and mean it, if she'd only agree to come back to Glory so they could start over? It was because, deep down, he didn't really think she *would.* But Jeremiah was dead right; he'd never forgive himself if he didn't make the effort.

Cal drove into the small village of Ladner's Landing midafternoon the second day after he'd left the Rocking Bar S. He'd spent the night with the Basarabas in the Steeple Mountains and had made a deal on two good-looking young bulls. Cal had used a Maine Anjou bull on some of his Hereford cows three years before and had liked the results. Small calves with plenty of crossbred vigor. The cows had no trouble birthing them, unlike a lot of the big-framed exotic crosses that had been tried by other ranchers and eventually abandoned.

He was pleased with his purchase. He always felt good when he bought or sold stock; after all, it was a critical part of his business. Now, he thought, gripping the steering wheel and making sure he didn't miss the overpass over Highway 99, if the rest of his trip turned out half as well…

Ladner's Landing was right out on the Fraser River delta, about as far as you could go before reaching the Gulf of Georgia. Cal had studied the road map when he'd had lunch back in Chilliwack and he knew exactly how to reach the village. When he arrived, he stopped for gas and asked how to find River Road, where Nina had lived. The gas jockey told him, but he got twisted up a few times before he finally found her address, the one he'd written to all winter.

When he'd parked and switched off the ignition, breathing deeply to fill his lungs with the old-water smell of the river and the coastal air, deeper and denser than the bright dry air of the prairies, Cal realized he had major misgivings. *What was he doing here? What if she really didn't want to see him again? What did he plan to say?*

Well, he definitely hadn't come all this way just to sit here in his vehicle. He got out and stretched. The day was soft with a misty kind of fog, the kind of day they never saw around Glory. He'd left home with the poplars all brilliant yellow, and here, hardly a tree had changed color yet. He saw one red maple. The rest were cedars, big oaks and horse chestnuts, a few holly trees. There was a weird-looking monkey-tail tree across the road. He didn't see one poplar or cotton-wood.

He walked around the Suburban and took a good look at the place where she'd lived. He didn't really expect to find her here, but he thought somebody might be able to tell him where she'd gone. He could see the tops of fishing-boat masts on the far side of the building, and his heart thudded. She'd told him so much about that view, the view from her window; it was almost as though he'd been here before. The building was low and stretched along the top of the dike, pale dirty-looking brick, not particularly attractive. He noticed an outside phone booth and directory and walked over to it. How likely was it that she'd been here? She'd probably gone straight back to that job she'd liked so much. Certainly she'd have had to find another place to stay, maybe in Vancouver.

He scanned the listings quickly. No Nina O'Shea. No Nina Blake, either, but he hadn't expected that.

Suddenly he wanted to see where she'd lived, as though seeing the number on her door would make that furious exchange of letters last winter real, not just something he'd dreamed up. He walked up the steps that led from a small landscaped terrace onto the second level. Apartment 246. He approached the door, which was partly open. The loud sound of a radio tuned to a hard-rock station came from inside. Cal took a deep breath, closed his eyes for a few seconds to center his emotions, then rapped loudly. When nothing happened, he knocked again.

The door was flung wide. "Yeah?" It was a man in housepainter's garb—white paint-spattered overalls and cap. Cal noted that the man's glasses, old-fashioned horn-rims, were finely spattered with dried-on paint, different colors. "What can I do for ya?"

"I'm looking for the lady who used to live here. Nina O'Shea." Cal glanced past the painter's shoulder. There was nothing in the apartment that he could see. Just a couple of ladders and paint cans and canvas drop sheets.

"Dunno who used to live here, man. You'll have to check with the manager. Upstairs." The painter nodded toward the stairs and moved the wad of gum from one side of his mouth to the other. "Just paintin' the place, that's all, man."

Cal looked into the room with a sinking feeling. He saw the off-white paint that was going over a deep red color. Nina had told him she'd painted her walls cranberry to make up for the fact that she had so little furniture. He definitely had the right place. But she was gone.

On the off chance the manager could tell him anything, he stopped at the building office.

"Nope. Don't know where the little lady went," the manager said. He didn't seem very interested. "She had her rent paid until end of this month when her lease was up, although she took off four or five months ago. Wished she'd told me she was gonna paint the place that godawful red," he complained. "I kept her deposit, but it's still costing me double to get it cleaned up."

Cal felt like punching him. *Cleaned up? Don't you know taste and class when you see it, mister? Don't you know my wife's no off-white beige kind of woman?*

He muttered his thanks and left. For a long time he sat in his vehicle and wondered what to do next. First, he'd check out the telephone book. Then, if he didn't get any leads there—and it was doubtful—he'd go over to Vancouver and find that fancy place where she used to work. Maybe they'd heard from her. As he recalled, she seemed to have a pretty high regard for her ex-boss. He frowned. What was the joint called? Swain and Company. That was it.

Suddenly Cal felt very tired. He'd had a long drive. His emotions were twisted up tighter than a hackamore knot. He'd just stuck his neck out on a couple of unproved bulls, which might not make his bank manager all that happy. His wife had left him and he didn't know where she was. Someone was stealing his goddamn steers from under his nose. It was suppertime—he glanced at his watch—at least on Alberta time, and he was hungry.

He made up his mind. He'd go and take a room in that hotel he'd passed a few blocks back on the main street. The Ladner Arms. He knew the type—along the lines of the Glory Hotel. Quite a lot of traffic downstairs in the tavern, but not too many guests upstairs, at least not the kind that came with luggage. He'd grab something to eat and get some sleep. Tomorrow, bright and early, he'd head across the river to Vancouver. He'd find her.

One way or another, he'd find her.

CHAPTER SEVENTEEN

"I'M LOOKING for Nina O'Shea."

The girl sitting at the desk gazed up at him and blinked behind thick wire-rimmed glasses, then slowly stood. She seemed a little scared. "Er, just a minute. I'll check."

She disappeared behind a glass-bricked partition that ran halfway across the back of the shop. Was this the person who'd taken over Nina's job? Cal straightened, hoping he hadn't frightened her by the way he'd burst into the shop just after the doors had opened for business. He'd waited outside for a while when he'd found the place in a busy stretch between Fourteenth and Fifteenth on Granville Street, shaken to see a display of several of Nina's Rocking Bar S paintings in the window. He'd stared at those antelope-gray stretches of hills run through with the deep green of the hidden coulees—places he recognized, *places that were his, damn it*. Somehow, seeing the pictures displayed for passersby to admire in a shop window had brought home the fact of her leaving him, as nothing else had.

Then, this morning...

Cal had been up early, showered and downstairs in the hotel dining room by seven. He'd picked up the *Vancouver Sun* to scan over breakfast and been surprised to see Nina's name—well, at least *O'Shea*—prominently displayed on the front page of the second section. Apparently this Meredith O'Shea, the legal type Ray Wallenstein had mentioned, was involved in some high-profile criminal trial that was going on. The coincidence—that the very person Wallenstein had mentioned should be featured in the newspaper the day after Cal arrived in town—had amazed him. Then it had angered him. Never mind this Meredith O'Shea, whoever the hell she was; it was Nina O'Shea he wanted to find.

"Perhaps I can be of some assistance."

A tall man dressed entirely in black had emerged from behind the glass-brick wall and spoken quietly. Cal halted. He'd been pacing the small front area of the store, avoiding dangerous-looking metal gargoyles and bolts of cloth draped artistically on tables, and brightly painted wooden animals and birds suspended on wires from the ceiling. It was a strange place; he didn't quite see what Nina had liked so much about it.

"I hope so." He met the man's curiously calm green eyes and felt some of his annoyance slip away. "I'm looking for someone who worked here a while back. Nina O'Shea."

The tall man said nothing, just continued to look at him steadily. Finally he spoke. "And who might you be?" The question could have sounded rude; oddly, from this man it didn't.

"I'm her husband."

The man in black stepped forward and offered his hand with a slight smile. "I thought you might be. I'm Leo Swain. I know Nina very well."

Cal nodded and shook his hand briefly. "McCallum Blake." Swain was a handsome man; in fact, a lot of women would probably consider him *very* handsome. But Cal had the distinct impression that he wasn't interested in Nina in a male-female kind of way. Maybe he wasn't interested in any woman that way.

"Could you tell me where I can find her?" No point going into details if he could help it. Cal hoped Swain wouldn't ask why, for instance, if he was her husband, he didn't know where she was. If Nina was back working in the shop, the guy would have said so. Or the receptionist would have. Obviously she wasn't.

The man frowned. "Nina hasn't told you?" he began slowly.

"Told me what?"

"Well...where she is?"

"No." That sounded bad. "Fact is, she doesn't exactly know I'm in town," he added.

"I see." Swain raised one eyebrow. "She's been in Vancouver for quite a while," he said matter-of-factly.

"I know. Over six weeks." Cal was beginning to feel exasperated. And more than a little embarrassed. "I haven't been able to get away before this. Summer's a busy season. I, uh…" Just how much did this guy know about what was happening between him and his wife? "Nina and I need to talk."

"Mmm." Swain nodded. He had an odd way of frowning at the same time as he regarded a person intently with those curious green eyes. It was starting to annoy Cal.

"I'd appreciate it if you'd tell me where I can find her," he said stiffly, aware of how stupid it was to be asking another man for his wife's whereabouts.

Swain bent to pick up a tablet of paper that was on the desk and pulled a pen from an inner pocket. A fountain pen, lustrous black and trimmed with gold. Who used a fountain pen in this day and age? He wrote quickly on the tablet of paper and tore off the top sheet, pocketing the pen and waiting a few seconds before folding the paper in half, and handing it to Cal.

Cal tucked the paper into his shirt pocket without looking at it. He felt relief. Incredible relief. "H-how is she?" He hadn't meant to ask. But this Swain guy seemed to know so much more about Nina than he did.

Swain frowned and rocked back slightly on his heels. "She's hurting, Blake."

Hot fear tore into Cal's chest. *Hurting?* He took a deep breath, but restrained himself from asking more. He'd find out what Swain meant soon enough.

"Letty's looking after her, doing what she can, but…" Swain shrugged. "Well, she's just not happy. What can I say?" He walked toward the door with Cal. As they reached it, he touched Cal briefly on the arm.

"Make her happy," he said enigmatically, with a small sad smile. "And don't be too hard on her. She didn't mean for any of this to happen, you know."

Didn't mean for any of *what* to happen? Cal felt as though he had walked onto the wrong planet when he'd come through the old-brass-and-beveled-glass Swain and Company door. Neptune, maybe Mars. At least he had her address now in his shirt pocket. As soon as he could track down where she lived, he was going to find out for himself what Swain was talking about. *Letty? Looking after her? What the hell was going on?*

Cal stepped out onto the street. "Those paintings for sale?" He indicated Nina's work in the shop window.

Swain glanced toward it. "Those? Yes, everything's for sale. For a price."

"I'll be back for them," Cal said. The thought of Nina's work in someone else's home, some stranger's...he didn't like it.

"Fine." Swain smiled. He looked genuinely pleased. "If I can help you any further, please don't hesitate to get in touch. Call me."

CAL DROVE SLOWLY down the tree-lined street, stunned. This was the Shaughnessy district, at the top of the hill. He didn't need a guided city tour to realize that this was where the rich people lived. Here there were trees that had begun to change color. Towering maples, elms, untouched by the disease that had claimed so many elsewhere, massive lindens, chestnuts—all cast their benevolent shadows on the winding pavement.

Cal passed ten-foot laurel hedges, cast-iron gates, gatehouses, coach houses, limestone mansions set well back from the street, velvety jade-colored lawns, towering gingerbread gables, turrets, cupolas, rose windows, all the nouveau riche excess of a former age. Railway tycoons, lumber barons, steamship owners— all the patriarchs had built their dynastic piles here.

He eased up to the address that Swain had given him. He couldn't see the number, but this had to be it, according to how the rest of the street was numbered. There was no gate. The rosy-bricked driveway beckoned, but after a few seconds of indecision, Cal decided to park on the street. He slumped in the Suburban for a moment and studied the massive old ivy-covered building through narrowed eyes. *This was where Nina lived?* He ran both hands over his face. Damn, he was tired. He felt the weariness right down to his bones.

Maybe this Letty that Swain had mentioned lived here. Maybe she was some friend of Nina's who'd taken her in when she'd come back from Alberta.

Cal cursed himself for not thinking of that before. He'd never thought about her needing money. She'd seemed so independent, so proud of what she'd earned and saved from her job at Swain and Company—but that must have run out long ago. They'd been married more than five months. And how much could she have made from selling a few paintings?

Forget that stuff, Blake. Think about what you're going to say to her, how you're going to convince her to come back to Glory. Think about your feelings, how you've missed her, how much you want her back....

Cal got out of the truck. He headed across the street to the building where Nina was supposed to be. When he started up the sidewalk, he realized the old mansion had been split into several apartments or condos. There was even a doorman, which surprised him.

"I'm looking for Nina O'Shea," he said, feeling that he'd begun to sound like a stuck record since he'd crossed the river that morning. "Is she here, do you know?"

"Your name, sir?"

"McCallum Blake." At least she'd have a chance

to prepare. He didn't want to shock her. After all, no one was on the run here. If she didn't want to see him, all she had to do was say so.

"I'll ring right up, sir." The uniformed doorman picked up a white phone on his desk and punched some buttons. Cal stuck his hands in his jacket pockets and looked around. Pretty swank. The floor was green-veined marble. There was a huge fireplace at one end, flanked by upholstered chairs and a low polished table. Fresh flowers filled the empty grate. Leaded windows by the fireplace spilled multicolored light into the foyer.

The doorman cleared his throat. "You're to go straight up, sir. Second floor, to the right."

Two apartments per floor. Cal tried to muster his thoughts in the elevator. He felt scared, as scared as he'd ever felt about anything. This was it—either she was going to be happy to see him, or she wasn't. Still, what could he do about it? Not a whole lot.

Cal got off the elevator and turned to the right. The door was large and very solid-looking dark oak, the carpets blood red and very thick. He pushed the door-bell and took a deep breath.

The door opened almost instantly. He saw an older woman, dark-complected and short, wearing a blue skirt, a white blouse and a checked apron. Cal could smell something good cooking somewhere in the apartment. The woman's dark eyes scanned him avidly. "You must be the husband."

"I...I'm McCallum Blake." Cal was completely taken aback. *The husband?* "You're...?"

"I'm Letty." She held out her hand; it felt firm and

small in his. "Letitia F. Espinoza. The 'F' stands for Florence. I'll tell Nina you've arrived."

It didn't sound as though Nina knew he was here. Cal took another deep breath. *Who in hell was this Letty?* Nothing was making any kind of sense today. First Leo Swain, now this…this Letty person.

"Yoo-hoo? Miss Nina?" He heard her call, just out of sight in the hallway. "You have a visitor. Someone's come to see you."

Cal heard low voices, then steps approaching. Nina turned the corner.

"Cal!"

She was as beautiful as he'd remembered, maybe more. She looked like she'd gained a little weight; her face was fuller, but there were dark shadows under her eyes. *She's hurting, Blake.* Swain's words echoed in his head. Her hair was loose and she had on some sort of long gown. For a few seconds he couldn't trust himself to speak. Finally he nodded. "Nina," he said. His voice sounded stiff, unnatural. The muscles of his face felt like rapidly hardening plaster. "How are you?"

"My God, Cal! What are you doing *here?*" Nina had put one hand to her mouth when she'd seen him and the other to her midriff. Her eyes were wide and blue. Cal could see her astonishment warring with something else. He had a good feeling about it; she was trying to hide the fact that deep down she was pleased to see him.

"I, uh, just thought I'd look you up," he said diffidently. He hadn't moved away from the door, had made no effort to come any farther into the apartment.

"You left in quite a hurry and I thought…well, I thought we should talk. That's all."

He couldn't drag his eyes from hers. He felt caught up in something he couldn't control. He knew he'd made the right decision to track her down. No matter what happened.

Suddenly, with a small shrill cry that went straight to his heart, Nina flew into his arms. "Oh, Cal, oh, Cal," she whispered brokenly. "Oh, I've missed you so much. I don't know what to do. I've been so stupid. I…"

Cal closed his eyes and wrapped his arms around her and buried his face in her hair. She felt bulky in her long gown. Her hair was fluffy and soft and smelled of something floral. *God, it felt good to hold her in his arms! It had been so long.*

"Oh, Cal, how can you ever forgive me? How can—"

He didn't want to talk. He silenced her, his mouth covering hers in a kiss that was so hungry and so alive and so endless—and so right. This was exactly what he should be doing, what he'd wanted to do all these past long weeks. This was his wife. Why hadn't he come for her before? Why had he taken so long to make up his damn-fool mind?

"Cal," she began breathlessly, pulling back slightly, "you don't know what I'm—"

"Shut up, Nina," he growled, and covered her mouth with his again. She moaned and sagged against him, her hands gripping the fabric of his shirt. He explored the dark familiar sweetness and felt his body harden. He tasted her willingness again, that perfect intoxicating blend of her need with his that he remembered so well. He wanted her; he'd always want her. No matter what happened. He couldn't just stand here and keep kissing her, though. This was crazy. His blood was exploding. In a minute he'd be so hot he'd take her right here on the tiled floor of the foyer, and what would Letitia F. Espinoza make of that?

"Let's get out of here," he whispered between kisses. "Let's go back to my hotel. We can talk there."

"I...I can't." Nina twisted her head back and he was horrified to see tears on her cheeks. "I can't leave."

"Why not?"

"I...I live here, Cal."

He looked at her. "Yeah, sure. I know, you've been living here. But..." He looked into her eyes and saw fear. What was she talking about? "Let's just go somewhere we can talk. Privately."

"We can talk here." Her eyes begged for understanding and he felt himself respond to that appeal. But he *didn't* understand. What was wrong with her?

"But what about—" he made an impatient gesture in the direction of the hall "—*her?*"

"She's okay. She's not a problem."

"Who *is* she? Is this her place?"

He could see Nina struggle to hold back tears. He felt terrible—he'd made her unhappy. Still, something was wrong here. Something was really wrong.

"Letty's my friend, Cal," she said finally, so softly he could barely hear her. "And my housekeeper. I've known her all my life. She helped raise me."

Cal felt like he'd been hit by a train. "Your *housekeeper?*"

She nodded and bit her lip to hold it still.

"You mean a *servant?*"

Nina nodded again.

"What are you talking about?"

"This isn't Letty's place, Cal. It's mine. I own it. I've told you a bunch of lies. That's why I ran away. I couldn't stand it anymore. I was going crazy. I couldn't stand not telling you and I just couldn't see any way to tell you the truth. I...I had to leave like I did."

Cal felt his face turn to stone. All his desire for her fell away from him like so many cold wet rags. He had an awful feeling in his stomach, in his brain—as though something ugly and silent had come out of a dark corner and he was having to face it for the first time. "All that stuff about being poor—you made that up."

"Yes," she whispered.

"That car." He paused. His chest hurt. He could barely look at her, yet at the same time couldn't take his eyes off her. He had to know. "The Porsche. It was yours."

She nodded. "Yes."

He took a step back. She leaned against the wall and shut her eyes. Fat tears leaked through to run down her cheeks.

"What about Leo?" His voice was hard.

Her eyes opened. "Leo?"

"I saw him this morning. He gave me your address." Cal barely recognized the harsh sound that came from his throat as laughter. "Did you work for him? Was that the truth at least?"

She shook her head. "We're partners. I bought into his company about five years ago."

"You *bought* into his company."

She looked at him and Cal was shocked at the pain in her eyes. She had both hands pressed to her waist in an odd way, one beside the other. "I'm from a very wealthy family, Cal. I've had everything money could buy all my life. When I met you, I…I just didn't want to tell you that. It was stupid of me, I know." Her eyes searched his. "You don't know how much I regret what I did. I didn't think anything would come of it. And then…then when we started writing back and forth, I—" Her voice broke off.

"Why didn't you tell me then?" he demanded. "You had plenty of chances to tell the truth."

"I know. I should have. I…I…" Nina suddenly covered her face with her hands and Cal saw her shoulders heaving. Pain wrenched at his heart, stabbed into his chest. He tried to harden himself against the emotions he felt. He tried to pretend he didn't want to pull her into his arms, stroke her hair, kiss her, tell her he'd forgive her anything. *God help him, he'd forgive her anything.…*

Then, to his horror, he noticed something else. Nina had put one hand back on her stomach as though in pain—or as though protecting something. *What?*

"Dear God," he said hoarsely. "You're pregnant. *You're pregnant with my child!*"

He stepped forward and seized her by the shoulders. *"Aren't you?"*

She nodded mutely.

He flung her from him and blindly reached for the door.

"Cal—don't go!" She grabbed his arm but he threw her hand off and wrenched the door open. *"Where are you going?"*

"Away from here," he managed to get out through clenched teeth. "Anywhere."

"No!"

"Don't worry—I'll be back. I don't know who the hell you used to be, but you're my wife now." Another thought struck him then, and his blood ran cold. "At least that part is true, isn't it? We're legally married?"

She nodded, one hand trembling over her mouth.

"So you can pack up your bags. You're coming home with me."

CHAPTER EIGHTEEN

NINA CRUMPLED onto a hall chair and burst into tears. That man! Now he'd gone somewhere. She might never see him again. They had to talk. They had to discuss things. She couldn't go back to Glory. Not like this. He had to come back. He had to!

"Miss Nina? Now, now. You know that's not going to help the baby a bit, you getting all upset," Letty said, brandishing the stainless-steel spoon she carried. "Lunch is ready...."

"Oh, I couldn't eat a thing," Nina sobbed.

"Yes, you could. And you will when you see what I've got for you." Letty inspected the empty foyer. "Where's Mr. Blake?"

"He's gone! He says he's coming back but I don't think he will. Not when he thinks about...about everything I've done and..." Nina wailed again.

"What a shame. I was hoping he'd stay for lunch," Letty said calmly. She brandished the spoon again. "Now, go wash your face, dear. You'll feel better." And she retreated down the hall, making disappointed muttering sounds.

Stay for lunch! That had to be the last thing on his mind. How could he sit at her table and eat lunch after what had just happened? Nina obediently got up and wiped her cheeks with the backs of her hands. She sniffed loudly and smoothed down the warm quilted robe she was wearing, her hands pausing at the small mound of her belly, as was her habit lately. *Her baby. Cal's baby.*

She shivered violently. She was so cold. She'd been so cold ever since she left Alberta. She looked critically in the mirror of the powder room just off the hall. What a mess. Her hair hung limply on her shoulders. Her nose was red. Her eyes—she looked like she hadn't slept in weeks, which was almost true. Her doctor was getting very impatient with her, but how could she help it? You could only expect so much from camomile tea and hot milk. Sometimes she couldn't get to sleep at all; sometimes she'd wake early to toss and turn. She missed Cal's large warm body beside her in bed, and she couldn't stop her brain from dwelling on all the things that had happened since that fateful day a year ago when she met him. Why hadn't she confessed everything in a letter last winter? How had she been so stupid as to end up pregnant accidentally? Why hadn't she told him the truth after she'd spoken to her mother last June?

Nothing helped. She never reached any new conclusions, except to know that she missed Cal more than she'd ever thought possible. And that she'd never ever be able to forgive herself for being so foolish. These weeks without him had been hell; she felt it even more now that she'd seen him, now that she'd felt his arms around her and tasted his kisses again.

If she could start over at the beginning, change everything, she would. But who could turn back the clock?

''Look. A nice Thai salad and some chicken soup

with dumplings,'' Letty announced with her usual quiet cheer when Nina entered the kitchen. "I think Mr. Blake should have stayed, don't you? I know he would have loved these little dumplings. Oh, well, I'm sure he'll be back soon.'' The small woman bustled around the immaculate kitchen, carefully ladling out two bowls of soup. Nina knew better than to say anything. Letty always worked out her thoughts aloud. It was a habit that had driven Nina's mother crazy when Letty had lived with Meredith and Jake. Nina didn't mind.

Letty had more or less raised Nina—she'd arrived from the Philippines as a young woman of twenty-three only two weeks after Nina was born—and Nina was glad when Letty had moved to the apartment, lock, stock and barrel three years earlier, tired of Meredith's bossy ways. Nina's view was that they were both, the two of them, the bossiest people she'd ever met. Leo had pointed that out years ago.

"Leo told him where I was," Nina blurted. Letty sat down opposite her at the little breakfast table in a sunny nook of the kitchen and shook out a napkin.

"Good for Leo. Have some of this crispbread?" Letty spread some cream cheese on a rye cracker and positioned it on Nina's side plate. "I have always regarded Leo Swain as a very sensible man," she said, picking up her spoon, then adding with a tiny smile, "not a view shared by your father."

No, Jake O'Sullivan had never thought much of Leo. What would he think of Cal if he knew him? Nina had told her parents she was expecting a baby in early March, but had said little about the baby's father. Predictably her father had hit the roof, while her mother had absorbed the news silently. Nina could practically see the wheels turning in her sharp legal mind as she examined every aspect of the situation before commenting. Then Meredith had quietly congratulated her. She'd asked no questions, and Nina had known she could count on Meredith to soothe her father.

It had always been like that. Nina had always known she could count on her mother. There'd been—still was—a genuine closeness between them. Meredith had exhibited a childlike curiosity and delight in all that interested her only child. Many of Nina's school friends had been awed at Meredith's stature in the community and had considered her cold and unapproachable. Nina knew, though, that her mother possessed an enormous capacity for focus. When her mind was on a legal problem, that was where she directed all her energies. Sometimes that made her seem distant. On the other hand, when she spent time with her daughter, she was there 110 percent. Nina recalled a private game the two of them had often played called Get Lost. They'd play it when Meredith was driving her somewhere and they had time to spare. Nina would suddenly order her mother to turn here, turn there, left, right, left again, until they were both giddy with laughter. The idea was to get lost and then find their way home. Nina never tired of the game. And neither, it seemed, did Meredith. Nina had often wondered what her mother's law partners would think if they'd seen her.

"How's the soup?"

"Soup? Oh, it's very nice. Very tasty." Just the thought of her old nanny taking such care of her, making sure she ate, caused the tears to flow again. Nina knew some of the tears could be attributed to the hormonal wash of pregnancy. But it wasn't all pregnancy. She drew a tissue from her pocket and blew her nose vigorously. "Sorry, Letty. I just can't seem to help it. I've been dreading this. I...I just don't know what's going to happen now..."

"I know, dear." Letty removed Nina's half-finished bowl of soup and busied herself at the counter preparing two plates of the noodle salad. "Don't worry. It'll pass. You'll see."

"It's j-just that I never expected to see him again. Not like that—right out of the b-blue!" Nina pulled out the tissue again. Then she frowned. Why *hadn't* Letty told her Cal was on his way when Earl had rung?

"I know you didn't. But I knew he would come. I've been expecting him any day now for several weeks, as a matter of fact," Letty said enigmatically as she carried over the two plates. "Haven't you?"

Nina stared at the older woman. "Of course I didn't expect him! He had no idea who I really was. He had no idea where to find me. He thought I lived somewhere in Ladner's Landing. I'd told him one stupid lie after another. About everything! If it hadn't been for Leo..."

"He'd have found some other way. Believe me, dear, he's that kind of man. I could tell right away. Now eat your salad."

Nothing perturbed Letty's equanimity. Nina knew better than to try. *What was she going to do?* He'd said he wanted her to return to the ranch with him. But the look on his face... *He hated her.* Nina shuddered. Even in her worst nightmare, she hadn't thought he'd ever look at her like that.

"Think of it this way," Letty said. Her bright black imperturbable gaze held Nina's. "Just think for a moment. What have you been most afraid of? What is the worst, the absolute *worst* possible thing you could imagine happening?"

"That he'd find out." Nina began to sob again, pressing one hand to her waist, just one poor hand to shelter her baby from so much. "That he'd find out somehow and…" *And that he'd hate me.*

"Well?" Letty went on, raising a delicate black eyebrow. "That's happened now, hasn't it? I'd say things are bound to get better, wouldn't you?"

CAL DIDN'T GO BACK to Ladner's Landing. He drove around for several hours; he had no idea how long. At one point, he realized he'd driven almost to Mission, heading up the Fraser Valley on the north side of the river. He stopped for gas, then turned around and went back to Vancouver.

Eventually he found himself at Granville Island in a crowd of theatergoers, although he couldn't have said how he'd ended up there. He sat through a play that had three women in it who talked about their relationships for two and a half hours. He tried hard to pay attention, but he felt like a zombie. Nothing made any sense. He had no idea why he was in the theater in the first place. Then, turning down several offers of paid companionship along the way, he walked to one of the clubs on the island and got drunk.

Stinking pissy-eyed drunk. After the club closed, he somehow managed to stumble over to the Pelican Ho-

tel, where some poor clerk must have taken pity on
him—a country boy, clearly way way off his turf—
and rented him a room.

*His baby. She was having his baby. And she'd lied
to him. Everything she'd told him was a lie.*

He lay on his rented king-size bed and stared at the
ceiling. Even drunk, he was so angry all he wanted
was to get back in his truck and head for the Rocking
Bar S. Go home. Stop at Basaraba's, pick up his bulls
and go back to the life he knew best. Alone. Just him
and his cows. To hell with women. To hell with finding a wife. Right from the very beginning everything
with Nina O'Shea had been one big mistake.

Good riddance.

Then he thought of her taking off, pregnant with his
child, not telling him—*his child!* No goddamn way
was she getting away with that. She was going back
to Glory with him if he had to drag her every inch of
the way.

She'd go back and pretend to be his loving wife—
she had the acting talent, they both knew that. They'd
pass off the time she'd spent out here in Vancouver
as a holiday or something. She'd have the baby and
then…well, he didn't care what happened then. If she
wanted to leave after that, she could goddamn well
leave. Make the whole thing look like your ordinary
garden-variety postpartum marriage breakup. It happened all the time.

Let her leave with his tiny son or daughter?

She'd tricked him and deceived him. She'd made a
fool of him. She'd manipulated and used him. Had that
been her plan all along—to use him as some sort of
no-name cowboy stud? Was she one of those hard-

boiled career types he'd heard about who decided to have a baby alone and raise it without a father? Had she used him *that* way?

Cal felt sickened to the bottom of his soul. Yet how could he punish the child for the sins of the mother? He couldn't. For the sake of their child, he'd have to do his best to work out something with her. No way was he going to be cut out of his child's life. If she stayed, well, there was that to deal with; if she left, he'd have to see her, talk to her from time to time....

Cal frowned, searching his fuzzy brain. Something didn't add up, but he couldn't quite wrap his mind around it. Deep down it didn't ring true that Nina had planned this cold-bloodedly and coldheartedly. How could she have faked her excitement and simple pleasure when he showed her things? The puppies, for instance. *Hell, Blake, everybody likes puppies.* But did it make sense that she would have sat so patiently through Lou's lectures on the correct way to make jam and put up fruit—or the garden, why would she have bothered to weed the garden?—if she'd planned all along to take off as soon as she was pregnant? How could she have faked that sweetness he found so attractive in her? The innocence, the vulnerability? She'd have to be a better actress than the three women he'd seen in the play last night rolled up in one. Maybe she was.

Last night? Had it only been last night that he'd been to some damn play he didn't know the name of?

Cal groaned and slowly raised himself to a sitting position. Dawn was starting to break. It was a new day. Rainy and miserable. Damn, he wished he was back in the Alberta hills. He was sore and he was dog-tired. Everything on him hurt, even his ears. Was that possible? He stood and methodically peeled off all his clothing, leaving it in a heap by the bed. Then he walked to the bathroom and stepped into the shower and turned on the cold faucet full blast. He stayed there for a long time, relishing the painful icy water on his too-sensitive skin. When he felt numb enough, he got out and scrubbed himself hard with one of the oversize fluffy white towels provided. Oh, yes, the Pelican was a considerable step up from where he'd stayed the night before, he thought with grim humor.

Yep, nothin' too good for a cowboy. The old-timers' expression generally referred to an experience along the lines of sleeping out in forty below with a wind chill, a bunch of jumpy steers to keep an eye on and just a dog to keep you warm—if you were lucky. Ha!

Right now he could think of worse things....

He tossed the balled-up towel into the tiled enclosure, closed the shower door and stepped over to the sink. He ran one hand over his jaw. He looked terrible. Bloodshot eyes, unshaven...old. Goddamn it—could he blame her for leaving?

He drank three big glasses of water and walked back into the room and threw himself onto the bed, naked. Within five minutes he was sound asleep.

CAL CAME BACK, as he'd promised, in the middle of the following afternoon. His timing could not have been worse.

Nina heard the faint flutter of the doorbell from the living room, but that was only because she was straining to hear it. Ever since Cal had arrived so unexpectedly the day before, she'd been both dreading and hoping for his return. She got up, then realized that Letty had gone to the door. She nervously moved to stand beside the window, hoping her father hadn't noticed her jumpiness. Cal's Suburban was parked on the street.

"Your mother says to tell you she's sorry she couldn't make it today. She had some kind of last-minute meeting to do with that trial," she heard Jake say behind her, then the unmistakable sound of him setting his coffee cup down on a marble-topped side table. He stood up and approached her from behind, lightly touching her shoulder. "I'd better go, sweetie. Sounds like you've got more company, anyway."

"Bye, Dad," Nina turned to kiss his whiskery cheek, hugging him a little longer and a little tighter than usual. "Take care of yourself."

He pulled back, sharp blue eyes examining her. "Something wrong, baby?"

"No, Dad." She smiled, knowing it for just about the biggest lie of her entire life. *Everything was wrong.* She had two suitcases packed and had canceled her Wednesday doctor's appointment. She'd made up her mind last night that she'd do her best to gather together and try to mend the tatters of her life. She'd write to her parents and explain everything once she got back to the ranch. "Everything's fine. Just fine."

When she turned toward the doorway that led to the hall, she saw Cal standing there. Letty, trust her, had disappeared. Cal had on a scarred cowhide-leather jacket—the one he'd worn when they'd met—jeans and a white T-shirt. His eyes were masked by wrap-around sunglasses. She couldn't stop staring at him.

Slowly he raised one hand and pushed his sunglasses onto his forehead. His eyes held no expression.

He looked straight at her, ignoring her father. From the corner of her eye, Nina noted Jake's surprise.

"Have you decided?" His voice sounded raw, as though he'd been smoking too much. Nina knew he didn't smoke.

"Do I have an option?" she asked faintly.

"No," was the flat response. "Are you ready to come with me? Now?"

"Yes," she whispered. When he frowned, she repeated it more loudly, "Yes. I am."

Jake cleared his throat loudly. "Look here. Could somebody please have the courtesy to tell me what's going on?"

Cal gave him a level stare. "Who the hell are you?"

"Me?" Jake paled. "Why, I'm Jake O'Sullivan, young man. I'll have you know I'm Nina's father. And if I might ask—just who the hell are *you?*"

Cal made no effort to step forward or offer his hand. Nina could hardly blame him, considering the way Jake had spoken. Damn, she'd managed to mess things up again—and with the two men who mattered most in her life.

"McCallum Blake," Cal answered with a swift glance at Nina. His eyes challenged the older man. "I'm your daughter's husband."

"Her husband?" Jake swung around to glare at Nina. *"This* is the mystery man you married, honey? And never bothered to tell any of us?"

Nina nodded. "Yes, Dad."

He swung back to glare at Cal. "Well, where the hell have *you* been all this time while my little girl's been down here in Vancouver crying her eyes out? Where the hell have *you* been when you shoulda been right alongside of her here, looking after her? We've been worried sick, her mother and me, wondering what the *hell* was going on with our girl.''

"Dad, please,'' Nina protested. She knew it was no use. Jake always managed to make her seem like she was eight years old. Once he got started...

"Seems to me a man's number-one job is to look after his wife—''

"That's just what I've been doing,'' Cal interrupted, his jaw hard. "Making a living. I've finished my summer work and now I've come to get my wife.'' Cal replaced the sunglasses. "Ready, Nina?''

"I'll just get my suitcases—'' she began.

"You're not carrying any suitcases!'' Jake burst out. "A woman in your condition? Where's he taking you? And what do you mean, get your suitcases? You going with this man, sweetheart, after he's abandoned you and...and talked to me like that?''

"Yes, Dad, I am,'' Nina said firmly. "Cal didn't abandon me. I'm the one who left. He's the man I married for better or worse, and he's the father of my baby, and yes, I've made up my mind I'm going home with him. Back to Alberta, where I belong.'' Nina couldn't be certain, but she thought she caught a glimmer of respect on Cal's face.

Suddenly he moved toward her. "Okay. Where's your stuff? I'll get it.''

"Well!'' Jake settled his dove-gray fedora carefully on his head. "I guess I'll say goodbye, sweetie. Sounds like I'm just in the way here.'' He sounded fretful and confused. Nina hadn't realized how old he was starting to look. His skin was shiny; his freshly barbered hair was thin. Where was the big hearty bull-dozer of a father she'd always known? He looked hurt, too, as though she'd done something to let him down. "If you need anything or you want to talk, you just call us collect, pumpkin. Day or night. I'll come and get you if you want, anytime. Or Murray will."

He glowered at Cal. "And you damn well take bet-ter care of my daughter than you've been doing, young fellow—I don't care what she says about who's to blame. Or you'll have me to answer to." Jake bran-dished a meaty finger, then disappeared down the hall. A second or two later Nina heard him giving Letty what-for about something. Probably his daughter, Nina thought.

Nina glanced at Cal. He still stood there, a foot or two away, presumably waiting to be told where her luggage was. She led him to her bedroom. As soon as they were inside, Cal shut the door and leaned against it.

"So that's the old man of the sea come back to life, huh?"

"Cal!" She must have been mistaken to think his attitude had softened toward her.

"Where's the gin-soaked mama? The one who— let's see, wasn't she supposed to have died of grief? She wouldn't happen to be *the* Meredith O'Shea I keep reading about in the papers, would she? The one you told Ray Wallenstein you'd never heard of?"

His grim smile hurt her to the soul. But she knew she deserved it, all of it. "Yes, she's the one," she said wearily, indicating the two suitcases that stood by her bed. "There they are. Cal, I already told you I lied. I've said I'm coming back with you, haven't I? Could we discuss the details later?"

Cal hesitated, then stepped forward to pick up her luggage. "I guess we could."

She moved to open the door for him, then paused with her hand on the glass knob. "Oh, there's one more thing I haven't told you...."

"What's that, darlin'?"

The casual endearment made her face burn. "Letty's coming back with us."

"Oh, Lord."

NINA FELT SICK from all the curves in the road. Cal was a fast driver. She got him to stop at a service station once and bought some peppermints, which seemed to help. Letty lay down on the back seat of the Suburban—she could, she was short enough—and covered her eyes with a damp cloth. She said the mountains made her nervous. She said it didn't seem right for a road to be so close to mountains like that. She didn't want to see them, and this way, she said, she wasn't even tempted to peek.

Nina also discovered how hard it was to talk to someone wearing sunglasses, especially someone who obviously didn't want to talk. After a while she gave up and wadded her sweater against the window, adjusted her seat-back as low as it would go and tried to nap. At first she didn't think she'd be able to, but she must have drifted off. The next thing she knew it was nearly dark and she was completely disoriented and her neck was stiff and sore. Cal had taken off his sunglasses and hooked them on the visor. His face looked drawn and tired in the dim light from the dash.

Nina heard the unmistakable sound of gentle snoring from the back seat. She smiled. *Dear Letty...*

"You awake?"

"I...I guess I drifted off for a while." Nina peered out the window. Trees, rocks, more trees and rocks. The mountains seemed a little more distant. "Where are we?"

"East of Grand Forks." He gazed steadily out the windshield. "We're stopping soon. Cranbrook. I've got two young bulls to pick up in the morning."

"Oh." What could she say? She was married to a rancher. Bulls were now part of her life—and cows and dogs and muddy boots and hanging out clothes and dust in the summer...and soon a baby.

Cal flicked a glance into the back seat. Letty was sound asleep. "I want to ask you something," he said.

Nina turned toward him, sorry to see the flat dead look in his eyes. It scared her. It made her think her dreams for the future had no possibility of ever coming true, no matter what she did. "Sure."

"Why did you come back with me?"

"Why?" She stared at him. "You asked me to!"

"I did. But you didn't have to. You're a free agent."

"I asked you, did I have an option? And you said no." What was he getting at?

"That was true. To a degree. I was prepared to raise hell to force you to come back with me. Whatever it took. I don't think your father was too thrilled to find out who you'd married so secretly, was he? Not quite what he had in mind for his high-society daughter. Am I right?"

Nina refused to answer. His bitterness was understandable. There was nothing she could say to change that.

"But you could have told me to go straight to hell," he went on. His attention was on the road. "You didn't. Why not?"

Nina took a deep breath. She had resolved that she'd tell no more lies. Unconsciously her hand went to cover the mound of her unborn child. She realized he'd noticed the gesture and forced herself not to remove her hand. The baby was part of who she was now, part of the truth. Cal had to realize that. "I wanted a second chance, Cal," she said quietly.

"What do you mean, a second chance?"

"I wanted to come back, like you asked, and try to start over."

There was a long silence. They must have gone nearly a mile before Cal spoke. "I don't see how that's possible anymore. Do you?"

Shocked, she looked at him. Heart sinking, she made herself go on, "What exactly do you have in mind?"

"When's the baby due?"

"March."

"How in hell did that happen, anyway? I thought you were taking care of—"

"I was!" Nina hadn't known a man's words could hurt so much.

"So?"

He looked at her and Nina's face burned. She was glad it was dark in the cab. Memories of him and her together flooded through her. They'd made love so many times, so many places. He knew that. She remembered the afternoon he'd waylaid her in the barn and they'd gone up to the loft and made love like a couple of crazy teenagers. How could he blame her for what had happened? "I...I was careless, I guess. It just...happened."

"I see." Cal was silent for a long time. "Well. We'll just have to deal with it, won't we?"

She nodded, but he didn't even look at her. Instead, he concentrated on the road, winding and dark, ahead of them. "Okay," he said finally. "You asked me what I had in mind. This is it. You'll come back to Glory and make out to be happily married to me—or as happily as you can manage to fake it," he said with a sideways glance at her. "See if you can fool the neighbors. Lou. You're a pretty good actress, we already know that."

Nina flinched at the derision in his voice.

"Have the baby and then after a month or so, when you're feeling all right and the baby's okay and everything, I want you to make up your mind what you plan to do. Go back to Vancouver if you want. Whatever. I don't care what you do. We can get a divorce. I realize I wouldn't have a snowball's chance in hell of getting custody, nor would I drag you through something like that. But I intend to be part of my son or daughter's life. I'll fight you tooth and nail if you try to prevent me."

Nina stared at him, horrified.

"And I'll pay the bills," he went on grimly. "Whether you've got a rich father or a dead fisherman for a daddy doesn't matter to me. I intend to support my own goddamn child."

"What if I...I decided to stay?"

He didn't say anything and after a mile or two Nina realized he wasn't going to.

"You want me to go?"

He stared at her, then flicked his gaze back to the road. "I don't know," he said flatly. "Right now I have to be honest and say, yes, I do. I don't think you realize what's happened here, do you?" He took a deep breath. "All the garbage about the car and your family and all that? Well, to some degree I could understand how it could happen. You're an impulsive kind of person—obviously or you never would've married me. That I could maybe handle."

He shrugged and looked at her again. Then, as though he couldn't help himself, he glanced at her belly. "But I can't believe you wouldn't tell me about the baby. *My* baby. Running away like that..." He studied the road ahead, his jaw granite hard. Nina felt his anger grow and expand to fill the space between them.

Nina couldn't believe what she was hearing. Was there no chance at all for them? Was her return to Glory just...just a form of revenge for him? "You must really hate me," she whispered.

"Hate you?" He was silent for another long long mile, until Nina thought she'd scream. "No. I don't hate you. In a way, I wish I did."

CHAPTER NINETEEN

October 20
Dear Leo,
I've picked up my pen many times this month to sit down and write you, but this is the first time I've actually put words on the page.

Am I glad to be back? Yes, I am. It was the right thing for me to do, to come back here with Cal. I never should have run away as I did—I see that now. I was a coward. I should have stuck it out, no matter what. At the time, though, it seemed like I *had* to do it. Isn't that so often the way? You think one thing's happening when really something altogether different is. Last year at this time, I thought I was busy and happy and successful, traveling and doing a great job for Swain and Co., and now I see that really I was falling in love with a man I didn't think I'd ever see again!

So much has happened since then. Some of it's been bad—these last few weeks with Cal have been very hard—and some of it's been wonderful.

I feel the baby move now, and I'm so thrilled and excited about it. I can tell Cal is, too, but he has a hard time letting me see that he does. He won't share his feelings with me. He won't share his thoughts, either, except the ordinary day-to-day stuff. It hurts me so much to see such a fine sensitive loving man all tied up in knots, even though I know a lot of it's my fault.

Are all men like that? Lou says yes, but I don't think you are, Leo. I wonder what you'd think of Lou and Jeremiah and Henry and all the other people who are so much a part of my life now. Letty's been a lifesaver. I think I would've gone crazy this last month living with this silent stubborn man if it hadn't been for Letty. She's so serene and optimistic about everything. You know Letty! I think Cal's foreman, Henry, is sweet on her. Can you believe it?! He's always coming around after dinner—supper, as they say here—and hanging around in the kitchen, hat on his knees. He doesn't say much, but Letty talks enough for both of them, as you know.

The doctor says things are going very well for me and the baby. The baby's growing. I'm huge—you should see me! I feel about eighty percent sure it's going to be a girl, but I won't care either way, as long as he or she is healthy. I love being pregnant—I just wish things were right between Cal and me. I'm beginning to wonder, Leo, if they'll ever be really right again. It breaks my heart to think he'll feel this way when the baby's born. If things don't change soon, I don't know how I can continue on here

Nina put the pen down and slowly reread what she'd written. Should she be this frank with Leo? But if she wasn't, she'd burst. She had to tell somebody. She couldn't confide her doubts to Meredith and Jake. They'd been through enough the first time she'd left Cal. If it happened again, this time for good...

Nina put her left hand on the swell of her belly and smiled. *Well.* The baby didn't like *that* thought much. Neither did she. She picked up her pen again.

> although I've made up my mind I'm going to give it my absolute best. We'll see. Do you remember that game I told you I used to play with Meredith, where we'd take this corner and that and try to get lost? Half the fun was finding your way back. I feel like that, Leo, except somehow I've forgotten how to get home again.
>
> In my heart, I think the baby's going to make a big difference. I hope so. I know Cal wants children, and although he doesn't act like it these days, deep down he's a reasonable man. If he gave me even the slightest hope that we had a chance, the two of us, I'd stick it out forever. I love him, Leo. I don't think I could ever feel the way I do about another man.

Nina gazed out the window, across the pasture with its dusting of snow on frost-stiffened grass. Several saddle horses huddled under a big tree at the far end. She could see Babe and Blackjack. And Tibbles, the new palomino quarter-horse yearling Cal had brought back from the High River auction a week ago and said they'd have to rename. She'd laughed—Tibbles!—and for a split second had seen the answering humor in his eyes. Then he'd abruptly left the house, as he did so often these days—to avoid spending time with her, she was sure.

Nina sighed and looked around the room. The kitchen was cozy and warm since she'd lit the small cast-iron woodstove in the corner this morning. Cal had told her they often used it in the winter to take the chill off the room they used most and to save on the heating bills. The pound cake she'd put in the oven before she'd sat down to write her letter was beginning to smell heavenly. Letty was upstairs having her afternoon nap. She'd urged Nina to do the same, but Nina had felt it was high time she wrote to Leo and wanted an hour or two alone in which to do it. This room had become so familiar to her. Nothing could have been more different from the up-to-the-minute space-age kitchen in her condo....

I've been doing a lot of thinking, Leo. I'd like to ask you a favor, since it isn't something I want to have to explain to Mother and Dad. Could you take care of selling the Porsche for me? And I'd like to put the condo on the market. I think part of my problem this past year has been trying to live two lives at once, and it's time I made the choice. This is the life I want, here on the ranch with Cal and my baby. Even if this doesn't last, I'm not about to go back to my old life and just take up where I left off. I'll be a mother, for one thing. Everything will be different. If it comes down to that—and I hope and pray it never will—I'll find a new place. Let me know if you'll take this on for me....

Nina finished up, filling Leo in on some of the other details of her life: how she hadn't felt much like painting since she'd been back but that she'd try to get started again after the baby came. How she'd invited Meredith and Jake to the ranch for Christmas—extending an invitation to him, too—determined to continue at the Rocking Bar S as though nothing was wrong. How grateful she was to Leo for being such a kind and wonderful and faithful friend. Then she sealed the letter, stamped and addressed it. Finally she put it in the wire basket reserved for outgoing mail, on top of some bills Cal had paid and a subscription to an interior-design magazine Nina had filled out.

That meant something, didn't it? When you took out a magazine subscription, surely it meant you planned to stick around?

CHAPTER TWENTY

"WHOA, BABE."

Cal shushed the mare, who'd thrown her head up and down a couple of times, jingling bridle and bit. The sound seemed to crack like a pistol shot through the frost and darkness. He shifted in the saddle. Damn, it was cold. He couldn't blame the mare. He was antsy, too. They'd been waiting for something to happen since just after dark. So far nothing had.

Somewhere just out of sight, Henry and Jeremiah and Adam waited on other Rocking Bar S horses. Jeremiah had finally talked him into it. Either they'd toss a spanner into the rustlers' plans tonight or they'd be riding home in the morning hungry and cold and in one hell of a cranky mood.

Earlier that afternoon Cal had found seven prime steers blocked into the canyon he'd discovered last spring and had realized tonight was the night. Just as he'd guessed, the rustlers had thrown up a rudimentary brush-and-windfall fence to contain the steers until they could load them. That meant riders. How else did they plan to put seven spooky steers into the back of a trailer?

Something didn't make sense, though. Why would rustlers go to all that trouble? Were they bringing horses in on the trailer? How would they get the horses back once the steers were loaded? Unless no one would ever suspect those particular ponies and riders, and they'd just drift back to wherever they'd come from, nobody the wiser....

Babe snorted again and Cal heard another horse approach slowly over the frozen grass. "Hold up," he ordered quietly, tugging on the reins. The brown mare obeyed.

"Any sign?" It was Jeremiah. He and Henry had stationed themselves at the top of the canyon. Adam Garrick was on the other side of the draw. Jeremiah's black gelding blended completely into the background. Clouds scudded across the new moon.

"Nothing yet."

"Damn, it's colder than a well digger's butt out here tonight," Jeremiah said, clapping his leather-gloved hands together. The gelding rubbed noses with the mare.

"Keep it down, Jeremiah. Those steers are plenty skittish, wondering what's going on." Cal pushed back the cuff of his sheepskin jacket. It was twenty minutes past midnight.

"Think anybody tipped 'em off?"

Cal considered for a moment. "Can't see how. We kept it pretty close. Just you and me and Henry and Adam. You never said anything to your boys, did you?" Lewis Hardin and Johnny Baines, the other Rocking Bar S hands, were both away for a couple of days. Cal had given them time off so they'd be ready for roundup in a week or so.

"What d'you think I am, crazy?" Jeremiah hunched his shoulders and craned his neck, trying to look into the box canyon. "Don't answer that," he added irritably. The steers, Cal knew, were impossible to see with only a new moon but there was no question that they were there, all right. Eight thousand pounds at sixty-five dollars a hundredweight. Rocking Bar S Grade A beef.

Cal had come into this plan late. His inclination had always been to let the Mounties handle the rustlers. But Adam had convinced him that the men in red serge could use some help. "What have they done so far, Cal? Nothing. Let them chase paper—that's what they're good at," Adam had advised. The Mounties were looking for suspicious sales records. "We'll take care of the livestock."

The plan was simple and based on some luck. Keep an eye on that little box coulee and, when it seemed another play was about to be made, interrupt it. Keep the plan quiet in case there were locals involved. And get a good look at whoever was doing this so the Mounties could arrest their man. Or men.

They'd had luck when Cal had spotted the steers that day.

"The bad guys better get here if they're going to try to load this stock tonight," Cal grumbled. He wished now that they'd left the entire operation, start to finish, to the RCMP. How'd he let himself get mixed up in such a damn-fool scheme, anyway?

"Yeah. Bet you want to get back to that warm house," his brother teased softly. "And that nice warm bed, huh? Can't blame you, man."

Cal frowned. He didn't respond to Jeremiah's comment. It was true; he wished he was home. He didn't like being away, especially at night. Nina still had more than three months to go before the baby was due, but anything could happen. The warm house and the warm bed applied. And Nina?

He'd reserve judgment on that. Irritated, he spoke sharply to the mare when she tossed her head again. Everything concerning his wife was driving him wild these days. He didn't know what to do. He didn't know which way to turn or what was right anymore. He wanted her as much as he'd ever wanted her, maybe more. He couldn't bear the thought of that house empty again if she left after the baby came. But then he'd think of all the lies she'd told him and the way she'd run away when she found out she was pregnant and... He didn't think he knew her anymore, didn't know who she was. And he wasn't sure how he could get beyond that.

It wasn't her fault. She'd been gentle and sweet since he'd brought her back. Just watching her trying to do everything the way she thought he wanted it done made him hurt inside. That wasn't right. That wasn't the way it was supposed to be between a man and a woman, her trying to please him all the time. He didn't want that. They were supposed to be partners, damn it. *That's what marriage is, isn't it?* She hadn't touched her paints since she'd been back; she hadn't even been into her studio, as far as he knew. Why? She wasn't the one who needed to change; *he* was.

She still wanted that second chance. She wanted him to trust her again. He just couldn't do it. She'd said she was sorry—why couldn't he accept that and go on? He didn't know. Something important had dried up, had died, back there in Vancouver. No, the bubble had burst. The magic was gone. That was all there was to it. It was over.

The baby. He barely allowed himself to think about the baby.

Yet all he seemed to do these days was hurt her more. He'd seen her eyes look all bruised when he'd been cool with her. But he couldn't seem to help himself. Thank God they'd brought Letty back. At first he'd been reluctant—he'd thought she was the flakiest little oddball of a woman he'd ever met—but now he didn't know how he'd have coped without her. She knew Nina better than anyone on earth, probably even her own mother. She was company for Nina in the evenings—when that old fool Henry wasn't up at the house making eyes. She catered to Nina's every whim, which was fine by Cal.

Even more amazing, Letty steadfastly believed that everything would work out—somehow. She'd told him so several times. He didn't see how it was possible.

"Hear that?" Jeremiah gathered his reins and sat up.

Cal froze. He hadn't heard anything.

"Truck coming," Jeremiah said tersely, and eased his gelding forward. "I'll head back up and tell Henry. Remember—wait until they start loading."

Cal knew the drill. They were to wait until the rustlers unloaded their horses—if they'd brought horses—and started to load the steers. Then they were to ride down and catch them in the act. Cal hoped that was all it would amount to; if everything went the way it should, the Mounties would take care of the rest. He didn't expect the rustlers would try anything except to

get away. Let them, he'd told the others. All they had
to do was catch them trying to steal the steers. Just
get a good look—horses, men, make of the truck,
plates. Cal glanced at the sky. A little more moon
would have helped.

Of course it was going to be tough to keep the others from giving chase. If they grabbed one or two of
the bastards, all the better, was Jeremiah's way of
thinking. Maybe they'd even end up with the truck
and trailer, Henry had said. Jeremiah and Adam carried rifles in their saddle scabbards, but there'd be no
gunfight. A couple of rounds fired in the air, maybe.
It wasn't likely they'd be armed since they had no
cause to be suspicious. Most of their heists had obviously been a piece of cake. Besides, this wasn't the
Wild West. People these days didn't go around pack-
ing rifles outside of hunting season.

Cal tensed. A truck appeared around the corner of
the hill, moving slowly on the frozen ground. Cal held
Babe well back, afraid the truck's headlights might
pick out the mare if she moved. Lights blazing, the
vehicle stopped in a clear space a hundred yards from
the canyon and turned around. Cal heard the steers
below bawl nervously. Then he watched while three
men spilled out of the cab and went around to the back
of the trailer. They threw down a ramp and led out
some saddled mounts. They were laughing, and one
stopped to light a cigarette.

Cal was sprung tight. He hoped Jeremiah and Adam
wouldn't make their moves too soon. He thought he
could count on Henry for caution. One minute, then
another ticked by. Four minutes. The rustlers didn't
expect any surprises. They hadn't even bothered to

douse the truck lights. Cal could see the passenger door hanging open as the truck backed slowly toward the draw, guided by one of the men on horseback. Back, back… He saw the man shout and gesture for the driver to stop.

Then the men disappeared for a moment, below him in the coulee. One emerged on a saddle pony. The moon was starting to glimmer a little more brightly as the clouds moved off, and Cal could see a rope dallied to the horn. Cal realized the horse was dragging off one of the trees that had been pushed up into the canyon to hide the steers.

These boys had this down like clockwork, he thought with grim admiration. They'd had plenty of practice unfortunately. Well, it'd be the last play they made on Rocking Bar S beef.

Then with a few expert moves they started the confused steers toward the dark opening at the back of the truck. Cal held his breath and waited until one steer, a second, then a third went up the ramp, bawling mightily, hooves thundering on the wooden deck of the trailer. He squeezed Babe's side gently and eased the mare forward. Branches snapped and there was sudden movement in the brush to his left—Jeremiah or Henry moving in. The men below would never hear them in the general mayhem of loading the steers. Cal heard a shout of laughter from one and the snap of a lariat.

Then all hell broke loose. Cal kept to his flank. No way they wanted to allow an opening down the hill and lose not only the rustlers, but have the steers scatter. Those steers were evidence. He heard Jeremiah and Henry shouting as they rode down the middle. Adam, he hoped, was protecting his flank on the left.

The rustlers were surprised. One ran for his mount, but the horse spooked and took off, snorting and bucking with fear, stirrup leathers swinging crazily. The man ducked behind the barricade and Cal lost him as a cloud covered the moon again.

Cal cursed. Goddamn bad luck. The other two cowboys spurred their horses and rode off. Cal saw Adam set off after one of them and Jeremiah shout and give chase to the other, but the rustlers already had fifty yards on them. Cal didn't give much for their chances.

The driver must have realized something had gone wrong, because he suddenly revved his engine and started to move forward. The ramp, still lowered, snagged on a rock and the truck's engine stalled. Cal saw the man who'd lost his horse make a run for the truck. Just as he reached the passenger door, the truck's engine caught again and the driver gunned it.

Cal heard shots in the distance and hoped it was only Jeremiah and Adam firing off a warning to the two men they were chasing. Where the hell were the Mounties? Hadn't they gotten his message? He put the spurs to Babe and the mare leaped ahead.

The truck. He'd get to the truck and stop the driver and then they'd have them for sure. Cal kicked his feet out of the stirrups, ready to make a leap for the side of the trailer or for the still-swinging open door of the truck. The steers were making a hell of a racket inside the trailer, and just as Cal came even with it, one lost its balance and toppled off the back.

"Damn it!" Cal gripped the saddle with his knees and grabbed the horn as the quarter horse gathered

herself on her haunches and leaped over the downed steer. He glanced quickly behind, saw the dazed animal stagger to its feet and disappear into the blackness, bawling.

The truck picked up a little speed on the rough terrain, and Cal swore under his breath. Urging Babe close to the hitch, he threw himself onto the front of the trailer and grunted with pain as his left shoulder slammed into the corner. Both doors to the truck still swung wide open and the cab's inside lights were on. That was to his advantage, Cal realized. They couldn't see him in the darkness. He gripped the rough wooden corner of the trailer and hung on. If only he could work his way into the cab…

Just then the truck hit a side hill and the trailer bounced up and began to tilt dangerously. Cal swore and looked behind him. There was nowhere he could pitch off that would be clear of the trailer if it overturned. He saw Henry in the distance, racing to catch up. Metal screamed on metal. The steers inside were panicking, their hooves sliding and drumming on the timbers. Everything seemed stuck in slow motion, as though it were happening underwater.

Nina…sweet Nina. All he could see was her face. How foolish he'd been. Her smile, her blue eyes, her sweet promises… It hadn't been all bad. No, it hadn't been all bad.

Just as the trailer went over, he got a glimpse into the brightly lit cab and saw the terrified face of the young driver. *Lewis Hardin.*

Then something hot burst in his side, and darkness swam up at him from the frozen ground and down from the pale cold moon and swallowed him whole.

NINA GLANCED UP at the clock in the kitchen, dimly lit by the light over the stove. Midnight. She opened the refrigerator and took out a carton of milk and poured some into a saucepan. She couldn't sleep. She hated it when Cal wasn't home at night. And now, with the baby so active, sometimes she had a hard time getting comfortable enough to sleep. Partly she missed Cal's large warm presence beside her. Partly, well, she just liked knowing he was home. Nights were the only time she felt the way she had before, when she'd first married him and come to the Horsethief Valley.

If he hadn't wanted her the way he did—at least physically—Nina would have given up on McCallum Blake long ago. She hadn't got where she had in the business world by ignoring the facts. There was a time in every venture to move forward and take risks, and there was a time to hold off and regroup.

This past month and a half at the Rocking Bar S she'd been doing both. Was it possible to be in heaven and hell at the same time? Nina didn't think there'd ever been so much at stake at once in her life. The future she wanted with Cal and the Rocking Bar S, her baby's right to belong to a family and to grow up with a father... Cal's happiness, if he only knew it.

Nina frowned and poured the hot milk into a mug and stirred a brimming spoonful of honey into it. Her own happiness?

She'd already forfeited that. She'd played the wild card and lost. She'd risked her happiness when she made the choice not to tell him the truth right at the beginning. She'd traded honesty and the possibility of losing him then—when he'd asked her to marry him— for the hope that something real and genuine would

happen between them and then she'd be able to tell
him everything. She'd clung to the belief that he'd
forgive her. She'd been wrong.

Still, despite what he'd said, she'd realized a second
chance was possible that first night after they'd left
Vancouver. He'd started out in his own bed at the
Bluebird Motel in Cranbrook, his back turned. He'd
ended up in hers, making love to her with a fierceness
and passion and intensity that took her breath away.
She'd wept afterward. She'd wept for her foolishness
and for being given—God only knew why or how—
another chance, faint as it was, to keep him. This part
of him, at least. Of them. *He desired her.*

That was something to build on. It meant he wasn't
as indifferent to her as he seemed. Maybe that, and
the baby when it came, would be steps toward building
a new life together. If only she could get past his mon-
umental stubbornness.

Nina blew on her milk to cool it. She glanced at the
clock again. Nearly half past. Why wasn't he home
yet? Surely if there'd been any rustlers tonight, they
would have come for the steers before now. What
could they do in the dark?

She didn't like the idea of Cal's being out there with
rustlers. She'd tried to tell him, but it had been hard,
so hard. What could she say? *I love you and I don't
want you to risk getting hurt over this? I need you,
the baby needs you?*

Well, maybe if she took that chance one of these
days and said what she really felt, things would get
better. *Or worse.*

Nina took a sip of the hot milk and leaned back in
the rocking chair in a corner of the kitchen. Letty's

favorite chair. Dear Letty—what would she have done without her? Nina thought of the way Letty's eyes brightened whenever that taciturn old cowpoke Henry showed up at the door after supper, clean shirt on, hair freshly slicked down. Love? Who knew what love looked like when it happened? Hadn't Leo warned her? Told her to answer the door when fortune knocked? That playing it safe wasn't all people said it was?

She'd found out that not playing it safe could hurt, too. Still, she had the baby. Even if everything possible went wrong between her and Cal—and it seemed sometimes that it already had—she still had their child to love.

Nina smoothed the round hummock of her lap and closed her eyes. This baby was one of the best things to come out of the whole experience—something she'd never ever regret.

Why couldn't they talk anymore? At one time it seemed they'd hardly needed to put their thoughts and feelings into words. Now? Cal avoided her. He worked harder than he had to, she was sure of it, just to stay away from the house. He took on crazy things like this rustling business—mostly Jeremiah and Henry's idea, she knew, and that other rancher friend of theirs, Adam Garrick. Sometimes it seemed as though Cal was just putting in time until she had the baby. That he really truly didn't care anymore. If he hadn't slept with his arms around her as he did every night—unaware, Nina often thought sadly, of what he was doing—she'd have given up. But there was no way she was quitting yet.

Nina looked at the silent telephone on the counter

nearby, and the pad of paper lying there for messages. *Why not write him a letter? Tell him how she really felt, what was in her heart?*

Once, their letters to each other had been everything. How she'd loved receiving a letter from him and then sitting down in that apartment in Ladner's Landing and writing him back. She'd put on her shoes and rush out to post it. That was when she'd fallen in love with him. She'd known she *could* love him, as she'd told Leo, but she hadn't realized that it had already happened. She hadn't known what love was then.

Nina got up clumsily and rinsed her mug, then set it in the sink. She glanced at the clock—yet again. Quarter past one. There was no way she'd sleep now until Cal was back. She walked to the counter and opened a drawer and pulled out a pad of lined yellow paper and a pen. She didn't need fancy stationery; she just needed to tell Cal the truth. The whole truth.

The words flowed onto the paper as though a dam had burst. Nina wrote until her fingers were cramped and her shoulders were stiff and sore. Then she folded the pages and stuffed them into an envelope and wrote Cal's name on the outside. She'd give this to him tomorrow when he was rested up from all this rustler nonsense. Maybe then, maybe when he knew how she really felt…

She closed her eyes to rest them for a few moments. She must have dozed, because suddenly she was wideawake and frightened at the sound of a low but persistent knocking at the outside door. One of the dogs barked a couple of times, not very enthusiastically, then quit. Nina hauled herself up. It must be Cal knocking. Why didn't he come straight in? She hadn't locked the door....

But it wasn't Cal.

"Mrs. Blake? Ma'am?" Adam Garrick stood under the porch light, tall and dark and forbidding. "May I come in? I need to talk to you."

"Cal?" Nina fumbled with the door. *Omigod, if something had happened to Cal...* "Please, come in."

Adam came in. He looked drawn and tired and his shirt was ripped on one sleeve. He reached out to put his hand on Nina's shoulder. She shook it off.

"What's wrong? Where's Cal?"

"Uh, I'd like you to sit down, ma'am, please, if you don't mind. Woman in your condition—"

"For God's sake—say what you have to say!" Nina grabbed his shirtfront. "It's Cal, isn't it? *Where is he?"*

"Yeah. It's Cal. He's in the hospital in Glory. He's been hurt pretty bad."

CHAPTER TWENTY-ONE

"Psst! Wake up!"

Letty awoke instantly. "Are you having the baby?"

"No, I'm all right. I'm going to Glory to the hospital. Cal's been hurt. Adam Garrick's taking me."

"Is Mr. Blake hurt bad?"

"Adam doesn't know." Nina tried to keep the tremor out of her voice as she bent and kissed the older woman's cheek. "I just wanted to let you know so you wouldn't worry."

"I never worry, dear," Letty said softly. "You know that. Will you be okay? Take care of yourself. I suppose a hospital is not a bad place for you in case anything does happen."

"It's half-past four in the morning," Nina whispered. "I just hope they let me in to see Cal."

"They will."

"Go back to sleep." Nina couldn't help smiling a little in the darkness. Letty was right—Nina knew she never worried. Her faith in what she called "things working out" was too great. That was probably why she didn't ask for details; she knew Cal was in the hospital, where there were competent doctors, and Nina would soon be with him. In Letty's world, those where the kinds of things that mattered.

"What happened?" Nina said as soon as she got

into Adam's pickup. She'd stuffed a few things in her carryall and hoped she had everything she needed. Money. ID. Her toothbrush, just in case. At the last minute she'd scooped up the letter she'd written Cal, mainly so Letty wouldn't find it in the morning and wonder. She adjusted the seat belt cautiously, making sure the strap was under the baby.

"We caught the rustlers. Cal tried to jump onto the trailer and somehow—" Adam glanced at her, but she couldn't make out his expression in the dark cab "—somehow the trailer turned over—"

"My God!"

"I don't think it really fell on him, but he was pinned under it. Lewis and Henry got him out and—"

"Lewis?" Nina's shock turned to bewilderment. "I thought he was away. I'm sure Cal gave him and Johnny a few days off."

Adam glanced at her again, then turned his attention back to the road. "Lewis was driving the truck."

"You mean, Lewis was *one of the rustlers?*"

"That's right. It hit Cal pretty hard."

"He was conscious, then…." Nina's head was spinning. No sleep, Cal injured—how badly she had no idea but she could only pray he'd be all right—and now Lewis? Cal must be devastated. How many times had he spoken of the admiration he had for the Hardin boy looking after his crazy mother and sister the way he did? To have Lewis turn on him like this— Nina covered her mouth with one hand. Betrayed…again.

"I was there when they got Cal out," Adam said hesitantly, as though unsure how much to tell this woman his friend had married. "Cal told Lewis, uh—" Adam paused and cleared his throat "—he told him he'd be going to jail for this but not to worry, he'd make sure his mother and sister were taken care of.''

"Cal said *that?*" Nina felt the tears run hot and welcome down her cheeks.

"Yeah. Blake's a hell of a guy. I guess you know that," Adam said with a sideways look at her. "Just like him to hire the bastard on again when he gets out, too."

Nina said nothing. All the love she had for Cal and their baby was focused on his getting better. She dug the heels of her hands into her eyes, trying hard to stem the flood of silent tears. She knew she unsettled the tough-looking rancher beside her. "How'd h-he get to the hospital from up there?"

"The Mounties. Cal tipped them off. Told them to be there tonight." Adam frowned at her. "Damn." He sounded concerned and awkward, as though he didn't know quite what to do with this very pregnant woman in his truck, the wife of his friend, who couldn't seem to stop crying. "Look…you okay, ma'am?"

"I'm f-fine, Adam. I'm going to be okay. The b-baby's okay, don't worry. Please. I just want to see my husband. That's all." It was the truth—every word.

LIGHT SEEPED into his brain from somewhere beyond his eyelids. He didn't want to open his eyes. Not yet. He wasn't one-hundred-percent sure he *could* open them.

He started to take a slow deep breath— Damn! His chest felt like he had one of Basaraba's Maine Anjous standing on it. He wiggled his toes. No problem there.

His hands seemed fine; he could move his fingers okay. His shoulder hurt, though, his left one. And the left side of his head felt like it was on fire. Goddamn it. What happened?

He remembered the trailer toppling so slowly—just like in some Peckinpah movie. He remembered hitting the cold ground and then he didn't remember much.

Lewis Hardin.

He remembered seeing Lewis's face in the cab of the truck. Later, when he'd come to, he remembered someone carrying him to the Mounties' car. There were lights flashing and the sound of strange men's voices. And above it all…the cold crescent moon.

Nina. His wife. The mother of his child.

What kind of fool had he been? He'd dreamed all night that she was there beside him, as always, only this time he held her close and whispered all the small private things he longed to tell her, and made her the promises he should have made a long long time ago.

The light must mean it was morning. He knew from the distant sounds, the low voices and smell of disinfectant that he was in a hospital. The Mounties must have brought him to Glory.

Has anybody told Nina yet? He tensed, then groaned as red-hot iron sliced into his chest and shoulder.

"Cal?"

Her voice. He'd know it anywhere.

"Cal? Are you awake?" she whispered, and he felt her hand, cool and smooth, on the side of his face. The side that didn't hurt quite as bad. He opened his eyes a crack.

He wasn't dreaming. Nina was here. Beside him.

He opened his mouth to say something—what? He had no idea.

"You're awake." He saw tears in her eyes. "Oh, Cal!" Her face wavered in front of him. Then he felt her put something to his mouth. A glass. "Do you want some water?" she whispered. "Here's some water." She slid her arm beneath his head, and he tilted his head forward and drank. It was cool and sweet and he was so thirsty....

"Oh, dear, oh, dear," he heard her mutter worriedly, as though she was talking to herself. "Maybe I should call a nurse—"

"No!" Somehow he found the strength to raise his good hand. She clasped it in both of hers and held it tight against her. It was a simple gesture. He closed his eyes, savoring the sweetness. Her soft small hands holding his. Did she realize that their entwined hands rested on her belly? *On their child?* Cal was sure he'd imagined it, but he could swear he felt the new life there, his son or daughter, vigorously protesting the sudden weighty intrusion from the outside world. He wanted to smile, but it hurt too much.

"Shall I call the nurse?" Nina's face loomed in front of him, earnest and worried, although she hadn't let go of his hand. He willed her closer, wanting to kiss her, but she didn't move.

"No," he managed, amazed by the pain of speaking, at the harsh croak that was his voice. He swallowed a couple of times. "Don't call the nurse." After a long while—at least it seemed like a long while to him—he spoke again. "You okay?"

"I'm all right. Adam came for me. I've been sitting

here for hours worried sick about you. Jeremiah's worried sick.''

He focused on her face. "Jeremiah?"

"He's not hurt. You're the only one who got hurt, Adam told me. He said it figures, thinking you could bulldog a stock trailer.''

Cal smiled then; he couldn't help it. How come when the last thing you wanted to do was laugh because it hurt so much, everything seemed so damn funny?

"What's bulldogging, Cal? No, don't answer, I can see it hurts you to talk. You shouldn't talk. The nurse said you had a couple of broken ribs.''

He felt her squeeze his hand, and he squeezed hers back. "Bulldogging's another word for steer wrestling." He paused, eyes closed, breathing steadily. "Adam's a rodeo man. I guess he knows what he's talking about. You heard about—" it still hurt him to think of it "—about Lewis?"

"Oh, Cal, I'm so sorry. I know how much you thought of him. Adam says he helped pull you out from under that trailer, him and Henry.''

Cal heard the pain in her voice. Oddly, the sound of it soothed him and took away some of the sting of Lewis' betrayal. "He did it because...well, for his mother. And his crazy sister. I guess. Damned if I know—I suppose he needed the money.''

"Don't talk about it, Cal," she whispered.

"He should have come to me." Cal closed his eyes for a few seconds. "What about Henry?"

"He's okay. He's driving in later to bring me home. The doctor says maybe you'll be able to go home tomorrow, but I think they must be crazy to think about letting you out like this—''

Cal squeezed her hand to interrupt her. ''I'd rather be home. With you.'' He withdrew his hand from hers and slipped it behind her neck and pulled her close and kissed her, ever so gently. ''I love you, Nina.''

Nina bent her head and didn't say anything for a long time, and when she spoke again, Cal realized she'd been weeping silently.

''Oh, C-Cal…'' He pulled her to him roughly then and she collapsed and buried her face on his shoulder. He felt the tears on his bare chest—he'd been taped up from beneath his armpits to the bottom of his ribs— and held her tightly against him with his one good arm. He wished she could get up on this bed beside him and he could hold her properly and comfort her.

He thought of all the things that had happened since they'd met. The lies… Who hadn't lied? Who hadn't been tempted to tell a fantastic story to a passing stranger? He'd always known she was an impulsive passionate person. It was part of what he loved about her. Most people lied to make themselves out to be more important and more deserving than they were; he'd married a woman who'd turned the Cinderella story on its head. She'd been the princess who wanted to be a farmer's wife. *A rancher's wife.*

As for running away when she knew the baby was coming… Well, yes, that had hurt more than Cal had thought possible. It had seemed as though all his dreams, all his hopes for a solid marriage and a family one day had come to nothing.

But now he could see that she'd painted herself into such a corner by not telling him the truth about her family that she hadn't known which way to turn. Like a wounded creature, she'd gone to ground. She'd run to Letty and Leo and her parents—people she knew she could trust. The fact that she hadn't felt she could trust *him* still hurt. No question. But…who could say what he'd have done in the same situation. What anyone would have done. If he was going to make allowances for a hired hand stealing his goddamn steers, he sure as hell was going to forgive his own wife for whatever foolishness had occurred.

He held her tighter, cursing his wounded left arm that wouldn't permit him to hold her properly.

"Cal?"

"Yes, darlin'?" The endearment came naturally to his lips. It loosened something tight and aching in his chest.

"Am I…is this hurting you?" She tried to sit straight, but he wouldn't let her.

"What hurts me is *not* holding you like this, Nina." Her eyes were swimming and her nose was a dull red. He'd never seen and never would see a woman who was more beautiful to him. "Nina…"

"Yes, Cal?" she whispered, and he felt her relax against him so that her head was heavy on his arm. He turned to look at her. Her eyes, only inches from his, were wide.

"We've made a hell of a mess of things, haven't we, darlin'?"

She nodded, her eyes brimming again.

He took a deep breath, as deep as he could with his ribs hurting the way they did. "Up there last night while we were waiting for the rustlers to show, I decided I'd let you go if you wanted, even before the baby was born. I don't know what I was thinking of, dragging you back here like I did——''

"I wanted to come," Nina broke in. "You couldn't drag me *away!*"

Cal smiled. It didn't hurt quite so much anymore. He ran one finger down the curve of her cheek—soft, sweet, beloved. How had he ever gotten things so damn mixed-up and wrong? When had he fallen in love with this woman? Did it matter? "I've changed my mind. I want to start over if you'll give me the chance. I want to start over with you and with this babe and with everything. Our marriage. Being together. I want you to give me another shot at being the husband I promised I'd be back in April. I've let you down and——''

"You've let me down? How can you *say* that? I'm the one who's botched everything, Cal," she said fervently. He tightened his arm around her, but she didn't stop. "This mess is all *my* fault. I can't begin to tell you how much I regret the way everything's happened.''

"Forget that." He placed his thumb against her lip. "Does this mean we're going to get that second chance, you and me?"

"Oh, Cal, you *know* it does," she said, her voice tremulous. "I...I wrote you a letter last night while I was waiting for you to come home. I couldn't sleep. I tried to put everything in it....''

"A letter, huh?" He couldn't help laughing faintly. Damn, it hurt!

"I brought it with me. You can read it if you want." Nina dug in her bag and pulled out a tissue. She blew her nose.

He thought about that for a few seconds. *Letters. That's what had brought them together.* He didn't feel like reading now. Maybe later. All he wanted was to kiss her and hold her and show her how much he cared. "What's it about?"

"It's about love, Cal." Her eyes were serious on his. He felt he was drowning in those clear blue depths, tumbling over and over. *The joy of it...* "Love. About how much I love you. And how much I love our child and the Rocking Bar S. And everyone here. Lou, Letty, your brother—"

"Henry?" He couldn't resist.

"Even Henry!" She inched forward, smiling, leaning over him.

"Nina," he whispered, looking up into her eyes.

"Yes?"

"I love you. You know that, don't you?"

She nodded, lower lip trembling.

"I don't know when it happened, but it did," he went on. "I've never been in love before, but I am now. I love you. I always will. I'm sorry it's taken me so long to figure that out."

"Oh, Cal—"

"Now don't start crying again."

"I won't." She smiled down at him. *She loved him.* Maybe he'd always known that.

"You know I've already got a reputation for being hopeless with women...."

"I know. I won't cry. Promise." She smiled, and he wished again he could pull her up onto this hospital bed and really kiss her.

"Promise me something else." He held her face close to his.

"What's that?"

"Promise you'll start your painting and drawing again, the way you did before. I know how much it means to you."

"Oh, Cal…" Her voice was suspiciously wobbly. "I will. *I will*."

"And something else…"

"Yes?"

"Climb up here and kiss me."

And she did.

Themed Collections

Looking for great value and a great read?

Enjoy Big Savings and Free Books at
www.themedcollections.com

Western Cowboys   *Sizzling Suspense*

Nora Roberts's Classics

Debbie Macomber's Latest

Forbidden Love   *Sexy Lovers*

Our editors have handpicked books
from the most popular themes
and bestselling authors to create
fabulous collections—*all at discounted prices.*

Some of our collections are not available
in stores, so come by to check out these
and other compelling collections!

Visit **www.themedcollections.com** today.

THEMAD

Harlequin Romance®

Delightful
Affectionate
Romantic
Emotional

    Tender
    Original

      Daring
      Riveting
      Enchanting
      Adventurous
      Moving

Harlequin Romance® —
capturing the world you dream of...

HARLEQUIN®
Makes any time special ®

Visit us at www.eHarlequin.com   HROMDIR1

Harlequin® Historical

From rugged lawmen and valiant knights to defiant heiresses and spirited frontierswomen, Harlequin Historicals will capture your imagination with their dramatic scope, passion and adventure.

Harlequin Historicals...
they're too good to miss!

passionate powerful provocative love stories that fulfill your every desir

Desire ®

Silhouette Desire delivers strong heroes, spirited
heroines and stellar love stories.

Desire features your favorite authors, including

Diana Palmer, Annette Broadrick, Ann Major, Anne MacAllister and Cait London.

Passionate, powerful and provocative
romances *guaranteed!*

For superlative authors, sensual stories and
sexy heroes, choose Silhouette Desire.

Available at your favorite retail outlet.

Silhouette ®
TM
Where love comes alive™

passionate powerful provocative love stories that fulfill your every desire

Visit us at www.eHarlequin.com   SDGEN00

Where love comes alive™

From first love to forever, these love stories are
for today's woman with traditional values.

A highly passionate, emotionally powerful
and always provocative read.

SPECIAL EDITION™

Emotional, compelling stories that capture the
intensity of living, loving and creating a family in
today's world.

INTIMATE MOMENTS™

A roller-coaster read that delivers romantic thrills
in a world of suspense, adventure and more.

Visit Silhouette at www.eHarlequin.com

SDIR2

eHARLEQUIN.com

The eHarlequin.com online community is *the* place to share opinions, thoughts and feelings!

- Joining the community is easy, fun and **FREE!**

- Connect with **other romance fans** on our message boards.

- Meet your **favorite authors** without leaving home!

- **Share opinions** on books, movies, celebrities…and *more!*

Here's what our members say:

"I love the friendly and helpful atmosphere filled with support and humor."
—Texanna (eHarlequin.com member)

"Is this the place for me, or what? There is nothing I love more than 'talking' books, especially with fellow readers who are reading the same ones I am."
—Jo Ann (eHarlequin.com member)

Join today by visiting
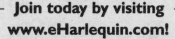
www.eHarlequin.com!

INTCOMM

HARLEQUIN®
Presents

The world's bestselling romance series...
The series that brings you your favorite authors,
month after month:

Helen Bianchin...Emma Darcy
Lynne Graham...Penny Jordan
Miranda Lee...Sandra Marton
Anne Mather...Carole Mortimer
Susan Napier...Michelle Reid

and many more uniquely talented authors!

Wealthy, powerful, gorgeous men...
Women who have feelings just like your own...
The stories you love, set in exotic, glamorous locations...

HARLEQUIN®
Presents

Seduction and Passion Guaranteed!

www.eHarlequin.com

HPDIR104

eHARLEQUIN.com

The Ultimate Destination for Women's Fiction

For FREE online reading, visit
www.eHarlequin.com now and enjoy:

Online Reads
Read **Daily** and **Weekly** chapters from
our Internet-exclusive stories by your
favorite authors.

Interactive Novels
Cast your vote to help decide how these
stories unfold...then stay tuned!

Quick Reads
For shorter romantic reads, try our
collection of Poems, Toasts, & More!

Online Read Library
Miss one of our online reads?
Come here to catch up!

Reading Groups
Discuss, share and rave with other
community members!

For great reading online,
visit www.eHarlequin.com today!

INTONL04